SONS OF

The PRIEST

a novella

ENCOURAGEMENT

FRANCINE RIVERS

TYNDALE HOUSE PUBLISHERS, INC.
WHEATON, ILLINOIS

Visit Tyndale's exciting Web site at www.tyndale.com

TYNDALE is a registered trademark of Tyndale House Publishers, Inc.

Tyndale's quill logo is a trademark of Tyndale House Publishers, Inc.

Check out the latest about Francine Rivers at www.francinerivers.com

"Seek and Find" section written by Peggy Lynch.

Edited by Kathryn S. Olson

Designed by Alyssa Force

Library of Congress Cataloging-in-Publication Data

Rivers, Francine, date.
   The priest / Francine Rivers.
      p. cm. — (Sons of encouragement ; 1)
   ISBN 0-8423-8265-8
   1. Aaron (Biblical priest)—Fiction.   2. Bible. O.T. Exodus—History of Biblical events—
Fiction.   3. Priests—Fiction.   I. Title.
PS3568.I83165P75 2004
813'.54—dc22   2003026586

Printed in the United States of America

10   09   08   07   06   05
9   8   7   6   5   4   3

*To men of faith who serve
in the shadow of others.*

✦　✦　✦

I want to thank Peggy Lynch for listening
to my ideas and challenging me to dig
deeper and deeper. I also want to thank
Scott Mendel for sending me materials on
the Jewish perspective. And Danielle Egan-
Miller, who calmed the turbulent waters of
sorrow when my friend and agent of many
years, Jane Jordan Browne, passed away.
Jane taught her well, and I know I'm in
good hands. I also want to thank my editor,
Kathy Olson, for all her hard work on these
projects, and the entire Tyndale staff for all
the work they do in presenting these stories
to readers. It's a team effort all the way.

I also want to thank all those who have
prayed for me over the years and through
the course of this particular project. May
the Lord use this story to draw people close
to Jesus, our beloved Lord and Savior.

DEAR READER,

This is the first of five novellas on biblical men of faith who served in the shadows of others. These were Eastern men who lived in ancient times, and yet their stories apply to our lives and the difficult issues we face in our world today. They were on the edge. They had courage. They took risks. They did the unexpected. They lived daring lives, and sometimes they made mistakes—big mistakes. These men were not perfect, and yet God in His infinite mercy used them in His perfect plan to reveal Himself to the world.

We live in desperate, troubled times when millions seek answers. These men point the way. The lessons we can learn from them are as applicable today as when they lived thousands of years ago.

These are historical men who actually lived. Their stories, as I have told them, are based on biblical accounts. For a more thorough reading of the life of Aaron, see the books of Exodus, Leviticus, and Numbers. Also compare Christ, our High Priest, as found in the book of Hebrews.

This book is also a work of historical fiction. The outline of the story is provided by the Bible, and I have started with the facts provided for us there. Building on that foundation, I have created action, dialogue, internal motivations, and in some cases, additional characters that I feel are consistent with the biblical record. I have attempted to remain true to the scriptural message in all points, adding only what is necessary to aid in our understanding of that message.

At the end of each novella, we have included a brief study section. The ultimate authority on people of the Bible is the Bible itself. I encourage you to read it for greater understanding. And I pray that as you read the Bible, you will become aware of the continuity, the consistency, and the confirmation of God's plan for the ages—a plan that includes you.

Francine Rivers

ONE

AARON sensed someone standing close as he broke loose a mold and put the dried brick aside. Skin prickling with fear, he glanced up. No one was near. The Hebrew foreman closest to him was overseeing the loading of bricks onto a cart to add on to some phase of Pharaoh's storage cities. Wiping the moisture from his upper lip, he bent again to his work.

Through the area, sunburned, work-weary children carried straw to women who shook it out like a blanket over the mud pit and then stomped it in. Sweat-drenched men filled buckets and bent beneath the weight as they poured the mud into brick molds. From dawn to dusk, the work went on unceasingly, leaving only a few twilight hours to tend small garden plots and flocks in order to sustain life.

Where are You, God? Why won't You help us?

"You there! Get to work!"

Ducking his head, Aaron hid his hatred and moved to the next mold. His knees ached from squatting, his back from lifting bricks, his neck from bowing. He set the bricks in stacks for others to load. The pits and plains were a hive of workers, the air so close and heavy he could hardly breathe for the stench of human misery. Sometimes death seemed preferable to this unbearable existence. What hope had he or any of his people? God had forsaken them. Aaron wiped the sweat from his eyes and removed another mold from a dried brick.

Someone spoke to him again. It was less than a whisper, but it made his blood rush and the hair on the back of his neck stand on end. He paused and strained forward, listening. He looked around. No one paid him any notice.

Maybe he was suffering from the heat. That must be it. Each year became harder, more insufferable. He was

eighty-three years old, a long life blessed with nothing but
wretchedness.

Shaking, Aaron raised his hand. A boy hurried over with
a skin of water. Aaron drank deeply, but the warm fluid did
nothing to stop the inner quaking, the feeling of someone
watching him so closely that he could feel that gaze into the
marrow of his bones. It was a strange sensation, terrifying in its
intensity. He leaned forward on his knees, longing to hide from
the light, longing to rest. He heard the overseer shout again and
knew if he didn't get back to work he would feel the bite of the
lash. Even old men like him were expected to fulfill a heavy
quota of bricks each day. And if they didn't, they suffered for
it. His father, Amram, had died with his face in the mud, an
Egyptian foot on the back of his neck.

Where were You then, Lord? Where were You?

He hated the Hebrew taskmasters as much as he hated the
Egyptians. But he gave thanks anyway—hatred gave a man
strength. The sooner his quota was filled, the sooner he could
tend his flock of sheep and goats, the sooner his sons could
work the plot of Goshen land that yielded food for their table.
*The Egyptians try to kill us, but we go on and on. We multiply.
But what good does it do us? We suffer and suffer some more.*

Aaron loosened another mold. Beads of sweat dripped from
his brow onto the hardened clay, staining the brick. Hebrew
sweat and blood were poured into everything being built in
Egypt! Raamses' statues, Raamses' palaces, Raamses' storage
buildings, Raamses' city—everything was stained. Egypt's ruler
liked naming everything after himself. Pride reigned on the
throne of Egypt! The old pharaoh had tried to drown Hebrew
sons in the Nile, and now Raamses was attempting to grind
them into dust! Aaron hoisted the brick and stacked it with
a dozen others.

When will You deliver us, Lord? When will You break the yoke of slavery from our backs? Was it not our ancestor Joseph who saved this foul country from starvation? And look at how we're treated now! Pharaoh uses us like beasts of burden, building his cities and palaces! God, why have You abandoned us? How long, oh, Lord, how long before You deliver us from those who would kill us with labor?

Aaron.

The Voice came without and within, clear this time, silencing Aaron's turbulent thoughts. He felt the Presence so acutely that all else receded and he was cupped silent and still by invisible hands. The Voice was unmistakable. His very blood and bone recognized it.

Go out into the wilderness to meet Moses!

The Presence lifted. Everything went back to the way it had been. Sound surrounded him again—the suck of mud from stomping feet, the groan of men lifting buckets, the call of women for more hay, the crunch of sand as someone approached, a curse, a shouted order, the hiss of the lash. Aaron cried out as pain laced his back. He hunched over and covered his head, fearing the overseer less than the One who had called him by name. The whip tore his flesh, but the Word of the Lord ripped wide his heart.

"Get up, old man!"

If he was lucky, he would die.

He felt more pain. He heard voices and drifted into blackness. And he remembered . . .

How many years since Aaron had thought of his brother? He had assumed he was dead, his dry bones forgotten somewhere in the wilderness. Aaron's first memory was of his mother's angry, anguished weeping as she covered a woven basket she had made with tar and pitch. "Pharaoh said we have to give our sons to the Nile, Amram, and so I will. May the Lord preserve him! May the Lord be merciful!"

And God had been merciful, letting the basket drift into the hands of Pharaoh's daughter. Miriam, at eight, had followed to see what became of her baby brother, and then had had enough boldness to suggest to the Egyptian that she would have need of a wet nurse. When Miriam was sent for one, she ran to her mother.

Aaron had been only three years old, but he still remembered that day. His mother pried his fingers loose. "Stop holding on to me. I have to go!" Gripping his wrists tightly, she had held him away from her. "Take him, Miriam."

Aaron screamed when his mother went out the door. She was leaving him. "Hush, Aaron." Miriam held him tight. "Crying will do no good. You know Moses needs Mama more than you do. You're a big boy. You can help me tend the garden and the sheep. . . ."

Though his mother returned with Moses each night, her attention was clearly on the infant. Every morning, she obeyed the princess's command that she take the baby to the palace and stay nearby in case he needed anything.

Day after day passed, and only Aaron's sister was there to comfort him. "I miss her, too, you know." She dashed tears from her cheeks. "Moses needs her more than we do. He hasn't been weaned yet."

"I want Mama."

"Well, wanting and having are two separate things. Stop whining about it."

"Where does Mama go every day?"

"Upriver."

"Upriver?"

She pointed. "To the palace, where Pharaoh's daughter lives." One day Aaron snuck away when Miriam went out to see about their few sheep. Though he had been warned against it, he went along to the Nile and followed the river away from the village. Dangerous things lived in the waters. Evil things. The reeds were tall and sharp, making small cuts on his arms and legs as he pressed through. He heard rustling sounds and low roars, high-pitched keens and frantic flapping. Crocodiles lived in the Nile. His mother had told him.

He heard a woman laughing. Pushing his way through the reeds, he crept closer until he could see through the veiling green stalks to the stone patio where an Egyptian sat with a baby in her lap. She bounced him on her knees and talked low to him. She kissed his neck and held him up toward the sun like an offering. When the baby began to cry, the woman called out for "Jochebed." Aaron saw his mother rise from a place in the shadows and come down the steps. Smiling, she took the baby Aaron now knew was his brother. The two women talked briefly, and the Egyptian went inside.

Aaron stood up so that Mama could see him if she looked his way. She didn't. She had eyes only for the baby she held. As his mother nursed Moses, she sang to him. Aaron stood alone, watching her tenderly stroke Moses' head. He wanted to call out to her, but his throat was sealed tight and hot. When Mama finished nursing his brother, she rose and turned her back to the river. She held Moses against her shoulder. And then she went back up the steps into the palace.

Aaron sat down in the mud, hidden among the reeds. Mosquitoes buzzed around him. Frogs croaked. Other sounds, more ominous, rippled in deeper water. If a snake got him or a crocodile, Mama wouldn't care. She had Moses. He was the only one she loved now. She had forgotten all about her older son.

Aaron ached with loneliness, and his young heart burned with hatred for the brother who had taken his mother away. He wished the basket had sunk. He wished a crocodile had eaten him the way crocodiles had eaten all the other baby boys. He heard something coming through the reeds and tried to hide.

"Aaron?" Miriam appeared. "I've been looking all over for you! How did you find your way here?" When he raised his head, her eyes filled with tears. "Oh, Aaron . . ." She looked toward the palace, yearning. "Did you see Mama?"

He hung his head and sobbed. His sister's thin arms went around him, pulling him to her. "I miss her, too, Aaron," she whispered, her voice breaking. He rested his head against her. "But we have to go. We don't want to cause her trouble."

He was six when his mother came home alone one night, grieving. All she could do was cry and talk about Moses and Pharaoh's daughter. "She loves your brother. She'll be a kind mother to him. I must take comfort in that and forget she's a heathen. She'll educate him. He will grow up to be a great man someday." She balled up her shawl and pressed it to her mouth to stifle her sobs as she rocked back and forth. "He will come back to us someday." She was fond of saying that.

Aaron hoped Moses would never come back. He hoped never to see his brother again. *I hate him,* he wanted to scream. *I hate him for taking you away from me!*

"My son will be our deliverer." All she could talk about was her precious Moses, Israel's deliverer.

The seed of bitterness grew in Aaron until he couldn't stand to hear his brother's name. "Why did you come back at all?" he sobbed in rage one afternoon. "Why didn't you just stay with him if you love him so much?"

Miriam cuffed him. "Hold your tongue or Mama will think I've let you run wild while she was gone."

"She doesn't care about you any more than she cares about me!" he yelled at his sister. He faced his mother again. "I bet you didn't even cry when Papa died with his face in the mud. Did you?" Then, seeing the look on his mother's face, he ran. He ran all the way to the mud pits, where his job was to scatter straw for the workers to stomp into the mud in the making of bricks.

At least, she had spoken less of Moses after that. She had hardly spoken at all.

Now Aaron roused from the painful memories. He could see the heat through his eyelids, a shadow falling over him. Someone put a few drops of precious water to his lips as the past echoed around him. He was still confused, the past and present mingling.

"Even if the river spares him, Jochebed, whoever sees he's circumcised will know he is condemned to die."

"I will not drown my own son! I will not raise my hand against my own son, nor can you!" His mother wept as she placed his sleeping brother in the basket.

Surely God had mocked the Egyptian gods that day, for the Nile itself, the life's blood of Egypt, had carried his brother into the hands and heart of the daughter of Pharaoh, the very man who commanded all Hebrew boy babies be drowned. And furthermore the other Egyptian gods lurking along the shores of the Nile in the form of crocodiles and hippopotamuses had also failed to carry out Pharaoh's edict. But no one laughed. Far too many had died already and continued to die every day. Aaron sometimes thought the only reason the edict had eventually been lifted was to make sure Pharaoh had enough slaves to make his bricks, chisel his stone, and build his cities!

Why had his brother been the only one to survive? Was Moses to be Israel's deliverer?

Miriam had ruled Aaron's life, even after their mother had returned home. His sister had been as protective of him as a lioness over her cub. Even then, and despite the extraordinary events regarding Moses, the circumstances of Aaron's life didn't change. He learned to tend sheep. He carried straw to the mud pits. At six, he was scooping mud into buckets.

And while Aaron lived the life of a slave, Moses grew up in a palace. While Aaron was tutored by hard labor and abuse at the hands of taskmasters, Moses was taught to read and write and speak and live like an Egyptian. Aaron wore rags. Moses got to wear fine linen clothes. Aaron ate flat bread and whatever his mother and sister could grow in their small plot of hard, dry ground. Moses filled his belly with food served by slaves. Aaron worked in the heat of the sun, up to his knees in mud. Moses sat in cool stone corridors and was treated like an Egyptian prince despite his Hebrew blood. Moses led a life of ease instead of toil, freedom instead of slavery, abundance instead of want. Born a slave, Aaron knew he would die a slave.

Unless God delivered them.

Is Moses the one, Lord?

Envy and resentment had tormented Aaron almost all his life. But was it Moses' fault he had been taken from his family and raised by idol-worshiping foreigners?

Aaron didn't see Moses until years later when Moses stood in the doorway of their house. Their mother had come to her feet with a cry and rushed to embrace him. Aaron hadn't known what to think or feel, nor what to expect from a brother who looked like an Egyptian and knew no Hebrew at all. Aaron had resented him, and then been confused by Moses' desire to align himself with slaves. Moses could come and go as he pleased. Why had he chosen to come and live in Goshen? He could have been riding a chariot and hunting lions with other young men from Pharaoh's household. What did he hope to gain by working alongside slaves?

"You hate me, don't you, Aaron?"

Aaron understood Egyptian even though Moses didn't understand Hebrew. The question had given him pause. "No. Not hate." He hadn't felt anything but distrust. "What are you doing here?"

"I belong here."

Aaron had found himself furious at Moses' answer. "Did we all risk our lives so you could end up in a mud pit?"

"If I'm to try to free my people, shouldn't I get to know them?"

"Ah, so magnanimous."

"You need a leader."

Their mother defended Moses with every breath. "Didn't I tell you my son would choose his own people over our enemies?"

Wouldn't Moses be of more use in the palace speaking on behalf of the Hebrews? Did he think he would gain Pharaoh's respect by working alongside slaves? Aaron didn't understand Moses, and after years of disparity in the way they lived, he wasn't sure he liked him.

But why would he? What was Moses really after? Was he Pharaoh's spy sent to learn whether these wretched Israelites had plans to align themselves with Egypt's enemies? The thought may have occurred to them, but they knew they would fare no better at Philistine hands.

Where is God when we need Him? Far off, blind and deaf to our cries for deliverance!

Moses might have walked the great halls as the adopted son of Pharaoh's daughter, but he had inherited the Levite blood and the Levite temper. When he saw an Egyptian beating a Levite slave, he became a law unto himself. Aaron and several others watched in horror as Moses struck the Egyptian down. The others fled while Moses buried the body in the sand.

"Someone has to defend you!" Moses said as Aaron helped him hide the evidence of his crime. "Think of it. Thousands of slaves rising up against their masters. That's what the Egyptians fear, Aaron. That's why they load you down and try to kill you with work."

"Is this the kind of leader you want to be? Kill them as they kill us?" Was that the way to deliverance? Was their deliverer to be a warrior leading them into battle? Would he put a sword in their hands? The rage that had built over the years under slavery filled Aaron. Oh, how easy it would be to give in to it!

Word spread like fine sand blown before a desert wind, eventually reaching the ears of Pharaoh himself. When Hebrews fought among themselves the next day, Moses tried to intercede and found himself under attack. "Who appointed you to be our prince and judge? Do you plan to kill me as you killed that Egyptian yesterday?" The people didn't want Moses as their deliverer. In their eyes, he was an enigma, not to be trusted.

Pharaoh's daughter couldn't save Moses this time. How long could a man survive when he was hated and hunted by Pharaoh, and envied and despised by his brethren?

Moses disappeared into the wilderness and was never heard from again.

He didn't even have time to say good-bye to the mother who'd believed he had been born to deliver Israel from slavery. And Moses took their mother's hopes and dreams with him into the wilderness. She died within the year. The fate of Moses' Egyptian mother was unknown, but Pharaoh lived on and on, continuing to build his storage cities, monuments, and grandest of all, his tomb. It was scarcely finished when the sarcophagus containing Pharaoh's embalmed body was carried to the Valley of the Kings, followed by an entourage of thousands bearing golden idols, possessions, and provisions for an afterlife thought to be even grander than the one he had lived on earth.

Now Raamses wore the serpent crown and held a sword over their heads. Cruel and arrogant, he preferred grinding his heel into their backs instead. When Amram could not rise from the pit, he was smothered in the mud.

Aaron was eighty-three, a thin reed of a man. He knew he would die soon, and his sons after him, and their sons down through the generations.

Unless God delivered them.

Lord, Lord, why have You abandoned Your people?

Aaron prayed out of desperation and despair. It was the only freedom he had left, to cry out to God for help. Hadn't God made a covenant with Abraham and Isaac and Jacob? *Lord, Lord, hear my prayer! Help us!* If God existed, where was He? Did He see the bloody stripes on their backs, the worn-down, worn-out look in their eyes? Did he hear the cries of Abraham's children? Aaron's father and mother had clung to their faith in the unseen God. *Where else can we find hope, Lord? How long, O God, how long before You deliver us? Help us. God, why won't You help us?*

Aaron's father and mother had long since been buried beneath the sand. Aaron had obeyed his father's last wishes and married Elisheba, a daughter from among the tribe of Judah. She had given him four fine sons before she died. There were days when Aaron envied the dead. At least they were at rest. At least their unceasing prayers had finally stopped and God's silence no longer hurt.

Someone lifted his head and gave him water. "Father?"

Aaron opened his eyes and saw his son Eleazar above him. "God spoke to me." His voice was scarcely a whisper.

Eleazar leaned down. "I couldn't hear you, Father. What did you say?"

Aaron wept, unable to say more.

God had finally spoken, and Aaron knew his life would never be the same.

✦   ✦   ✦

Aaron gathered his four sons—Nadab, Abihu, Eleazar, and Ithamar—and his sister, Miriam, and told them God had commanded him to go to meet Moses in the wilderness.

"Our uncle is dead," Nadab said. "It was the sun speaking to you."

"It's been forty years, Father, without a word."

Aaron held up his hand. "Moses is alive."

"How do you know it was God who spoke to you, Father?" Abihu leaned forward. "You were out in the sun all day. It wouldn't be the first time the heat got to you."

"Are you sure, Aaron?" Miriam cupped her cheeks. "We have been hoping for so long."

"Yes. I'm certain. No one can imagine a voice like that. I cannot explain, nor do I have the time to try. You must all believe me!"

They all spoke at once.

"There are Philistines beyond the borders of Egypt."

"You can't survive in the wilderness, Father."

"What will we tell the other elders when they ask after you? They will want to know why we didn't stop our father from such folly."

"You won't make it to the trade route before you're stopped."

"And if you do, how will you survive?"

"Who will go with you?"

"Father, you're eighty-three years old!"

Eleazar put his hand on Aaron's arm. "I'll go with you, Father."

Miriam stamped her foot. "Enough! Let your father speak."

"No one will go with me. I go alone, and God will provide."

"How will you find Moses? The wilderness is a vast place. How will you find water?"

"And food. You can't carry enough for that kind of journey."

Miriam rose. "Would you try to talk your father out of what God instructed?"

"Sit, Miriam." His sister merely added to the confusion, and Aaron could speak for himself. "God called me to this journey; surely God will show me the way." Hadn't he prayed for years? Maybe Moses would know something. Maybe God was finally going to help His people. "I must trust in the God of Abraham, Isaac, and Jacob to lead me." He spoke with more confidence than he felt, for their questions troubled him. Why should they doubt his word? He must do as God said and go. Quickly, before courage failed him.

+   +   +

Carrying a skin of water, seven small loaves of unleavened barley bread, and his staff, Aaron left before the sun came up. He walked all day. He saw Egyptians, but they paid him no attention. Nor did he allow his steps to falter at the sight of them. God had given him purpose and hope. Weariness and desolation no longer oppressed him. He felt renewed as he walked. *God exists. God spoke.* God had told him where to go and whom he was to meet: Moses!

What would his brother be like? Had he spent all forty years in the wilderness? Did he have a family? Did Moses know Aaron was coming? Had God spoken to him as well? If not, what was he to say to Moses when he found him? Surely God would not send him so far without purpose at the end. But what purpose?

His questions made him think of other things. He slowed his steps, troubled. It had been easy to walk away. No one had stopped him. He had taken up his staff, shouldered a skin of water and a pouch of bread, and headed out into the desert. Maybe he should have brought Miriam and his sons with him.

No. No. He must do exactly as God said.

Aaron walked all day, day after day, and slept in the open at night, eyes on the stars overhead, alone in silence. Never had he been so alone, or felt so lonely. Thirsty, he sucked on a small flat stone to keep his mouth from going dry. How he wished he could raise his hand and have a boy run to him with a skin of water. His bread was almost gone. His stomach growled, but he was afraid to eat until later in the afternoon. He didn't know how far he had to go and whether his supply of bread would hold out. He didn't know what to eat out here in the desert. He didn't have the skills to hunt and kill animals. He was tired and hungry and beginning to wonder if he really had heard God's voice or just imagined it. How many more days? How far? The sun beat down relentlessly until he looked for escape in a cleft of rocks, miserable and exhausted. He couldn't remember the sound of God's voice.

Was it all his imagination, birthed by years of misery and a dying hope that a Savior would come and deliver him from slavery? Maybe his sons were right and he'd been suffering from the heat. He was certainly suffering now.

No. He had heard God's voice. He had been on the point of exhaustion and heatstroke many times in his life, but he had never heard a voice like that one:

Go out into the wilderness to meet Moses. Go. Go.

He set off again, walking until nightfall and finding a place to rest. The inexorable heat gave way to a chill that gnawed at his bones and made him shiver. When he slept, he dreamed of his sons sitting with him at the table, laughing and enjoying one another while Miriam served bread and meat, dried dates and wine. He awakened in despair. At least in Egypt, he had known what to expect; every day had been the same with overseers to regulate his life. He had been thirsty and hungry many times, but not as he was now, with no respite, no encouraging companion.

God, did You bring me out into the wilderness to kill me? There is no water, just this endless sea of rocks.

Aaron lost count of the days, but he took hope in that every day there seemed to be just enough water and food to keep him going. He headed north and then east into Midian, sustained by infrequent oases, and leaning more heavily on his staff with each day. He didn't know how far he had come, or how far he had to go. He only knew he would rather die in the wilderness than turn back now. What hope remained was fixed on finding his brother. He longed to see Moses as intently as he had longed for a long draught of water and hunk of bread.

When his water was down to a few drops and his bread was gone, he came to a wide plain before a jagged mountain. Was that a donkey and a small shelter? Aaron rubbed the sweat from his eyes and squinted. A man sat in the doorway. He stood, staff in hand, and came out into the open, his head turned toward Aaron. Hope made Aaron forgot his hunger and thirst. "Moses!" *Oh, Lord, Lord, let it be my brother!* "Moses!"

The man came toward him at a run, arms outstretched. "Aaron!"

It was like hearing the voice of God. Laughing, Aaron came down the rocky slope, his strength renewed like an eagle's. He was almost running when he reached his brother. They fell into one another's arms. "God sent me, Moses!" Laughing and sobbing, he kissed his brother. "God sent me to you!"

"Aaron, my brother!" Moses held tight, weeping. "God said you would come."

"Forty years, Moses. Forty years! We all thought you were dead."

"You were glad to see me go."

"Forgive me. I am glad to see you now." Aaron drank in the sight of his younger brother.

Moses had changed. He was no longer dressed like an Egyptian, but wore the long dark robes and head covering of a nomad. Swarthy, face lined with age, his dark beard streaked with white, he looked foreign and humbled by years of desert life.

Aaron had never been so glad to see anyone. "Oh, Moses, you are my brother. I am glad to see you alive and well." Aaron wept for the lost years.

Moses' eyes grew moist and tender. "The Lord God said you

would be. Come." He took Aaron by the arm. "You must rest and have something to eat and drink. You must meet my sons."

Moses' dark and foreign wife, Zipporah, served them. Moses' son Gershom sat with them, while Eliezer lay pale and sweating on a pallet at the back of the tent.

"Your son is ill."

"Zipporah circumcised him two days ago."

Aaron winced. *Eliezer* meant "my God is help." But in which God did Moses place his hope? Zipporah sat beside her son, dark eyes downcast, and dabbed his forehead with a damp cloth. Aaron asked why Moses had not done it himself when his son was eight days old as the Jews had done since the days of Abraham.

Moses bowed his head. "It is easier to remember the ways of your people when you dwell among them, Aaron. As I learned when I circumcised Gershom, Midianites consider the rite repugnant, and Jethro, Zipporah's father, is a priest of Midian." He looked at Aaron. "In deference to him, I did not circumcise Eliezer. When God spoke to me, Jethro gave me his blessing, and we left the tents of Midian. I knew my son must be circumcised. Zipporah argued against it and I delayed, not wanting to press my ways on her. I didn't see it as rebellion until the Lord Himself sought to take my life. I told Zipporah that unless my sons both bore the mark of the Covenant on their flesh, I would die and Eliezer would be cut off from God and His people. Only then did she herself take the flint to our son's flesh."

Troubled, Moses looked at the feverish boy. "My son would not even remember how the mark came to be on his flesh had I obeyed the Lord instead of bending to others. He suffers now because of my disobedience."

"He will heal soon, Moses."

"Yes, but I will remember the cost to others of my disobedience." Moses looked out the doorway to the mountain and then at Aaron. "I have much to tell you when you are not too tired to listen."

"My strength returned the moment I saw you."

Moses took up his staff and rose, and Aaron followed. When they stood in the open, Moses stopped. "The God of Abraham, Isaac, and Jacob appeared to me in a burning bush on that mountain," Moses said. "He has seen the affliction of Israel and is come to deliver them from the power of the Egyptians, to bring them into a land flowing with milk and honey. He is sending me to Pharaoh so that I may bring His people out of Egypt to worship Him at this mountain." Moses gripped his staff and rested his forehead against his hands as he spoke all the words the Lord had spoken to him on the mountain. Aaron felt the truth of them in his soul, drinking them in like water. *The Lord is sending Moses to deliver us!*

"I pleaded with the Lord to send someone else, Aaron. I said who am I to go to Pharaoh? I said my own people will not believe me. I told him I have never been eloquent, that I'm slow of speech and tongue." He let out his breath slowly and faced Aaron. "And the Lord whose name is I AM THE ONE WHO ALWAYS IS said you will be my spokesman."

Aaron felt a sudden rush of fear, but it subsided in the answer of a lifetime prayer. The Lord had heard the cry of His people. Deliverance was at hand. The Lord had seen their misery and was about to put an end to it. Aaron was too filled with emotion to speak.

"Do you understand what I'm saying to you, Aaron? I'm afraid of Pharaoh. I'm afraid of my own people. So the Lord has sent you to stand with me and be my spokesman."

The question hung unspoken between them. Was he willing to stand with Moses?

"I am your older brother. Who better to speak for you than I?"

"Are you not afraid, Brother?"

"What does a slave's life matter in Egypt, Moses? What has my life ever mattered? Yes, I'm afraid. I have been afraid all my life. I've bent my back to taskmasters, and felt the lash when I dared look up. I speak boldly enough in the privacy of my own house and among my brethren, but it comes to naught. Nothing changes. My words are but wind, and I thought my prayers were, too. Now, I know better. This time will be different. It won't be the words of a slave that are heard from my lips, but the Word of the Lord, the God of Abraham, Isaac, and Jacob!"

"If they don't believe us, the Lord has given me signs to show them." Moses told him how his staff had become a snake and his hand had become leprous. "And if that is not enough, when I pour water from the Nile, it will become blood."

Aaron didn't ask for a demonstration. "They will believe, just as I believe."

"You believe me because you are my brother, and because God sent you to me. You believe because God has changed your heart toward me. You have not always looked at me as you do now, Aaron."

"Yes, because I thought you were free when I wasn't."

"I never felt at home in Pharaoh's house. I wanted to be among my own people."

"And we scorned and rejected you." Perhaps it was living among two separate peoples and being accepted by neither that made Moses so humble. But he must do as God commanded, or the Hebrews would go on as before, toiling in the mud pits and dying with their faces in the dust. "God has chosen you to deliver us, Moses. And so you shall. Whatever God tells you, I will speak. If I have to shout, I will make the people hear."

Moses looked up at the mountain of God. "We will start for Egypt in the morning. We will gather the elders of Israel and tell them what the Lord has said. Then we will all go before Pharaoh and tell him to let God's people go into the wilderness

to sacrifice to the Lord our God." He shut his eyes as though
in pain.

"What is it, Moses? What's wrong?"

"The Lord will harden Pharaoh's heart and strike Egypt with
signs and wonders so that when we leave, we will not go empty-
handed, but with many gifts of silver, gold, and clothing."

Aaron laughed bitterly. "And so God will plunder Egypt as
Egypt plundered us! I never thought to see justice prevail in my
lifetime. It will be a joyous sight!"

"Do not be eager to see their destruction, Aaron. They are
people like us."

"Not like us."

"Pharaoh will not relent until his own firstborn son is dead.
Then he will let us go."

Aaron had been beneath the heel of Egyptian slave drivers
too long and had felt the lash too many times to feel pity for any
Egyptian, but he saw Moses did.

They set off at daylight, Zipporah taking charge of the donkey
carrying provisions and pulling a litter. Eliezer was improved,
but not well enough to walk with his mother and his brother.
Aaron and Moses walked ahead, each with a shepherd's staff
in hand.

✦   ✦   ✦

Heading north, they took the trade route between Egypt and
southern Canaan, traveling by way of Shur. It was more direct
than traveling south and west and then north through the
desert. Aaron wanted to hear everything the Lord had said to
Moses. "Tell me everything again. From the beginning." How
he wished he had been with Moses and seen the burning bush
for himself! He knew what it was to hear the sound of God's
voice, but to stand in His presence was beyond imagining.

When they reached Egypt, Aaron took Moses, Zipporah,

Gershom, and Eliezer into his house. Moses was overcome with
emotion when Miriam threw her arms around him and Aaron's
sons surrounded him. Aaron almost pitied Moses, for he saw
that Hebrew words still did not come easily to his brother, so he
spoke for him. "God has called Moses to deliver our people from
slavery. The Lord Himself will perform great signs and wonders
so that Pharaoh will let us go."

"Our mother prayed you were the promised one of God."
Miriam embraced Moses again. "She was certain when Pharaoh's daughter saved you that God was protecting you for
some great purpose."

Zipporah sat with her sons, watching from the corner of the
room, dark-eyed and troubled.

Aaron's sons went back and forth through Goshen, the
region of Egypt that had been given to the Hebrews centuries
earlier and in which they now lived in captivity. The men carried the message to the elders of Israel that God had sent them
a deliverer and the elders were to gather and hear his message
from God.

Meanwhile, Aaron talked and prayed with his brother. He
could see him struggling against fear of Pharaoh and the people
and the call of God on him. Moses had little appetite. And he
looked more tired when he rose in the morning than when he
had retired to bed the evening before. Aaron did his best to
encourage him. Surely that was why God had sent him to find
Moses. He loved his brother. He was strengthened at his presence and eager to serve.

"You give me the words God speaks to you, Moses, and I
will speak them. You will not go alone before Pharaoh. We go
together. And surely the Lord Himself will be with us."

"How is it you have no fear?"

No fear? Less perhaps. Moses had not grown up suffering physi-
cal oppression. He hadn't lived longing for the promise of God's

intervention. Nor had he been surrounded by fellow slaves and
family members who relied on each other for strength just to survive each day. Had Moses ever known love other than those first
few years at his mother's breast? Had Pharaoh's daughter regretted
adopting him? In what position had her rebellion against Pharaoh
placed her, and what repercussions had it caused Moses?

It occurred to Aaron that he had never thought of these
things before, too caught up in his own feelings, petty resent-
ments, and childish jealousies. Unlike Moses, he hadn't grown
up as the adopted son of Pharaoh's daughter among people who
despised him. Had Moses learned to keep out of sight and say
little in order to survive? Aaron hadn't been caught between
two worlds and accepted in neither. He hadn't sought to align
himself with his people, only to find they hated him as well.
Nor had he needed to run away from Egyptian and Hebrew
alike and seek refuge among foreigners in order to stay alive.
Nor had he spent years alone in the desert tending sheep.

Why had he never thought of these things before? Was it
only now that his mind and heart were open to consider what
Moses' life must have been like? Aaron was filled with compassion for his brother. He ached to help him, to press him
forward to the task God had given him. For the Lord Himself
said Moses was to be Israel's deliverer, and Aaron knew God
had sent him to stand beside his brother and do whatever
Moses could not do.

Lord, You have heard our cry!

"Ah, Moses, I've spent my life in fear, bowing and scraping
before overseers and taskmasters, and still getting the lash
when I failed to work fast enough for them. And now, for the
first time in my life, I have hope." Tears came in a flood. "Hope
casts out fear, Brother. We have God's promise that the day of
our salvation is at hand! The people will rejoice when they hear,
and Pharaoh will cower before the Lord."

Moses' eyes were filled with sorrow. "He won't listen."

"How can he not listen when he sees the signs and wonders?"

"I grew up with Raamses. He is arrogant and cruel. And now that he sits on the throne, he believes he is god. He won't listen, Aaron, and many will suffer because of him. Our people will suffer and so will his."

"Pharaoh will see the truth, Moses. Pharaoh will come to know that the Lord is God. And that truth will set us free."

Moses wept.

+   +   +

Israel gathered, and Aaron spoke all the words the Lord gave to Moses. The crowd was dubious, some outspoken and some derisive. "This is your brother who murdered the Egyptian and ran away, and he is to deliver us from Egypt? Are you out of your mind? God would not use a man such as he!"

"What's he doing back here? He's more Egyptian than Hebrew!"

"He's a Midianite now!"

Some laughed.

Aaron felt the rush of hot blood. "Show them, Moses. Give them a sign!"

Moses threw his staff on the ground and it became a huge cobra. The people cried out and scattered. Moses reached down and took the snake by the tail and it became his staff again. The people closed in around him. "There are other signs! Show them, Moses." Moses put his hand inside his cloak and drew it out, leprous. The people gasped and recoiled from him. When he tucked his hand inside his cloak and drew it out as clean as a newborn child's, they cried out in jubilation.

There was no need for Moses to touch his staff to the Nile and turn it to blood, for the people were already shouting with joy. "Moses! Moses!"

Aaron raised his arms, his staff in one hand and shouted,

"Praise be to God who has heard our prayers for deliverance! All praise be to the God of Abraham, Isaac, and Jacob!"

The people cried out with him and fell to their knees, bowing low and worshiping the Lord.

But when asked, the elders of Israel refused to go before Pharaoh. It was left to Aaron and Moses to go alone.

✦ ✦ ✦

Aaron felt smaller and weaker with each step inside Thebes, Pharaoh's city. He had never had reason to come here amid the bustle of markets and crowded streets that stood in the shadow of the immense stone buildings that housed Pharaoh, his counselors, and the gods of Egypt. He had spent his life in Goshen, toiling beneath overseers and toiling to eke out his own existence through crops and a small flock of sheep and goats. Who was he to think he could stand before mighty Pharaoh and speak for Moses? Everyone said that even as a small boy, Raamses had shown the arrogance and cruelty of his predecessors. Who dared thwart the ruling god of all Egypt? Especially an old man of eighty-three, as he was, and his younger brother of eighty!

I am sending you to Pharaoh. You will lead my people, the Israelites, out of Egypt.

Lord, give me courage, Aaron prayed silently. *You have said that I am to be Moses' spokesman, but all I can see are the enemies around me, the wealth and power everywhere I look. Oh, God, Moses and I are like two old grasshoppers come to the court of a king. Pharaoh has the power to crush us beneath his heel. How can I give Moses courage when my own fails me?*

He could smell the rankness of Moses' sweat. It was the smell of terror. His brother had hardly slept for fear of standing before his own people. Now he was inside the city with its thousands of inhabitants, its enormous buildings and magnificent statues of Pharaoh and the gods of Egypt. He had come to speak to Pharaoh!

"Do you know where to go?"

"We are almost there." Moses said nothing more.

Aaron wanted to encourage him, but how, when he was fighting the fear threatening to overwhelm him? *Oh, God, will I be able to speak when my brother, who knows so much more than I do, is shaking like a bruised reed beside me? Don't let any man crush him, Lord. Whatever comes, please give me breath to speak and the spine to stand firm.*

He smelled smoke laden with incense and remembered Moses talking about the fire that burned without consuming the bush, and the Voice that had spoken to him from the fire. Aaron remembered the Voice. He thought of it now and his fear lessened. Had not Moses' staff turned to a snake before his eyes and his hand shriveled with leprosy, only to be healed as well? Such was God's power! He thought of the cries of the people, cries of thanksgiving and jubilation that the Lord had seen their affliction and had sent Moses to deliver them from slavery.

Still . . .

Aaron looked up at the enormous buildings with their massive pillars and wondered at the power of those who had designed and built them.

Moses paused before a huge stone gate. On each side were carved beasts—twenty times the size of Aaron—standing guard.

Oh, Lord, I am but a man. I believe. I do! Rid me of my doubts!

Aaron tried not to stare around him as he walked beside Moses to the entrance of the great building where Pharaoh held court. Aaron spoke to one of the guards and they were brought inside. The hum of many voices rose like bees amid the huge columns. The walls and ceilings were resplendent with colorful scenes of the gods of Egypt. Men stared at him and Moses, frowning in distaste and drawing back, whispering.

Aaron's palm sweated as he held tight to his staff. He felt conspicuous in his long robe and woven sash, the woven shawl that covered his head dusty from their journey. He and his brother looked strange among these other men in their short fitted tunics and elaborate wigs. Some wore long tunics, ornate robes, and gold amulets. Such wealth! Such beauty! Aaron had never imagined anything like this.

When Aaron saw Pharaoh sitting on a throne flanked by two huge statues of Osiris and Isis, he could only stare at the man's magnificence. Everything about him announced his power and wealth. He glanced disdainfully at Aaron and Moses and said something to his guard. The guard straightened and spoke. "Why have you come before mighty Pharaoh?"

Moses lowered his eyes, trembling, and said nothing.

Aaron heard someone whisper, "What are these stinking old Hebrew slaves doing here?" Heat filled him at their contempt. Uncovering his head, he stepped forward. "This is what the Lord, the God of Israel, says: 'Let My people go, for they must go out into the wilderness to hold a religious festival in My honor.'"

Pharaoh laughed. "Is that so?" Others joined in. "Look at these two old slaves standing before me, demanding that their people be released." The officials laughed. Pharaoh waved his hand as though brushing aside a minor irritation. "And who is the Lord that I should listen to Him and let Israel go? Let you go? Why would I do that? Who would do the work you were born to do?" He smiled coldly. "I don't know the Lord, and I will not let Israel go."

Aaron felt the anger rise in him. "The God of the Hebrews has met with us," he declared. "Let us take a three-day trip into the wilderness so we can offer sacrifices to the Lord our God. If we don't, we will surely die by disease or the sword."

"What does it matter to me if a few slaves die? Hebrews reproduce like rabbits. There will be more to replace those who die of pestilence." Counselors and visitors laughed as Pharaoh continued to mock them.

Aaron's face burned, his heart thundered.

Pharaoh's eyes narrowed as Aaron stared up at him. "I have heard about you, Aaron and Moses." The ruler of Egypt spoke quietly, his tone filled with threat.

Aaron felt chilled that Pharaoh knew him by name.

"Who do you think you are," Pharaoh shouted, "distracting the people from their tasks? Get back to work! Look, there are many people here in Egypt, and you are stopping them from doing their work."

As the guards moved closer, Aaron's hand clenched his shepherd's staff. If any man tried to take hold of Moses, he would receive a clubbing.

"We must go, Aaron," Moses said under his breath. Aaron obeyed.

Standing in the hot Egyptian sun once again, Aaron shook his head. "I thought he would listen."

"I told you he wouldn't." Moses let out his breath slowly and bowed his head. "This is only the beginning of our tribulation."

✦   ✦   ✦

An order came quickly from the taskmasters that straw would no longer be given them to make bricks, but that they would have to scrounge for their own. And the quota of bricks would not be lessened! They were told Pharaoh's reason. The ruler of Egypt thought them lazy because Moses and Aaron had cried out to let them go and sacrifice to their god.

"We thought you were going to deliver us, and all you asked was that we be allowed to go for a few days and sacrifice!"

"Away with you!"

"You have made our lives even more unbearable!"

When the foremen among the sons of Israel were beaten for

not completing their required number of bricks, they went to
Pharaoh to beg for justice and mercy. Moses and Aaron went to
meet them. When they came out, the foremen were bloodied
and worse off than before.

"Because of you Pharaoh believes we are lazy! You have
caused us nothing but trouble! May the Lord judge you for getting us into this terrible situation with Pharaoh and his officials.
You have given them an excuse to kill us!"

Aaron was appalled at their accusations. "The Lord will
deliver us!"

"Oh, yes, He will deliver us. Right into Pharaoh's hands!"

Some spit at Moses as they walked away.

Aaron despaired. He believed the Lord had spoken to Moses
and promised to deliver the people. "What do we do now?" He
had thought it would be easy. One word from the Lord and the
chains of slavery would fall away. Why was God punishing
them again? Hadn't they been punished enough all these long
years in Egypt?

"I must pray." Moses spoke quietly. He looked so old and
confused, Aaron was afraid. "I must ask the Lord why He ever
sent me to Pharaoh to speak in His name, for He has only done
harm to this people and not delivered them at all."

✦   ✦   ✦

The people Aaron had known all his life glared at him and
whispered as he walked by. "You should have kept your mouth
shut, Aaron. Your brother was out in the desert too long."

"Speaking to God! Who does he think he is?"

"He's mad. You should've known better, Aaron!"

God had spoken to him as well. Aaron knew he had heard
the voice of God. He knew. No one would make him doubt that!

But why hadn't Moses thrown down his staff and shown
Pharaoh the signs and wonders the moment they were in the

ruler's presence? He asked Moses about it. "The Lord will tell us what to say and what to do, and when we are not to do anything less or more than that."

Satisfied, Aaron waited, ignoring the taunts and watching over Moses while he prayed. Aaron was too tired to pray, but he found himself distracted by concerns about the people. How could he convince them that God had sent Moses? What could he say to make them listen?

Moses came to him. "The Lord has spoken again: 'Now you will see what I will do to Pharaoh. When he feels my powerful hand upon him, he will let the people go. In fact, he will be so anxious to get rid of them that he will force them to leave his land!'"

Aaron gathered the people, but they wouldn't listen. Moses tried to speak to them, but stammered and then fell silent when they shouted at him. Aaron shouted back. "The Lord will deliver us! He will establish a covenant with us, to give us the land of Canaan, the land we came from. Isn't this what we have waited for all our lives? Have we not prayed for a deliverer to come? The Lord has heard our groaning. He has remembered us! He is the Lord and He will bring us out from under the burdens the Egyptians have put on us. He will deliver us from slavery and redeem us with great judgments with an outstretched arm!"

"Where is his outstretched arm? I don't see it!"

Someone shoved Aaron. "If you say anything more to Pharaoh, he will kill us all. But not before we kill you."

Aaron saw the rage in their eyes and tasted fear.

"Send Moses back where he came from!" another shouted.

"Your brother has caused us nothing but trouble since he came here!"

Despondent, Aaron gave up arguing with them and followed Moses out into the land of Goshen. He stayed close, but not too close, listening intently for God's voice and hearing only Moses speaking low, beseeching God for answers. Aaron covered his head and squatted, his staff held across his knees. However long it took, he would wait for his brother.

Moses stood, face to the heavens. "Aaron."

Aaron raised his head and blinked. It was near twilight. He sat up, gripped his staff, and rose. "The Lord has spoken to you."

"We are to speak to Pharaoh again."

Aaron smiled grimly. "This time—" he instilled confidence into his voice—"this time, Pharaoh will listen to the Word of the Lord."

"He will not listen, Aaron. Not until the Lord has multiplied His signs and wonders. God will lay His hand on Egypt and bring out His people by great judgments."

Aaron was troubled, but tried not to show it. "I will say whatever words you give me, Moses, and do whatever you command. I know the Lord speaks through you."

Aaron knew, but would Pharaoh ever realize it?

✦   ✦   ✦

When they returned to the house, Aaron told their families they were going to stand before Pharaoh again.

"The people will stone us!" Nadab and Abihu argued. "You haven't been to the brick fields lately, Father. You haven't seen how they treat us. You're only going to make things worse for us."

"Pharaoh didn't listen the last time. What makes you think he'll listen now? All he cares about is bricks for his cities. Do you think he'll let his laborers go?"

"Where is your faith?" Miriam was angry with all of them. "We have been waiting for this day since Jacob set foot in this country. We don't belong in Egypt!"

As the arguments swirled around him, Aaron saw Moses

drawn away by his wife. Zipporah was as upset as the rest of them and speaking low. She shook her head, drawing her sons close.

Miriam reminded Aaron's sons again of how the Lord had protected Moses when he was put into the Nile, how it had been a miracle that the old pharaoh's own daughter had found him and adopted him. "I was there. I saw how the Lord's hand has been on him since he was born."

Abihu was unconvinced. "And if Pharaoh doesn't listen this time, how do you suppose we'll all be treated?"

Nadab stood, impatient. "Half of my friends won't even speak to me now."

Aaron blushed at his sons' lack of faith. "The Lord has spoken to Moses."

"Did the Lord speak to *you?*"

"The Lord told Moses we are to go to Pharaoh, and to Pharaoh we must go!" He waved his hand. "All of you, out! Go tend the sheep and goats."

Zipporah went out quietly behind them, her sons close at her side.

Moses sat at the table with Aaron and folded his hands. "Zipporah is returning to her father, and taking my sons with her."

"Why?"

"She says she has no place here."

Aaron felt the rush of blood to his face. He had noticed how Miriam treated Zipporah. He had talked with her about it already.

"Let her share your work, Miriam."

"I don't need her help."

"She needs something to do."

"She can do as she wishes and go where she likes."

"She is Moses' wife and the mother of his sons. She is our sister now."

"She is not our sister. She is a foreigner!" Miriam said in hushed tones. "She is a Midianite."

"And what are we but slaves? Moses had to flee Egypt and Goshen. Did you expect him not to marry or have children of his own? She is the daughter of a priest."

"And that makes her suitable? Priest of what god? Not the God of Abraham, Isaac, and Jacob."

"It is the Lord God of Abraham, Isaac, and Jacob who has called Moses here."

"A pity Moses didn't leave his wife and sons where they belong." She rose and turned her back.

Angry, Aaron stood. "And where do you belong, Miriam— you without a husband and sons to take care of you?"

She faced him, eyes hot and moist. "*I* was the one who watched over Moses while he drifted on the Nile. *I* was the one who spoke to Pharaoh's daughter so our brother was given back to Mother until he was weaned. And if that is not enough, who became mother to your sons when Elisheba died? Lest you forget, Aaron, I am your *older* sister, firstborn of Amram and Jochebed. I had much to do with taking care of you as well."

Sometimes there was no reasoning with his sister. It was better to let her think things through for herself and keep peace in the family. Given time, Miriam would accept Moses' sons, if not his wife.

"I will speak with Miriam again, Moses. Zipporah is your wife. Her place is here with you."

"It is not only Miriam, Brother. Zipporah is afraid of our people. She says they blow hot and change direction like the wind. She has already seen that the people won't listen to me. Nor are they willing to listen to you. She understands that I must do as God tells me, but she is afraid for our sons and says she will be safer living in her father's tents than in the houses of Israel."

Were their women destined to make trouble? "Is she asking you to return with her?"

"No. She only asks that I give my blessing. And I have. She will take my sons, Gershom and Eliezer, back to Midian. She has spent her life in the desert. They will be safe with Jethro." His eyes filled with tears. "If God is willing, they will be returned to me when Israel has been delivered from Egypt."

Aaron knew from his brother's words that worse times were ahead. Moses was sending Zipporah home to her people, home to safety. Aaron would not have that luxury. Miriam and his own sons would have to remain and endure whatever hardships came. Hebrews had no alternative but to hope and pray that the day of deliverance would come swiftly.

"SHOW me a miracle!" Pharaoh raised his hand and smirked. The laughter rippling in the great chamber left a hollow echo in Aaron's chest. The ruler's smug pride was evidence he felt no threat from an unseen God. After all, Raamses was the divine child of Osiris and Isis, wasn't he? And, indeed, Raamses looked godlike in all his finery as he rested his hands on the arms of his throne. "Impress us with the power of your invisible god of slaves. Show me what your god can do."

"Aaron." Moses' voice quavered. "Th-throw . . ."

"Speak up, Moses!" Raamses mocked him. "We can't hear you."

"Throw d-down your shepherd's staff."

The laughter grew louder. Those closest imitated Moses' stammer.

Aaron's face went hot. Furious, he stepped forward. *Lord, show these mockers that You alone are God and there is no other! Let Israel's oppressor see Your power!*

Aaron moved in front of Moses to shield his brother from the sneering crowd and looked straight at Pharaoh. He would not cower before this despicable tyrant who laughed at God's anointed prophet and ground his heel into Hebrew backs!

Pharaoh's eyes narrowed coldly, for who dared look Pharaoh in the face? Aaron did not look away as he held his staff up in challenge, and then tossed it to the stone floor in front of the ruler of all Egypt. The moment it hit, it transformed into a cobra, the very symbol of power Pharaoh wore on his crown.

Gasping, servants and officials drew back. The snake moved with ominous grace, head rising as the cape of skin spread and revealed a mark on the back of its head, a mark unlike any other. The snake hissed and the sound filled the chamber. Aaron's skin prickled from head to foot.

"Are you all afraid of this sorcerer's trick?" Pharaoh looked around the room in disgust. "Where are my magicians?" The cobra moved toward Pharaoh. At a flick of his hand, four guards moved in front of their ruler, spears down and ready to jab if the snake came any closer. "Enough of this! Send for my magicians!" Running footsteps echoed off the stone as several men entered from each side, bowing low to Pharaoh. He waved his hand imperiously. "Deal with this farce. Show these cowards it is a trick!"

Uttering incantations, the sorcerers came toward the snake. They tossed their staffs on the floor, and their staffs also transformed into snakes. The floor teemed with serpents! But as each raised its evil head, the Lord's struck hard and fast, swallowing one after another.

"It's a trick!" Pharaoh paled when the great cobra seemed to fix its dark, unblinking eyes on him. "A trick, I say!" It moved toward him.

Moses gripped Aaron's arm. "Take hold of it."

Aaron longed to see that cobra strike Pharaoh, but he did as his brother said. Heart thumping, sweat trickling down the back of his neck, he stepped forward, leaned down, and grasped the snake in the middle. The cool scaly skin and muscle of the cobra hardened into wood, straightening into his staff. Aaron stood tall before Pharaoh, staff raised, his fear gone in the rush of awe. "The Lord God says, *'Let My people go!'*"

"Escort them out." Pharaoh waved them away like flies. "We've had enough entertainment for today."

Guards flanked them. Moses bowed his head and turned away. Aaron followed, teeth clenched. He heard the whispered insults as the Egyptians blasphemed God.

"Whoever heard of an invisible god?"

"Only slaves would think of anything so ridiculous."

"One god? Should we fear one god? We have *hundreds* of gods!"

Resentment and bitterness over the years of slavery and abuse filled Aaron. *It's not over!* He wanted to shout back at them. *"Many signs and wonders,"* Moses had told him. This was only the beginning of the war God was waging on Egypt. His father, Amram, had waited for this day, and his father before him and his father before him. The day of deliverance!

The guard left them at the entrance. Aaron put his hand on Moses' shoulder. His brother was trembling! "I know fear, too, Moses. I've lived with it all my life." How many times had he cowered before a taskmaster's whip or looked at the ground rather than allow those above him to see his true feelings? Aaron squeezed tightly, wanting to give comfort. "They will mourn the day they treated God's anointed with such contempt."

"It is God they reject, Aaron. I am nothing."

"You are God's prophet!"

"They do not understand, any more than our own people understand."

Aaron knew the Hebrews treated Moses with as much contempt as Pharaoh had. He bowed his head and let his hand hang at his side. "God speaks through you. I *know* He does. And God *will* deliver us." He was as certain of that as he was that the sun would go down tonight and come up again in the morning. The Lord would deliver Israel by signs and wonders. He didn't know how or when, but he knew it would happen just as the Lord had said it would.

Aaron shuddered at the power that had turned his staff into a cobra. He ran his thumb over the carved wood. Had he imagined what had just happened? Everyone in that great chamber had seen the Lord's cobra swallow those brought forth by Pharaoh's sorcerers, and *still* they dismissed God's power as nothing.

Moses stopped along the road to Goshen. The hair prickled on the back of Aaron's neck. "The Lord has spoken to you."

Moses looked at him. "We are to go to the Nile and wait near

Pharaoh's house. We will speak with him again tomorrow morning. This is what you are to say. . . ."

Aaron listened to Moses' instructions as they walked along the riverbank. He did not question his brother or press him for more information once the command was given. When they came near Pharaoh's house, Moses rested. Weary, Aaron squatted and covered his head. The heat was intense this time of day, making him lethargic. He watched as shimmering light danced on the surface of the river. Across the way, men were cutting reeds that would be woven into mats and pounded and soaked into papyrus. On this side of the river, near Pharaoh's house, the reeds were left untouched.

Frogs croaked. An ibis stood motionless, feet spread, head down, waiting for prey. Aaron remembered his mother weeping as she placed Moses in the basket. Eighty years had passed since that morning, and yet Aaron remembered it now as clearly as if it had happened this morning. He could almost hear the echo of other weeping mothers as they obeyed the old pharaoh's law and gave up their infant sons to the river. The Nile, Egypt's river of life, controlled by the god Hapi, had run with Hebrew blood as crocodiles grew fat during those years. His eyes filled with tears as he looked out over the Nile. He doubted Pharaoh would feel any remorse over what had happened to the Hebrew babies eighty years ago on the banks of this river. But perhaps his historians would remember and explain after tomorrow. If they dared.

God, where were You when the old pharaoh was making us cast our children into the brown, silt-rich waters of the Nile? I was born two years before the edict or I, too, would be dead. Surely, it was You who watched over Moses and allowed him to drift into the hands of one of the few who held sway over Pharaoh. Lord, I don't understand why You let us suffer so much. I never will. But I will do whatever You say. Whatever You tell Moses to do and he tells me, that will I do.

Moses walked along the shore. Aaron rose to follow. He did not want to think of those days of death, but they often came to him, filling him with helpless wrath and endless despair. But now, the Lord God of Abraham, Isaac, and Jacob had spoken to a man again. God had sent Aaron into the wilderness to find Moses, and He had told Moses to lead His people from Egypt. Finally, after centuries of silence, the Lord had promised an end to Israel's misery.

And revenge would come with freedom!

Help me stand tall beside my brother tomorrow, Lord. Help me not to give in to my fear before Pharaoh. You have said Moses is the one to deliver our people. So be it. But please, Lord, don't let him stammer like a fool before Pharaoh. Moses speaks Your words. Give him courage, Lord. Don't let him tremble for all to see. Please give him strength and courage to show everyone that he is Your prophet, that he is the one You have chosen to bring Your people out of bondage.

Aaron covered his face. Would the Lord hear his prayer?

Moses turned to him. "We will sleep here tonight." They were only a short distance from Pharaoh's house on the river, only calling distance from the platform where the barge would dock and board Egypt's ruler for a journey up the Nile to visit temples of lesser gods. "When Pharaoh comes out at first light to make his offerings to the Nile, you will speak to him again." Moses repeated the words the Lord had given him for Aaron to say.

Torn between fear and eagerness for morning, Aaron slept little that night. He listened to the crickets and frogs and the rustle of reeds. When he did finally sleep, he heard the dark voices of the river gods whispering threats.

Moses shook him awake. "It will be sunrise soon."

Bones aching, Aaron stretched and stood. "Have you been up all night?"

"I could not sleep."

They looked at one another and then went down to the river and drank their fill. Aaron walked shoulder to shoulder with his brother to the stone landing at the river's edge. The moon and stars shone overhead, but the horizon was turning lapis. Before the first golden beams emerged, Pharaoh emerged from his house, his priests and servants in attendance, all in readiness to welcome Ra, father of the kings of Egypt, whose chariot ride across the sky brought the sunlight.

Pharaoh paused when he saw them. "Why do you trouble your people, Aaron and Moses?" Pharaoh stood arms akimbo. "Why do you give them false hope? You must tell them all to go back to work."

Without his cape of gold and jewels and the double crown of Egypt, Pharaoh looked smaller, more like a man. Perhaps it was because he stood in the open rather than inside that huge chamber with its massive columns and vibrant paintings, surrounded by his finely dressed servants and sycophants.

Aaron's fear evaporated. "The Lord, the God of the Hebrews, has sent me to say, 'Let My people go, so they can worship Me in the wilderness.' Until now, you have refused to listen to Him. Now the Lord says, 'You are going to find out that I am the Lord.' Look! I will hit the water of the Nile with this staff, and the river will turn to blood. The fish in it will die, and the river will stink. The Egyptians will not be able to drink any water from the Nile."

Aaron struck the water with his staff, and the Nile ran red and smelled of blood.

"It is another trick, great Pharaoh!" A magician pressed his way forward. "I will show you." He called for his assistant to bring a bowl of water. Uttering incantations, the magician sprinkled granules and turned water to blood. Aaron shook his head. A bowl of water was not the Nile River! But Pharaoh had already made up his mind. Turning his back on them, he walked up the steps and went into his house, leaving his magicians and sorcerers to deal with the problem.

"We will return to Goshen." Moses turned away.

Aaron heard the priests making supplications to Hapi, calling on the god of the Nile to change the river back to water again. But the river continued to run blood and dead fish floated on the surface.

Every water vessel of stone or wood was filled with blood! All Egypt suffered. Even the Hebrews had to dig pits around the Nile to find water fit to drink. Day after day, Pharaoh's priests called to Hapi and then to Khnum, the giver of the Nile, to help them. They called to Sothis, god of the Nile floodwaters, to wash away the blood and fight against the invisible god of the Hebrews who challenged their authority. The priests made offerings and sacrifices, but still the land reeked of blood and rotting fish.

Aaron had not expected to suffer along with the Egyptians. He had been thirsty before, but never like this. *Why, God? Why must we suffer along with our oppressors?*

"The Egyptians shall know that the Lord is God," Moses said.

"But we know already!" Miriam paced in distress. "Why must we suffer more than we have already?"

Only Moses was calm. "We must examine ourselves. Are there any among us who have embraced other gods? We must cast out their idols and make ready for the Lord our God."

Aaron felt the heat flood his face. Idols! There were idols everywhere. After four centuries of living in Egypt, they had made their way inside Hebrew households!

The stench of blood turned Aaron's stomach. His tongue clove to the roof of his mouth as he stood at the edge of the pit his sons had helped dig. Moisture slowly seeped into cups. The water tasted of silt and sand, leaving grit between his teeth. His only solace was knowing that Egyptian taskmasters and overseers were now suffering the same thirst he had every day he had worked in the mud pits and brick fields.

The Israelites wailed in despair. "How long, Moses? How long will this plague last?"

"Until the Lord lifts His hand."

On the seventh day, the Nile ran clean.

But even Aaron's neighbors talked about which god or gods might have made the waters drinkable again. If not Hapi, then maybe Sothis, god of the Nile floodwaters, or perhaps the gods of each village had joined together!

"We are to return to Pharaoh."

"Signs and wonders," Moses had said. How many signs? How many wonders? And would Hebrews have to suffer everything the Egyptians suffered? Where was the justice in that?

A plague of frogs this time, dozens, then hundreds, then thousands.

Pharaoh was unimpressed. So were his sorcerers, who were quick to point out, "It is a small matter to make frogs come from the river."

Aaron longed to call out, "Yes, but can you stop them?" As the barge was poled out from the shore, the magicians and sorcerers remained beside the Nile, casting spells and calling on Heket, the frog goddess, to stop the plague of frogs. The frogs kept coming until they were a hopping, writhing mass along the shores of the Nile. They hopped into courts and houses and fields. They hopped up from streams. They hopped out of pools where no frogs had been. They hopped into kneading bowls and ovens.

Even in the land of Goshen.

Aaron could not stretch out on his mat without sweeping frogs away! The croak and rustle were maddening. He prayed as fervently as any Egyptian for respite from this plague, but the frogs kept coming.

Miriam flung another frog out the door. "Why did God see fit to send these frogs into our house?"

"I wonder." Aaron looked pointedly toward their neighbor, shrieking as she beat frogs to death with her statue of Heket.

✦ ✦ ✦

Flanked by soldiers, Aaron and Moses were escorted respectfully to the palace this time. Aaron heard Pharaoh before he saw him. Shouting curses, he kicked a frog away from the throne. Croaking and ribbeting echoed in the great chamber. Aaron smiled faintly. Clearly, Heket had failed to recall her frogs to the waters of the Nile.

Pharaoh glared. "Plead with the Lord to take the frogs away from me and my people. I will let the people go, so they can offer sacrifices to the Lord."

Triumphant, Aaron looked at Moses for the words to speak, but Moses spoke this time, quietly and with great dignity. "You set the time!" Moses replied. "Tell me when you want me to pray for you, your officials, and your people. I will pray that you and your houses will be rid of the frogs."

"Do it tomorrow!" Pharaoh leaned back in his throne and then jerked forward, snatched a frog from behind him and heaved it against the wall.

Perhaps the ruler still held out hope that his priests would prevail, though it was clear to all present that the number of frogs was increasing exponentially.

"All right," Moses replied, "it will be as you have said. Then you will know that no one is as powerful as the Lord our God."

The Lord answered Moses' prayer. The frogs stopped coming. But they didn't return to the waters from which they came. They died in the fields, streets, houses, and kneading bowls of

Egyptian and Hebrew alike. The people gathered the carcasses and piled them in heaps. The stench of rotting frogs lay like a cloud over the land.

The smell didn't bother Aaron. In a few days, he figured they would be out in the desert, breathing fresh air and worshiping the Lord.

Moses sat in silence, his prayer shawl over his head.

Miriam sewed sacks in which to carry grain. "Why are you so downcast, Moses? Pharaoh agreed to let us go."

The next morning, Pharaoh's soldiers arrived. When they left, the Hebrew taskmasters ordered the people back to work.

Joy quickly turned to rage and despair. The people blamed Moses and Aaron for giving Pharaoh an excuse to make their lives even more unbearable.

Go back . . .

Aaron and Moses obeyed the Lord.

Pharaoh sat smug. "Why should I let you go? It was Heket who stopped the plague of frogs, not your god. Who is your god that I should let the slaves go free? There is work to be done, and the Hebrew slaves will do it!"

Aaron saw his brother's calm ripple. "Stretch out your staff, Aaron, and strike the dust of the earth!"

Aaron obeyed, and swarms of gnats came up as numerous as the particles of dust he'd stirred, invading the flesh and clothing of those watching, including Pharaoh himself.

Aaron and Moses departed.

People poured into the shrines of Geb and Aker, gods over the earth, and gave offerings to pay for relief.

No relief came.

Aaron sat waiting with Moses near Pharaoh's palace. How long before the wretched man relented?

A pleading Egyptian official approached one afternoon.

"Great Pharaoh's magicians tried to bring forth gnats and couldn't. Pharaoh's sorcerers say this is the finger of your god who has brought this upon us." Shuddering, he scratched the hair beneath his wig. His neck showed angry welts and scabs. "Pharaoh won't listen to them. He has told them to keep offering to the gods." He uttered a frustrated groan and scratched at his chest.

Aaron cocked his head. "If this is but God's finger, consider what God's hand can do."

The man fled.

"We are to rise early in the morning," Moses said, "and present ourselves before Pharaoh as he goes down to the river."

Aaron was torn between dread and excitement. "Pharaoh will let us go this time, Moses. Pharaoh and his counselors will see that they and all the gods of Egypt cannot prevail against the God of our people."

"Raamses will not let us go, Aaron. Not yet! But only Egypt will suffer this time. The Lord will make a distinction between Egypt and Israel."

"Thanks be to God, Moses. Our people will listen now. They will see that the Lord has sent you to deliver us. They will listen to us and do as you say, for you will be as God to them."

"I do not want to be as God to them! It was never in my mind to lead anyone. I begged the Lord to choose someone else, to let another speak. You have seen how I tremble before Raamses. I am more afraid of speaking before men than I am of facing a lion or a bear in the wilderness. That's why the Lord brought you to stand beside me. When I saw you standing on the hill, I knew there would be no turning back. But the people must put their trust in the Lord, not in me. The Lord is our deliverer!"

Aaron knew why God had sent him to his brother. To encourage him, not just be his spokesman. "Yes, Moses, but you are the one to whom the Lord speaks. The Lord told me to go to you in the wilderness, and I did. When He speaks to me now, it is to affirm the word He has given you. You *are* the one who will lead us from this land of misery to the place God promised Jacob. Jacob is buried in Canaan, the land God gave him. And when we go from this place, we will carry his son Joseph's bones with us, because he knew the Lord would not leave us here forever. He knew the day would come when our people would return to Canaan."

Aaron laughed, exultant. "I thought never to see it happen in my lifetime, Brother, but I believe. However many plagues it takes, God will deliver us from bondage and take us home." Tears ran down his cheeks. "We're going home, Moses. Our real home, the home God will make for us!"

✦   ✦   ✦

Aaron stood with Moses before Pharaoh again. He felt the silence around them, the uneasiness of some, and the fear of others. More unnerving was the hatred in Pharaoh's dark glistening eyes as he listened, hands taut on his scepter.

"This is what the Lord says: 'Let My people go, so they can worship Me. If you refuse, I will send swarms of flies throughout Egypt. Your homes will be filled with them, and the ground will be covered with them.'"

Alarmed whispers surged around Aaron, echoing faintly in the massive chamber. Aaron did not stop. He looked straight at Pharaoh. "'But it will be very different in the land of Goshen, where the Israelites live. No flies will be found there. Then you will know that I am the Lord and that I have power even in the heart of your land!'"

Pharaoh did not listen, and the land was infested with armies of flies. They filled the air and scurried over the land. They swarmed up from the Nile, seeking warm human blood; they blanketed dung and infested the marketplace and houses. Bugs swarmed into sleeping mats. The Egyptians could not escape the torment.

Aaron felt little pity for the Egyptians. After all, when had the Egyptians ever shown pity to the Hebrews? While thousands cried out to Geb, god of the earth, or to their village gods for rescue, a few came to plead with him and Moses. Flies continued to swarm, sting, bite, and draw blood.

And then the Egyptian guards came again to usher Aaron and Moses to Pharaoh's house.

Counselors, magicians, and sorcerers thronged the great hall while Pharaoh, grim-faced and glowering, paced the dais. He stopped and glared at Moses and then at Aaron. "All right! Go ahead and offer sacrifices to your God," he said. "But do it here in this land. Don't go out into the wilderness."

"No," Moses said. Aaron felt his heart swelling with pride as his brother stood firm before the man who had once made him tremble. "That won't do! The Egyptians would detest the sacrifices that we offer to the Lord our God. If we offer them here where they can see us, they will be sure to stone us. We must take a three-day trip into the wilderness to offer sacrifices to the Lord our God, just as He has commanded us."

Pharaoh's face darkened. His jaw clenched. "All right, go ahead. I will let you go to offer sacrifices to the Lord your God in the wilderness. But don't go too far away." He lifted his hand. "Now hurry, and pray for me."

Aaron saw the armed guards move closer and knew death was close. If Moses prayed now, they would die the instant he finished. Clearly, Pharaoh thought killing two old men would stop the God of the universe from carrying out His will for His people. But Aaron had no wish to die. "Moses . . ."

Moses did not turn to him, but addressed Pharaoh again. "As soon as I go, I will ask the Lord to cause the swarms of flies to disappear from you and all your people. *Tomorrow.*"

Aaron breathed again. His brother had not been fooled.

Mouth tight, Pharaoh feigned confusion.

Moses looked from the guards to Pharaoh. "But I am warning you, don't change your mind again and refuse to let the people go to sacrifice to the Lord."

When they were safely outside, Aaron slapped Moses on the back. "They were closing in around us." He felt hope again. The prospect of freedom rising. "Once we are three days into the wilderness, we can keep going."

"You have not listened, Aaron. Remember what I told you when you met me at the mountain of God?"

Confused by his brother's frustration with him, Aaron bristled. "I listened. There would be signs and wonders. And so there have been. I remember."

"Raamses' heart is hard, Aaron."

"Then don't pray for him. Let the plague go on."

"And be like Pharaoh, who makes promises only to break them?" Moses shook his head. "The Lord is not like man, Aaron. He keeps His word. As I must keep mine."

Stung and ashamed, Aaron watched Moses go off by himself to pray. He followed Moses at a distance. Why should they keep their word to someone who broke his at every turn? It galled him that his brother was praying for relief for the Egyptians. Generations of them had abused and persecuted the Hebrews! Shouldn't they suffer? Shouldn't they learn what Israel had endured at their hands?

A group of Hebrew elders approached. Aaron rose to greet them. "We want to speak to Moses."

"Not now. He is praying."

"Praying for us or for Pharaoh?"

Aaron heard his own thoughts spoken back to him. He blushed. Who was he to question the Lord's anointed? Moses had not accepted the Lord's commission eagerly, and leadership still did not rest easily on his shoulders. As Moses' encourager, he must listen and learn rather than chafe at God's command.

"Aaron!" The elders demanded his attention.

He raised his head and faced them. "It is not for any of us to question the one God has sent to deliver us."

"We are still slaves, Aaron! And you say Moses will deliver us! When?"

"Am I God? Not even Moses knows the hour or the day! Let him pray! Perhaps God will speak and we will know more in the morning! Go back to your houses! When the Lord speaks to Moses, he will tell us what the Lord says."

"And what are we to do while we wait?"

"Pack for a long journey."

"What does a slave have to pack?" Grumbling, they went away.

Sighing, Aaron sat and watched his brother lying arms outstretched on the ground.

✦   ✦   ✦

As soon as God removed the flies, Pharaoh sent soldiers to Goshen and ordered the Hebrews back to work. The Egyptians knew Pharaoh's edict would bring more trouble upon them. Dread of the God of the Hebrews had filled them. They bowed their heads in respect when Aaron and Moses passed by. And no one dared abuse the slaves. People from the villages brought gifts to Goshen and asked the Hebrews to pray for mercy on them.

And still, Pharaoh did not let the Hebrews go.

Aaron no longer yearned to see the Egyptians suffer because of Pharaoh's stubbornness. He just wanted to be free! He stood beside his brother. "What next?"

"God is sending a plague on their livestock."

Aaron knew fear ran rampant among his people. Some said he should have left his brother in Midian. Frustrated and frightened, they wanted answers when none were to be had. Moses was in constant prayer, so it was left to Aaron to try to calm the elders and send them back to calm the people. "What will we sacrifice when we go into the desert to worship the Lord?" Would the plague fall on them? Was their lack of faith in God any less sinful than bowing down to idols?

But Moses continued to reassure him. "Nothing that belongs to the sons of Israel shall die, Aaron. The Lord set a time for the plague to start. Pharaoh and all his counselors will know the plague is of the Lord God."

✦   ✦   ✦

Buzzards circled the villages and came down to tear at the bloated flesh of dead sheep, cattle, camels, and goats rotting in the hot sun. In Goshen, the herds of cattle, flocks of sheep and goats, and the many camels, donkeys, and mules remained healthy.

Aaron heard the Voice again and bowed his face to the ground. When the Lord stopped speaking, he rose and ran to Moses. Moses confirmed the words and they went into the city, took handfuls of soot from a furnace, and tossed it into the air within sight of Pharaoh's seat of power. The dust cloud grew and spread like gray fingers over the land. Everywhere it touched, Egyptians suffered an outbreak of boils. Even their animals were afflicted. Within a few days, the city streets were empty of merchants and buyers. All were afflicted, from the lowly servant to the highest official.

No word came from Pharaoh. No soldiers came to order the Hebrews back to work.

The Lord spoke to Moses again. "Tomorrow morning, we stand again before Pharaoh."

✦   ✦   ✦

Dressed in splendor, Pharaoh appeared, two servants supporting him. Only a few counselors and magicians were present, all pale, their faces taut with pain. When Raamses tried to sit, he groaned and cursed. Two servants came forward quickly with cushions. Raamses clutched the arms of his chair and eased himself down. "What do you want now, Moses?"

"The Lord, the God of the Hebrews, says: 'Let My people go, so they can worship Me. If you don't, I will send a plague that will really speak to you and your officials and all the Egyptian people. I will prove to you that there is no other God like Me in all the earth. I could have killed you all by now. I could have attacked you with a plague that would have wiped you from the face of the earth. But I have let you live for this reason—that you might see My power and that My fame might spread throughout the earth. But you are still lording it over My people, and you refuse to let them go. So tomorrow at this time I will send a hailstorm worse than any in all of Egypt's history. Quick! Order your livestock and servants to come in from the fields. Every person or animal left outside will die beneath the hail.'"

Those in attendance whispered in alarm.

Pharaoh gave a bitter laugh. "Hail? What is hail? You have lost your mind, Moses. You speak nonsense."

When Moses turned away, Aaron followed. He saw the anxiety in men's faces. Pharaoh might not be afraid of the God of the Hebrews, but clearly others knew better. Several backed quickly between the pillars and headed for the doors, eager to see to their animals and protect their wealth.

Moses held his staff toward the sky. Dark, angry clouds swirled, moving across the land away from Goshen. A cold wind blew. Aaron felt a strange heaviness building in his chest. The darkening skies rumbled. Streaks of fire came from heaven, striking the land west of Goshen. Shu, the Egyptian god of the air, separator of earth and sky, was powerless against the Lord God of Israel.

Aaron sat outside all day and night listening and watching

the hail and fire in the distance, awestruck by the power of God. He had never seen anything like it. Surely Pharaoh would relent now!

Guards came again. Aaron saw the flattened and scorched fields of flax and barley. The land was in ruins.

Pharaoh, thought to be descended from the union of Osiris and Isis, Horus himself in man's form, looked cowed and cornered. Silence rang in the chamber, while the question pulsed: If Pharaoh was the supreme god of Egypt, why couldn't he protect his realm from the invisible god of Hebrew *slaves*? How could it be that all the great and glorious gods of Egypt were no match against the unseen hand of one unseen god?

"I finally admit my fault." Pharaoh cast a sallow look at his advisors clustered near the dais. "The Lord is right, and my people and I are wrong. Please beg the Lord to end this terrifying thunder and hail. I will let you go at once."

Aaron felt no triumph. Pharaoh's heart was not in his words. No doubt he had succumbed to pressure from his advisors. They still did not understand that it was God who was at war with them.

Moses spoke boldly. "As soon as I leave the city, I will lift my hands and pray to the Lord. Then the thunder and hail will stop. This will prove to you that the earth belongs to the Lord. But as for you and your officials, I know that you still do not fear the Lord God as you should."

Pharaoh's eyes gleamed. "Moses, my friend, how can you speak so to one you once called little cousin? How can you bring such heartache to the woman who lifted you from the river and reared you as a son of Egypt?"

"God knows you better than I, Raamses." Moses' voice was quiet but steady. "And it is the Lord who has told me how you harden your heart against Him. It is *you* who brings judgment on Egypt. It is *you* who makes your people suffer!"

Bold words that could bring a death edict. Aaron stepped closer to Moses, ready to protect him if any man should come close. Everyone moved back. Some lowered their heads just enough to show their respect to Moses, much to Pharaoh's ire.

Moses prayed, and the Lord lifted His hand. The thunder, hail, and fire stopped, but the quiet after the storm was even more frightening than the roaring winds. Nothing changed. Pharaoh wanted his bricks, and the Hebrew slaves were to make them.

The people wailed, "Pharaoh's sword is over our heads!"

"Have you no eyes?" Aaron shouted. "Have you no ears? Look around you. Can you not all see how the Egyptians fear what the Lord will do next? More come to our people every day bringing gifts. They hold Moses in great respect."

"And what good does that do us if we are still slaves?"

"The Lord will deliver us!" Moses said. "You must have faith!"

"Faith? That's all we've had for years. *Faith!* We want our *freedom!*"

Aaron tried to keep people away from Moses. "Leave him alone. He must pray."

"We are worse off now than we were before he came!"

"Cleanse your hearts! Pray with us!"

"What good have you done us when we are called back to the mud pits?"

Incensed, Aaron wanted to use his staff on them. They were like sheep, bleating in panic. "Have your gardens turned to ash? Are your animals sick?" The Lord has made a distinction between us and Egypt!"

"When will God get us out of here?"

"When we know *the Lord is God and there is no other!*" Hadn't they bowed down to Egyptian gods? They still turned this way and that! Aaron tried to pray. He tried to hear God's voice again, but the jumble of his own thoughts crowded in like a council of discordant voices. When he saw a scarab amulet around his son Abihu's neck, his blood ran cold. "Where did you get that thing?"

"An Egyptian gave it to me. It's valuable, Father. It's made of lapis and gold."

"It's an abomination! Take it off! And make certain there are no other idols in my house. Do you understand, Abihu? Not a scarab, nor a wooden Heket or the eye of Ra! If an Egyptian gives you something made of gold, melt it down!"

God was sending another plague, and it would only be by His grace and mercy that He didn't send it on Israel as well. Israel, so aptly named, "contender against God"!

God was sending locusts this time. Still, Pharaoh would not listen. Even as Aaron walked with Moses from the great hall, he could hear the counselors crying out to Pharaoh, pleading, begging.

"How long will you let these disasters go on?"

"Please let the Israelites go to serve the Lord their God!"

"Don't you realize that Egypt lies in ruins?"

Aaron turned sharply when he heard running footsteps behind them. No one would take Moses! Planting his feet, he gripped his staff in both hands. The servant bowed low. "Please. Great Pharaoh wishes you to return."

"*Great* Pharaoh can take a flying leap into the Nile!"

"Aaron." Moses headed back.

Tense with frustration, Aaron followed. Would Raamses ever listen? Should they go back and listen to another promise, knowing it would be broken before they stepped foot in Goshen? Hadn't God already said He was hardening Pharaoh's heart and the hearts of his servants?

"All right, go and serve the Lord your God!"

Moses turned away; Aaron fell into step beside him. They had not reached the door when Pharaoh shouted again. "But tell me, just whom do you want to take along?"

Moses looked at Aaron, and Aaron turned. "Young and old, all of us will go. We will take our sons and daughters and our flocks and herds. We must all join together in a festival to the Lord."

Pharaoh's face darkened. He pointed at Moses. "Thus *I* say to you, Moses: The Lord will certainly need to be with you if you try to take your little ones along! I can see through your wicked intentions. Never! Only the *men* may go and serve the Lord, for that is what you requested!" He motioned the guards. "Get them out of my palace!"

Pharaoh's servants came at them, shoving and pushing at them, shouting curses from their false gods. Aaron tried to swing his staff, but Moses held his arm back. They were both flung outside into the dust.

✦   ✦   ✦

All that day and night, the wind blew, and in the morning, locusts came with it. While Egyptians cried out to Wadjet, the cobra goddess, to protect her realm, locusts swarmed over all the land of Egypt, thousands upon thousands in ranks like an army devouring everything in its path. The ground was dark with creeping, leaping grasshoppers eating every plant, tree, and bush that the hail had left. The crops of wheat and spelt were consumed. The date palms were stripped bare. The reeds along the Nile were eaten down to the water.

By the time Pharaoh's soldiers summoned Moses and Aaron, it was too late. Every crop and source of food outside Goshen was gone.

Shaken, Pharaoh greeted them. "I confess my sin against the Lord your God and against you. Forgive my sin only this once, and plead with the Lord your God to take away this terrible plague."

Moses prayed for God's mercy, and the wind changed direction, blowing westward and driving the locusts away toward the Red Sea.

The land and all upon it was still and silent. The Egyptians huddled in their houses, afraid of what new catastrophe would come next if Pharaoh did not let the slaves go. Gifts appeared at Hebrew doorways. Gold amulets, jewelry, precious stones, incense, beautiful cloth, silver and bronze vessels were given to honor God's people. "Pray for us in the hour of our need. Intercede for us."

"They still don't understand!" Moses gripped his head covered by the prayer shawl. "They bow down to us, Aaron, while *it is God who holds the power.*"

Even Miriam was afire with frustration. "Why doesn't God kill Pharaoh and be done with it? The Lord has the power to reach inside that palace and crush Raamses!"

Moses raised his head. "The Lord wants the entire world to know He is God and there is no other. All the gods of Egypt are false. They have no power to stand against the Lord our God."

"We know that!"

"Miriam!" Aaron spoke sharply. Wasn't Moses plagued enough? "Be patient. Wait on the Lord. He will deliver us."

When Moses stretched out his hand again, darkness came over Egypt. The sun was blotted out by an inky darkness heavier than night. Sitting outside Pharaoh's palace, Aaron drew his robe around himself. Moses was silent beside him. They could both hear the priests crying out for Ra, the sun god, the father of the kings of Egypt, to drive his golden chariot across the sky and bring light again. Aaron gave a contemptuous laugh. Let these stubborn fools cry out to their false god. The sun would appear when God willed it—and not before.

Moses rose abruptly. "We must gather the elders, Aaron. *Quickly!*" They hastened to Goshen, where Aaron sent out messengers. The elders came, asking questions, grumbling.

"Be silent!" Aaron said. "Listen to Moses. He has the Word of the Lord!"

"Prepare to leave Egypt. All of us, men and women alike, are to ask their neighbors for articles of silver and gold. The Egyptians will give you whatever you ask of them, for the Lord has given us favor in their sight. The Lord says that this month will be the first month of the year for you. On the tenth day of this month, each family must choose a lamb or a young goat for a sacrifice. Take special care of these lambs until the evening of the fourteenth day of this first month. Then each family in the community must slaughter its lamb. . . ."

Moses told them of the plague to come and what they must do to survive. They all left in silence, the fear of the Lord upon them.

✦   ✦   ✦

For three days, Aaron waited with Moses near the palace entrance, before they heard Pharaoh's cry of fear and rage echo in the columned chambers. *"Moses!"*

Moses put his hand on Aaron and they rose together and entered. Aaron did not falter in the darkness. He could see his way as though the Lord had given him the eyes of an owl. He could see Moses' face, solemn and filled with compassion, and Pharaoh's eyes darting this way and that, searching, blind.

"I am here, Raamses," Moses said.

Pharaoh faced forward, leaning his head as though to hear what he could not see in the darkness that enfolded him. "Go and worship the Lord," he said. "But let your flocks and herds stay here. You can even take your children with you."

"No," Moses said, "we must take our flocks and herds for sacrifices and burnt offerings to the Lord our God. All our property must go with us; not a hoof can be left behind. We will have to choose our sacrifices for the Lord our God from among these animals. And we won't know which sacrifices He will require until we get there."

Pharaoh cursed them. "Get out of here!" he shouted. "Don't ever let me see you again! The day you do, you will die!"

"Very well!" Moses shouted back. "I will never see you again!" His voice changed, deepened, resonated, and filled the chamber. "This is what the Lord says: 'About midnight I will pass through Egypt. All the firstborn sons will die in every family in Egypt, from the oldest son of Pharaoh, who sits on the throne, to the oldest son of his lowliest slave. Even the firstborn of the animals will die.'"

Aaron's skin prickled and sweat broke out.

"Moses!" Pharaoh roared as he spread his arms and swept his hands back and forth, trying to find his own way out of the darkness. "Do you think Osiris will not defend me? The gods will not let you touch my son!"

Moses went on speaking. "'Then a loud wail will be heard throughout the land of Egypt; there has never been such wailing before, and there never will be again. But among the Israelites it will be so peaceful that not even a dog will bark. Then you will know that the Lord makes a distinction between the Egyptians and the Israelites. All the officials of Egypt will come running to me, bowing low. "Please leave!" they will beg. "Hurry! And take all your followers with you." Only then will I go!'" Face flushed with anger, Moses turned and strode from the great hall.

Aaron caught up and walked beside him. He had never seen his brother so angry. God had spoken through him. It had been *God's* voice Aaron heard in that immense hall.

Moses prayed fervently under his breath, eyes blazing as he strode through the streets of the city heading toward Goshen. People drew back and ducked into their houses or shops.

When they reached the edge of the city, Moses cried out. *"Oh, Lord! Lord!!"*

Aaron's eyes welled at the anguished cry. "Moses." His throat closed.

"Oh, Aaron, now we shall all see the destruction one man can bring upon a nation." Tears ran down his face. "We shall all see!"

Moses went down on his knees and wept.

THREE

THE LAMB struggled when Aaron held it firmly between his knees. He slit its throat and felt the small animal go limp as the bowl filled with its blood. The smell turned Aaron's stomach. The lamb had been perfect, without a blemish, and only a year old. He skinned the lamb. "Pierce it through and roast its head, legs, and inner parts."

Nadab took the carcass. "Yes, Father."

Taking up the bowl, Aaron dipped sprigs of hyssop into the blood and painted the door lintel of his house. He dipped again and again until the top of the doorway was stained red, and then he began to do the same on the doorposts on either side of the entrance into his home. All over Goshen and into the city, each Hebrew family was doing the same. Egyptian neighbors watched, confused and disgusted, whispering.

"They threw away all the yeast in their houses yesterday."

"And now they're painting their doorframes with blood!"

"What does it all mean?"

Some had come to Aaron and asked what they could do to be grafted in among the Hebrews. "Circumcise every male in your household, and then you may be like one born among us."

Only a few took his words seriously and went through with it. Afraid for their lives, they moved their families in among the dwellings of the Hebrews, and listened to whatever Aaron and Moses had to say to the people.

Aaron thought of what this night would hold for the rest of Egypt. In the beginning, he had wanted revenge. He had savored the thought of Egyptians suffering. Now he was filled with pity for those who still foolishly clung to their idols and bowed down before their empty gods. He longed to be away from this land of desolation. Finishing his task, he entered the

house and closed the door securely. Piled in one corner were
objects and jewelry of silver and gold that Miriam and his
sons had collected from their Egyptian neighbors. All his life,
Aaron had scratched out a meager living from the soil and his
small flock of sheep and goats, and now his family had silver
and gold to fill sacks! God had made the Egyptians look on
Aaron and Moses and all the Hebrews with favor, and they
had given whatever was asked for, even unto their wealth.
Without question, the Egyptians had given up things they
had prized only days before, hoping they could buy mercy
from the Hebrew God.

God's mercy was not for sale. Nor could it be earned.

On such a night as this, gold and silver did not matter, even
to Aaron, who had once thought wealth could bring him solace
and salvation from taskmasters and tyrants. Whatever he had
done in the name of the Lord in the past did not count on this
night. Had the Egyptians offered everything they owned to
their gods tonight, they could not buy the lives of their firstborn sons. Had they smashed their idols, it would not have
been enough. Pharaoh had brought this night upon Egypt, his
pride the people's bane.

God, who established the heavens, set the price for life, and
it was the blood of the lamb. The Angel of the Lord was coming, and he would pass over every house that had its lintels and
doorposts painted with the lamb's blood. The blood was a sign
that those inside the house believed in the God of Abraham,
Isaac, and Jacob, believed enough to obey His command and
trust His word. Only faith in the one true God would save them.

Aaron looked at his firstborn son, Nadab, as he sat at the
table with his brothers. Abihu sat alone, deep in thought, while
Ithamar and Eleazar sat with their wives and small children. Little Phinehas turned the spitted lamb over the fire. When he
tired, another took his place.

"Grandfather—" Phinehas slipped onto the bench beside Aaron—"what does this night mean?"

Aaron put his arm around the boy and looked at his sons, their wives, and the small children. "It is the Passover sacrifice to the Lord. The Lord will come tonight at midnight and see the blood of the lamb on our door and pass over us. We will be spared, but the Lord will strike down the firstborn sons of the Egyptians. From the firstborn of Pharaoh who sits on the throne, to the firstborn of the prisoner who is in the dungeon, to the firstborn of all the livestock as well."

The only sound in the house was the crackling fire and the pop and hiss of fat as it dropped onto the hot coals. Miriam ground wheat and barley to make bread without yeast. The hours wore by. No one spoke. Moses rose and closed the window openings, securing them as though for a sandstorm. Then he sat with the family and covered his head with his shawl.

The smell of roasting lamb filled the house, along with the bitter herbs Miriam had cut and put on the table. Aaron cut into the lamb. "It is finished." Miriam added oil to the ground flour and patted out thin cakes of bread that she laid over a round pan and set over some coals she had raked to one side.

Night was heavy upon them. Death was coming.

The men rose, girding their loins and tucking their cloaks into their belts. They put their sandals on again and stood at the table, staffs in hand, and the family ate of the lamb, the bitter herbs, and unleavened bread.

A scream rent the air. Aaron's skin crawled. Miriam stared at Moses, her dark eyes wide. No one spoke as they ate. Another scream was heard, closer this time, and then wailing in the distance. Outside someone cried out in anguish to Osiris. Aaron shut his eyes tightly, for he knew Osiris was nothing but an idol made by men's hands, his myth crafted by men's imaginings. Osiris had no substance, no power, other than the fictitious power men and women had given him over the centuries. Tonight, they would learn what men design cannot bring salvation. Salvation is in the Lord, the God of all creation.

The screams and wailing increased. Aaron knew by the sounds when the Angel of Death had passed over the house. He felt a rising joy, a thanksgiving that swelled his heart to bursting. The Lord was trustworthy! The Lord had spared His people Israel! The Lord was destroying His enemies.

Someone pounded on the door. "In the name of Pharaoh, open the door!"

Aaron looked to Moses and at his nod rose to open the door. Soldiers stood outside, and they bowed low when Aaron and Moses came through the door. "Pharaoh has sent us to bring you to him." As they went out, the soldiers fell in around them.

"Pharaoh's son is dead." The soldier to Moses' right spoke softly.

Another spoke to Aaron. "He was the first in the palace to die, and then others fell, many others."

"My son." A soldier wept behind them. "My son . . ."

All of Thebes was wailing, for every house suffered loss.

"Hurry! We must hurry before all Egypt dies."

They had barely crossed the threshold when Aaron heard Pharaoh's anguished cry. "Leave us! Go away, all of you!" He hunched on his throne. "Go and serve the Lord as you have requested. Take your flocks and herds, and be gone. Go, but give me a blessing as you leave."

Aaron stood in the flickering torchlight, hardly able to believe he had heard Pharaoh relent. Was it over? Was it really over? Or would they get no farther than the streets of Thebes and find out Pharaoh had changed his mind again?

Moses turned away without a word. "Go!" one of the guards urged Aaron. "Go quickly, or we will all die!"

As they hurried through the streets, Aaron shouted, "Israel! Israel! Your day of deliverance is at hand!"

+   +   +

Egyptians rushed from their houses, crying out to the Hebrews. "Hurry! Hurry! Go before Great Pharaoh changes his mind and we all die!" Some gave them donkeys and added gifts of goodwill as they helped to strap possessions to the animals' backs. Others gave portions of what little they had left from the plagues. "Take whatever you want and get out of Egypt! Hurry! Hurry before another plague falls upon us and we are no more!"

Aaron laughed in exultation, so full of emotion he couldn't think of anything but rushing, rushing. Miriam and his sons and their families caught up to him and Moses at the front of the congregation. The noise was deafening. People called out praises to the Lord and Moses and Aaron. Large flocks of bleating sheep and goats swirled alongside the mass of population. Herds of cattle followed so that the people would not choke in their dust. Six hundred thousand men left on foot as the sun came up, and headed for Succoth, accompanied by their wives and children.

Women carried their kneading bowls on their shoulders, while balancing a child on their hips and calling out to other children to stay close and keep up with the family. They had had no time to prepare food for the journey.

Aaron heard the cacophony of voices and tasted the dust stirred by over a million slaves hurrying away from Pharaoh's city. More joined them along the way. The tribes of Reuben, Simeon, Judah, Zebulon, Issachar, Dan, Gad, Asher, Nephtali, and Benjamin followed Moses and Aaron's tribe of Levi. Representatives of the half tribes of Ephraim and Manasseh traveled close to Moses, carrying with them the bones of their ancestor Joseph, who had once saved Egypt from famine. The elders of each tribe had made standards so that their relatives might gather together and march in divisions out of Egypt, every man armed for battle. And behind them and alongside came Egyptians who fled the desolation of their homeland and sought the provision and protection of the Lord God of Israel, the true God over all creation.

As the sun rose, Aaron watched the rising of a pillar of cloud. The Lord Himself was shielding them from the burning heat and leading them out of bondage, away from suffering and despair. Oh, life was going to be good! In a week, they would reach the Promised Land of milk and honey. In a week, they could pitch their tents and stretch out on their mats and revel in their freedom.

Men and women wept with joyful abandon. "Praise the Lord! We are free—free at last!"

"No son of mine will ever make another brick for Pharaoh!"

"Let him make his own bricks!"

People laughed. Women warbled in joy. Men shouted.

"I should have made more unleavened cakes! We have so little grain!"

"How far are we going today? The children are already tired."

Aaron turned, face hot at the sound of his own relatives grumbling. Would they rather have stayed behind? "This is the end of your captivity! Rejoice! We have been redeemed by the blood of the lamb! Praise the Lord!"

"We do, Father! We do, but the children are exhausted. . . ."

Moses raised his staff. "Remember this day! Tell your sons and daughters of what the Lord did for you when He brought you out of Egypt! Remember that you consecrated to the Lord every firstborn male, the offspring of every womb among Israel, whether man or beast, for the Lord made death pass over us! Commemorate this day! Never forget it was the Lord who with a mighty hand brought you out of Egypt!"

Because Pharaoh stubbornly refused to let God's people go, the Lord killed every firstborn in Egypt, both man and beast. Therefore, every first male offspring of every womb belonged to the Lord, and every firstborn son would be redeemed by the blood of a lamb.

"Praise the Lord!" Aaron raised his staff. He would not listen to the few grumblers among his people. He would not let them spoil this moment, this day. He would not listen to those who looked back over their shoulders like Lot's wife. He had dreamed all his life of what it would be like to live as a free man. And now he would know freedom firsthand. He wept in thanksgiving. *"Praise the Lord!"* A resounding shout came from men and women around him, spreading back until the praise rose thunderous to the heavens. The women sang.

Moses did not stop as the sun began its descent, for a pillar of fire appeared, leading them to Succoth, where they rested before moving on. They camped at Etham on the edge of the desert.

Korah and a delegation of other Levite elders came to Moses. "Why are you leading us south when there are two other routes to Canaan that are shorter? We could go by way of the sea."

Moses shook his head. "That would take the people through Philistine country."

"We are many and armed for battle. What about the way of Shur to southern Canaan?"

Moses stood firm. "We are armed, but untrained and untried. We go where the Angel of the Lord leads us. The Lord has said if the people face war, they might change their minds and return to Egypt."

"We will never return to Egypt!" Korah lifted his chin. "You should have more confidence in us, Moses. We have craved freedom as much as you. More so."

Aaron's head came up. He knew Korah was alluding to Moses

having lived forty years in the corridors of palaces and another forty among the free men of Midian. Others came, asking for Moses' attention. He rose to see what the problem was. Problems were already mounting.

"Aaron." Korah turned to him. "You understand us better than Moses. You should have some say about which road we travel."

Aaron saw through their flattery. "It is God's choice, Korah. God made Moses our leader. He is above us. He walks before us." Did they not see the Man who walked ahead of Moses, leading the way? Close enough to follow, but not close enough to see His face. Or could the people see Him?

"Yes." Korah was quick to agree. "We accept Moses as God's prophet. But Aaron, so are you. Think of the children. Think of our wives. Speak to your brother. Why should we go the long way rather than the short? The Philistines will have heard about the plagues. They will be in fear of us just as the Egyptians are now."

Aaron shook his head. "The Lord leads. Moses does not take one step without the Lord directing him. If you do not understand that, you have only to raise your eyes to see the cloud by day and the pillar of fire by night."

"Yes, but I'm sure if you asked the Lord, He would listen to you. Didn't He call you into the wilderness to meet Moses at Mount Sinai? The Lord spoke to you before He spoke to your brother."

Korah's words troubled Aaron. Did the man mean to divide brothers? Aaron thought of what jealousy had wrought between Cain and Abel, Ishmael and Isaac, Esau and Jacob, Joseph and his eleven brothers. No! He would not give in to such thinking. The Lord had called him to stand beside Moses, to walk with him, to uphold him. And so he would! "The Lord speaks through Moses, not me, and we will follow the Lord whatever way He leads us."

"You are Amram's firstborn son. The Lord continues to speak to you."

"Only to confirm what He has already said to Moses!"

"Is it wrong to ask why we must go the more difficult way?"

Aaron rose, staff in hand. Most of these men were his relatives. "Should Moses or I tell the Lord which way we are to go? It is for the Lord to say where we go and how long and how far we travel. If you set yourself against Moses, you set yourself against God."

Korah's eyes darkened, but he raised his hands in capitulation. "I do not doubt Moses' authority, or yours, Aaron. We have seen the signs and wonders. I was just asking . . ."

But even then, as the men turned away, Aaron knew there would be no end to the asking.

✦ ✦ ✦

Aaron joined Moses on a rocky hill overlooking the stretch of land to the east. Others were nearby, just down the hill, watching, but respecting Moses' need for solitude, waiting for Aaron to speak for him. Aaron realized Moses was becoming more accustomed to speaking Hebrew. "Soon you will have no need of me, my brother. Your words are clear and easily understood."

"The Lord called *both* of us to this task, Aaron. Could I have crossed the desert and stood before Pharaoh had the Lord not sent you to me?"

Aaron put his hand on Moses' arm. "You think too much of me."

"The enemies of God will do all they can to divide us, Aaron."

Perhaps the Lord had opened Moses' eyes to the temptations Aaron faced. "I don't want to follow in the ways of those who came before us."

"What is worrying you?"

"That one day, you will have no need of me, that I will be useless."

Moses was silent for so long, Aaron thought he did not intend to respond. Should he add to Moses' burdens? Hadn't the Lord called him to assist Moses, not to plague him with petty worries? How he longed to speak with Moses as they had when they were alone and crossed the wilderness together! The years of separation had fallen away. The imagined grievances dissolved. They were more than brothers. They were friends joined in one calling, servants of the Most High God. "I'm sorry, Moses. I will leave you alone. We can talk another time."

"Stay with me, Brother." He continued to look out over the people. "There are so many."

Relieved to be needed, Aaron stepped closer and leaned on his staff. He had never been comfortable with long silences. "All these descended from Jacob's sons. Sixty-six came into Egypt with Jacob, and Joseph's family made seventy in all. And from those few came this great multitude. God has blessed us."

Thousands upon thousands of men, women, and children traveled like a slow-moving sea into the desert. Clouds of dust rose from their feet and the hooves of their flocks and herds. Overhead was the heavy gray cloud canopy of protection, a shield from the burning heat of the sun. No wonder Pharaoh had feared the Hebrews! Look at them all! Had they joined with Egypt's enemies, they could have become a great military threat within the borders of Egypt. But rather than rebel, they had bent their necks to the pharaohs' will and served as slaves. They had not tried to break the chains of bondage, but had cried out to the Lord God of Abraham, Isaac, and Jacob to rescue them.

Egyptians traveled among the people. Most stayed on the outer edges of the mass of travelers. Aaron wished they had stayed behind in the Nile Delta or Etham. He didn't trust them.

Had they cast aside their idols and chosen to follow the Lord, or had they come along because Egypt was in ruins?

People waved. "Moses! Aaron!" Like children, they called. There was still jubilation. Maybe it was only Korah and his friends who questioned the route they traveled.

Moses began walking again. Aaron raised his staff and pointed in the direction he led. He did not ask why Moses headed south and then east into the heart of the Sinai. The gray cloud transformed into a swirling pillar of fire to light their way and keep them warm through the desert night. Aaron saw the Angel of the Lord walking ahead, leading Moses and the people deeper into the wilderness.

Why?

Was it right that he should even think such a question?

Moses did not make camp again, but continued traveling, resting for brief periods. Miriam and Aaron's sons' wives made enough flat bread to eat on the way while children slept using a stone for a pillow. Aaron sensed Moses' urgency—an urgency he also felt, but did not understand. Canaan was north, not east. Where was the Lord leading them?

The mouth of a great wadi opened ahead. Aaron thought Moses might turn north or send men ahead to see where the canyon led. But Moses did not hesitate or turn to the right or the left. He walked straight into the canyon. Aaron stayed at his side, looking back only to make certain Miriam, his sons, and their wives and children followed.

High cliffs rose on either side, the cloud remaining overhead. The wadi narrowed. The people flowed like water into a river basin cut for them. The canyon twisted and turned like a snake through the jagged terrain, the floor flat and easily traveled.

After a long day, the canyon opened wide. Aaron saw rippling water and smelled the salt-sea air. Whatever waters had come through the wadi during the times of Noah's flood had spilled a sandy pebbled beach wide enough for the multitude to encamp. But there was nowhere to go from here. "What do we do now, Moses?"

"We wait on the Lord."

"But there is no place to go!"

Moses stood in the wind facing the sea. "We are to encamp here opposite Baal-zephon as the Lord said. And Pharaoh will pursue us, and the Lord will gain glory for Himself through Pharaoh and his army, and the Egyptians will know that the Lord is God and there is no other."

Fear gripped Aaron. "Should we tell the others?"

"They will know soon enough."

"Should we make battle lines? Should we have our weapons ready to defend ourselves?"

"I don't know, Aaron. I only know that the Lord has led us here for His purpose."

A cry rose from among the Israelites. Several men on camel-back rode out onto the beach. Pharaoh's horses and chariots, horsemen and troops were coming up the canyon. Horns sounded in the distance. Aaron felt the rumble beneath his feet. An army that had never known defeat. Thousands of Hebrews wailed so loudly they drowned out the sound of the sea at their backs. People ran toward the sea and huddled in the wind.

Moses turned toward the deep waters and raised his arm, crying out to the Lord. The battle horns sounded again. Aaron shouted. "Come here to Moses!" His sons and their families and Miriam ran to them. "Stay close to us no matter what happens!" Aaron beckoned. "Do not be separated from us!" He took his grandson Phinehas up into his arms. "The Lord will come to our rescue!"

"Lord, help us!" Moses cried out.

Aaron closed his eyes and prayed for the Lord to hear.

"Moses!" the people cried out. "What have you done to us?"

Aaron handed Phinehas to Eleazar and stood between his brother and the people, staff in hand.

"Why did you bring us out here to die in the wilderness? Weren't there enough graves for us in Egypt?"

"We should've stayed in Egypt!"

"Didn't we tell you to leave us alone while we were still in Egypt?"

"You should've let us go on serving the Egyptians."

"Why did you make us leave?"

"Our Egyptian slavery was far better than dying out here in the wilderness!"

Moses turned to them. "Don't be afraid!"

"Don't be afraid? Pharaoh's army is coming! They're going to slaughter us like sheep!"

Aaron chose to believe Moses. "Have you forgotten what the Lord did for us already? He smote Egypt with His mighty hand! Egypt is in ruins!"

"All the more reason for Pharaoh to want to destroy us!"

"Where can we go now with our backs to the sea?"

"They're coming! They're coming!"

Moses raised his staff. "Just stand where you are and watch the Lord rescue you. The Egyptians that you see today will never be seen again. The Lord Himself will fight for you. You won't have to lift a finger in your defense!"

Aaron saw by Moses' expression that the Lord had spoken to him. Moses turned and looked up. The shining Angel of the Lord, who had been leading them, rose and moved behind the multitude, blocking the entrance of the great wadi that opened out upon Pi-hahiroth. Raising his staff, Moses stretched out his arm over the sea. The wind roared from on high and came down from the east, slicing the water in two, rolling it back and up so that walls of water rose like the sheer cliffs of the wadi from which the Israelites had come. A pathway of dry land sloped down where the depths of the sea had been and straight across and up to land on the other side of *yam suph*, the Red Sea.

"Move on!" Moses called out.

Heart leaping, Aaron took up the cry. "Move on!" Raising his staff, he pointed it forward as he followed Moses into the great, deep walls of water on either side.

The strong east wind blew all night as thousands upon thousands of Israelites raced for the other side. When Aaron and his family reached the eastern shore, they stood on the bluff with Moses, watching the multitude come through the sea. Laughing and crying, Aaron watched the people come out of Egypt. Impenetrable darkness was over the rocky terrain of the canyon through which they had come, but on this side, the Lord provided light so the Israelites and those traveling with them could see their way through the Red Sea.

When the last few hundred Israelites were hurrying up the slope, the fiery barrier holding the Egyptians back lifted and spread like a shimmering cloud over land and sea. The way opened for Pharaoh to pursue. Battle horns blasted in the distance. Chariots spread across the beach, then narrowed into ranks. Drivers whipped their horses down into the pathway into the sea.

Aaron continued standing on the bluff, leaning into the wind. Below him, Israelites struggled against exhaustion, hunched beneath the weight of their possessions. "They must hurry! They must . . ." He felt Moses' hand on his shoulder and drew back, submitting to the silent command to be calm. *"Don't be afraid,"* Moses had said. *"Just stand where you are!"* But it was so hard when he could see the charioteers coming, and the horsemen and troops behind. There were thousands of them, armed and trained, in a race to kill those who belonged to the God who had destroyed Egypt, the God who had killed their firstborn sons. Hatred drove them.

As the Egyptians neared the slope upward from the sea, a horse went down, overturning the chariot behind him, crushing the driver beneath. The chariots behind veered off. Horses screamed and reared. Some shook their riders loose and galloped back. The troops broke ranks in confusion. Some were trampled beneath the hooves of riderless horses.

The last few Israelites scrambled onto the eastern shore. The people screamed in terror of the Egyptians. "Israel!" Moses' voice boomed. He raised his hands. "Be still and know that the Lord is God!" He stretched out his hand and held his staff over the Red Sea. The east wind lifted. The waters spilled into the pathway, covering the panic-stricken Egyptians, the tumbling current drowning out their screams. A mighty flume of water rose skyward and then descended with a mighty splash.

The Red Sea rippled. All fell silent.

Aaron sank to the ground, staring at the azure water—tumultuous just seconds before, now tranquil. The waves lapped against the rocky shore and soft wind whispered.

Did they all feel as he did? Terror at seeing the power of the Lord visited upon the Egyptians, and exultation, for the enemy was no more! Egyptian soldiers washed up on the shore below him, hundreds facedown in the sand, their limbs gently lifting with the waves and resting again in the sand.

Aaron looked at his sons and daughters-in-law, his grandchildren gathered close around him. "Egypt boasted of its army and weapons, its many gods. But we will boast in the Lord our God." All the nations would hear what the Lord had done. Who would dare come against the people God had chosen to be His own? Look to the heavens! The God who laid the foundations of the earth and scattered the stars across the heavens was protecting them! The God who could call forth plagues and part the sea was overshadowing them! "Who will dare stand against a God like ours? We will live in security! We will thrive in the land

God is giving us! No one will stand against our God! We are free and no one will ever enslave us again!"

"I will sing to the Lord, for He has triumphed gloriously!" Moses' voice carried on the wind. "He has thrown both horse and rider into the sea."

Miriam took her tambourine and hit it, shaking it and singing out. "I will sing to the Lord, for He has triumphed gloriously!" She hit the tambourine again, dancing and shaking the instrument. "He has thrown both horse and rider into the sea!" Aaron's daughters-in-law joined her, laughing and crying out in abandon, "Sing praises to the Lord! Sing praises . . ."

Aaron laughed with them, for it was a wonderful sight to see his aged sister dancing!

Moses strode down the rise. The people parted for him as the sea had parted for all of them. Aaron walked with him, tears streaming down his cheeks, his heart bursting. He had to sing out with his brother. "The Lord is my strength and my song; He has become my victory!" He felt young again, full of hope and adulation. The Lord had fought for them! Aaron looked up at the cloud spread over them. Light streamed shimmering colors as though God was pleased with their praise. Aaron raised his hands and shouted his thanks and praise.

Thousands cried out in jubilation, hands reaching toward the heavens. Some knelt, weeping, overcome with emotion. Women joined in Miriam's dance until there were ten, a hundred, a thousand women spinning and dipping.

"He is my God!" Moses sang out.

"He is my God!" Aaron sang out. He strode alongside his brother. His family members fell in behind them. Others gathered around, raising their hands and singing out.

Miriam and the women danced and sang. "He is our God!"

Aaron's sons sang out, faces flushed, eyes bright, hands raised. Filled with triumph, Aaron laughed. Who could doubt the power of the Lord now? With His mighty hand, He had broken the chains of their captivity. The Lord had mocked the gods of Egypt and swallowed up in the depths of the sea the army of the most powerful nation on earth! All those who had boasted that they would draw their swords and destroy Israel were now dead along the shores. Man planned, but God prevailed.

Who among the gods is like You, Lord? There is no other so awesome in glory who can work wonders! The nations will hear and tremble. Philistia, Edom, Moab, Canaan will melt away before us because we have the Lord, the God of Abraham, Isaac, and Jacob on our side! By the power of Your arm, they will be as still as a stone until we pass by. When we reach the land God has promised our ancestors, we will have rest on all sides!

"The Lord will reign forever and ever!" Moses raised his staff as he led the people away from the Red Sea.

"Forever and ever." *Our God reigns!*

As the jubilation subsided, the people rejoined their divisions. Families clustered together and followed Moses inland. Aaron called his sons and daughters-in-law close. "Keep within the ranks of the Levites." The tribal leaders held up their standards, and family members fell in behind them.

Aaron walked beside Moses. "It will be easier now that the worst is behind us. Pharaoh has no one to send after us. His gods have proven weak. We are safe now."

"We are far from safe."

"We are beyond the borders of Egypt. Even if Pharaoh could muster another army, who would heed his commands and follow when they hear what has happened here today! Word will spread through the nations of what the Lord has done for us, Moses. No one will dare come against us."

"Yes, we are outside the boundaries of Egypt, Aaron, but we will see in the days ahead whether we have left Egypt behind."

✦ ✦ ✦

It was not long before Aaron understood what his brother meant. As the people followed Moses into the Desert of Shur and headed north through the arid land toward the mountain of God, their songs of deliverance ceased. There was no water. What they had brought out of Egypt was nearly gone, and there had been no springs at which to relieve their growing thirst or replenish their water bags. The people mumbled when they rested. They muttered on the second day when no water was found. By the third day, anger brewed.

"We need water, Aaron."

Aaron's tongue began to cleave to the roof of his mouth, but he tried to calm those who complained. "The Lord is leading Moses."

"Into the desert?"

"Have you forgotten the Lord opened the sea?"

"That was three days ago, and we are without water now. Would that it had been a body of freshwater so that we could have filled our bags! Why is Moses leading us into the desert?"

"We are going back to the mountain of God."

"We'll be dead of thirst long before we get there!"

Aaron tried to restrain his anger. "Should Moses' own kin grumble against him?" Perhaps it was thirst that lessened his patience. "The Lord will provide what we need."

"From your mouth to God's ears!"

They were like tired, cranky children, whining and complaining. "When will we get there?!" Aaron felt compassion for those who were sick. Some of the Egyptians traveling with them had boils; others still suffered from rashes and infections caused by insect bites. They were weary with hunger and thirst, sweating doubt and fear of what added miseries lay ahead. "We need water!"

Did they think he and Moses were God that they could produce water from the rocks? "We have no water to give you." Their bags were just as flat as everyone else's. They were just as thirsty. Moses had given the last of his water to one of Aaron's grandsons this morning. Aaron had a few drops left, but hoarded them in case his brother became weak from dehydration. What would they do without Moses to lead them?

When they came to a rise, Moses pointed. "There!" Like thirsty animals, they stampeded toward the growing pond, falling on their knees to drink. But they reared back and spit it out, wailing, "It is bitter!"

"Don't drink it! It's poison!"

"Moses! What have you done? Brought us out here into the desert to die of thirst?"

Children wept. Women wailed. Men shouted, faces twisted in wrath. Soon they would pick up stones to hurl at Moses. Aaron called for them to remember what the Lord had done for them. Had they forgotten so quickly? "Only three days ago we were singing His praises! Only three days ago, you were saying you would never forget the good things the Lord had done for you! The Lord will provide what we need."

"When? We need water *now!*"

Moses headed for the hills, and the people cried out louder. Aaron stood between them and his brother. "Leave him alone! Let Moses seek the Lord! Be still. Be quiet so he can hear the voice of the Lord."

Lord, we do need water. You know how weak we are. We are not like You! We are dust. The wind blows and we are gone! Have mercy on us! God, have mercy! "The Lord will hear Moses and tell him what to do. The Lord sent my brother to deliver us, and he has."

"Delivered us unto death!"

Angry, Aaron pointed to the sky. "The Lord is with us. You have only to look up and see the cloud over us."

"Would that the cloud would give us rain!"

Aaron's face went hot. "Do you think the Lord does not hear how you speak against Him? Surely the Lord has not delivered us from Egypt only to die of thirst in the desert! Have faith!" Aaron prayed fervently even as he spoke. *Lord, Lord, tell us where to find water. Tell us what to do! Help us!*

"What are we going to drink?"

"We will die without water to drink!"

Moses returned within minutes, a gnarled piece of wood in his hands. He tossed it into the water. "Drink!"

The people scoffed.

Aaron knelt quickly, cupped his hands, and drank. Smiling, he ran his wet hands over his face. "The water is sweet!" His sons and their families knelt and drank deeply.

People ran for the water, crowding around the edges, pushing, shoving, and clamoring to get their share. They drank until they could drink no more and then filled their water bags.

"Listen carefully," Moses called out to them. "If you will listen carefully to the voice of the Lord your God and do what is right in His sight, obeying His commands and laws, then He will not make you suffer the diseases He sent on the Egyptians; for He is the Lord who heals you."

Had anyone heard him? Was anyone listening? They all seemed so intent on taking care of their immediate needs that they scarcely looked up. Aaron shouted, "Listen to Moses! He has words of life to give us."

But the people weren't listening, let alone listening carefully. They were too busy drinking the water God had provided to stop and thank God for providing it.

+ + +

When they left the sweetened waters of Marah, the people followed Moses and Aaron to Elim and camped. They ate dates from the palm trees and drank from the twelve springs. When they were rested, Moses led them into the Sin Desert.

Aaron heard the complaints daily until he was worn down by them. They had come out of Egypt only one month and fifteen days ago, and it seemed years. They walked through the arid land, hungry and thirsty, vacillating between the dream of the Promised Land and the reality of hardship in getting there.

The Egyptians traveling among the people stirred up more complaints. "Oh, that we were back in Egypt!" a woman cried. "It would have been better if the Lord had killed us there! At least there we had plenty to eat."

"Do you remember how we sat around pots of meat and ate all the food we wanted?" Her companion tore off a bit of unleavened bread and chewed it with distaste. "This stuff is awful!"

The men were more direct in their rebellion. Aaron could not go anywhere without hearing someone say, "You and your brother have brought us into this desert to starve us to death!"

When the Lord spoke to Moses again, Aaron rejoiced. With Moses, he carried the message to the people, speaking before gatherings of the tribes. "The Lord is about to rain down food from heaven for you! You are to go out each day and gather enough for that day. In this way, the Lord will test us to see if we will follow His instructions. On the sixth day, you are to pick up twice as much as usual. In the evening you will realize that it was the Lord who brought you out of the land of Egypt. In the morning you will see the glorious presence of the Lord. He has heard your complaints, which are against the Lord and not against us!"

When Aaron looked out toward the desert, the glory of the Lord shone in the cloud. The people huddled together in fear, silent as Moses raised his hands. "The Lord will give you meat to eat in the evening and bread in the morning, for He has heard all your complaints against Him. Yes, your complaints are against the Lord, not against us!"

And so it was. When the sun began to set, quail flew into the camp, thousands upon thousands of them. Aaron laughed as he watched his grandchildren run and catch birds and bring them to their mothers. Before the stars shone, the camp smelled of roasting meat.

Stomach full, Aaron slept well that night. He did not have dreams of the people stoning him or his bag spilling out sand instead of water. He awakened to people's voices. "What is it?" When he went outside his tent, he saw the ground covered with flakes like frost, white like coriander seed. He put a few pieces to his mouth. "It tastes like wafers with honey."

"Manna? What is it?"

"It is the bread God promised you. It is the bread of heaven." Had they expected loaves to rain down on them? "Remember! Collect only what you need for the day. No more than that. The Lord is testing us." Aaron took a jar and went out with his sons, daughters-in-law, and grandchildren. Miriam shooed the family along.

Moses squatted beside Aaron. "Fill another jar and place it before the Lord to be kept for the generations to come."

When they set out again, they traveled from place to place in the desert, and the people complained again because they were thirsty. Each time their wants were not immediately met, they grew louder and more angry. When they camped at Rephidim, their frustration overflowed.

"Why are we camped here in this forsaken place?"

"There is no water here!"

"Where is the land of milk and honey you promised us!?"

"Why do we listen to these men? We have done nothing but suffer since we left Egypt!"

"At least in Egypt we had food to eat and water to drink."

"And we lived in houses rather than tents!"

Aaron could not silence their fears with words, nor cool their anger. He was afraid for Moses' life, and his own, for the people grew more demanding with each miracle the Lord performed.

"Why are you arguing with me?" Moses pointed to the cloud. "And why are you testing the Lord?"

"Why did you bring us up out of Egypt? To make us and our livestock die of thirst?"

Aaron hated their ingratitude. "The Lord is providing bread for you every morning!"

"Bread with maggots in it!"

Moses held out his staff. "Because you collected more than you need!"

"What good is bread without water?"

"Is the Lord among us or not?"

How could they ask such questions when the cloud was over them by day and the pillar of fire by night? Each day brought renewed complaints and doubts. Moses spent every day in prayer. And so did Aaron when he wasn't forced to quiet the people's fears and encourage them with what the Lord had already done. They stopped their ears. Didn't they have eyes to see? What more did these people expect of Moses? Several picked up stones. Aaron called out to his sons and they stood around Moses. Had these people no fear of the Lord and what God would do to them if they killed His messenger?

"Aaron, gather some of the elders and follow me."

Aaron obeyed Moses and called for representatives he trusted from each of the tribes. The cloud descended on the side of the mountain where the people were camped. Aaron's skin prickled, for he saw a Man standing within the rock. How could this be? He closed his eyes tightly and opened them again, staring. The Man, if man he be, was still there. *Lord, Lord, am I losing my mind? Or is this a vision? Who is it who stands at the rock by the mountain of God when You overshadow us in the cloud?*

The people saw nothing.

"This place shall be called Testing and Arguing!" Moses struck the rock with his staff. "For the Israelites argued here and tested the Lord!" Water gushed forth, as though from a broken dam.

The elders ran back. "Moses has given us water from a rock!"

"Moses! Moses!" The people rushed toward the stream.

Exhausted, Moses sat. "God, forgive them. They don't know what they are saying."

Aaron could see how the responsibility of these people weighed on his brother. Moses heard their complaints and beseeched God for provision and guidance. "We will tell them again, Moses. It is the Lord who has rescued them. It is the Lord who provides. He is the one who has given them bread and meat and water."

Moses raised his head, his eyes full of tears. "They are a stubborn people, Aaron."

"And so shall we be! Stubborn in faith!"

"They still think like slaves. They want their food rations on time. They have forgotten the whips and the heavy labor, the unrelenting misery of their existence in Egypt, their cries to the Lord to save them."

"We will remind them of the plagues, the parting of the Red Sea."

"The sweetened waters of Marah and the streams of water from the rock at Mount Sinai."

"Whatever you tell me to say, I will say, Moses. I will shout the words God gives you from the hilltops."

"Moses!" It was a cry of alarm this time. "Moses!"

Aaron pushed himself to his feet. Would trouble never depart from them? He recognized the voice. "It's Joshua. What is it, my friend? What's happened now?"

The young man sank to his knees before Moses, panting, red-faced, sweat pouring down his cheeks, his tunic soaked

through. "The Amalekites—" he gasped for breath—"they're
attacking at Rephidim! They've killed those who haven't been
able to keep up. Old men. Women. The sick . . ."

"Choose some of our men and go out to fight them!" Moses
swayed as he stood.

Aaron caught hold of him. "You must rest. You haven't eaten
all day, nor have you had so much as a cup of water." What
would he do if Moses collapsed? Guide the people himself? Fear
gripped him. "The Lord has called you to lead His people to the
Promised Land, Moses. A man cannot do that without food,
water, and rest. You can do nothing more today!"

"You are three years older than I, Aaron."

"But you are the one God has called to deliver us. You are the
one bearing the weight of responsibility for God's people."

"*God* will deliver us." Moses sank down again. "Go out and
fight them, Joshua. Call the Israelites to arms, and fight the
army of Amalek." He sighed, exhausted. "Tomorrow, I will
stand at the top of the hill with the staff of God in my hand."

✦   ✦   ✦

In the morning, Aaron and Moses went to the top of the hill
overlooking the battlefield. Hur came with them. Moses held
up his hands and Joshua and the Israelites gave battle cries
and launched attack. Aaron saw how they cut through the
Amalekites advancing on them. But after a while, the tide of the
battle turned. Aaron looked to his brother to call on the Lord
and saw Moses' hands at his side. He rested for a few moments
and raised his hands again, and immediately the Israelites
seemed to gain strength and advantage.

"I cannot keep this up long enough for the battle to be won."
Exhausted, Moses' hands dropped to his sides.

"Here!" Aaron called to Hur. "Help me move this rock."
They rolled and shoved the rock until it was at the crest of the

hill overlooking the battle. "Sit, my brother, and we'll hold your hands up!" Aaron took his right arm and Hur his left and they held them up. As the hours wore on, Aaron's muscles trembled and burned from the effort, but his heart remained strong as he watched the battle below. The Israelites were prevailing against their enemies. By sunset, Joshua had overcome the Amalekites and put them to the sword.

Moses rallied long enough to pile up rocks for an altar. "It will be called 'The Lord Is My Banner.' Hands were lifted up to the throne of the Lord today. They have dared to raise their fist against the Lord's throne, so now the Lord will be at war with Amalek generation after generation. We must never forget what the Lord has done for us!"

When they returned to camp, Moses went into his tent to write the events meticulously on a scroll to be kept and read to Joshua and future generations.

✦   ✦   ✦

When they set out from Rephidim and headed into the Desert of Sinai, a messenger came from Midian. Moses' father-in-law, Jethro, was on his way to meet him and was bringing Moses' wife, Zipporah, and his sons, Gershom and Eliezer.

Miriam came into Aaron's tent. "Where was Moses going in such a hurry?"

"His father-in-law is here with Zipporah and the boys."

She hung the water bag. "She would've been better off staying in Midian."

"A wife belongs with her husband, and sons belong with their father."

"Does Moses have time for a wife when the people are always clamoring for his judgments? What time do you have for your own sons?"

Aaron broke bread with his family members each evening.

He prayed with them. They talked about the events of the day and the blessings of the Lord. He rose, in no mood to listen to more of Miriam's complaints about what might happen in the days ahead. She liked managing his household. All well and good. He would leave her to her duties. But there was room enough for everyone beneath God's canopy.

Miriam made a sound of disgust. "The woman cannot even speak our language."

Aaron did not point out that Miriam had not helped Zipporah while they lived beneath the same roof in Egypt. Zipporah would learn Aramaic just as Moses had, and so would Moses' sons, Gershom and Eliezer.

Joshua came to Aaron's tent. "Moses' father-in-law has brought offerings and sacrifices to God. Moses said to come with all the elders of Israel to eat bread with them in the presence of God."

So, was Joshua now acting as Moses' spokesman?

When Aaron arrived at Jethro's camp, he was gratified to see Moses' smile. It had been a long time since his brother had been so happy. Zipporah did not take her eyes from Moses, but she looked thinner than Aaron remembered. Gershom and Eliezer were speaking rapidly in their mother's tongue as they vied for their father's attention. They looked more Midianite than Hebrew. That would change, given new circumstances. He watched his brother hug his sons against him, speaking tenderly to them.

For all the familiarity and affection between the brothers, there was an element of foreignness about Moses. Forty years with Egyptians and another forty years with Midianites set him apart from his people. Aaron sat among these people and felt uncomfortable. Yet, his brother was at ease now, speaking Midian and then Aramaic without faltering. Everyone understood him.

Aaron felt the difference between them. He still thought like a
slave and looked to Moses as his master, waiting on his instructions. And he was glad for Moses who spoke to God before
speaking to others. Sometimes Aaron wondered if Moses realized
how God had been preparing him to lead from the day of his
birth. Moses wasn't born to die in the Nile, but was saved by
God and given into the hands of Pharaoh's own daughter so the
son of Hebrew slaves would grow up a freeman in palace corridors, learning the ways of the enemy. Moses moved between
worlds, from palaces to poor brick houses to a nomad's tent. He
lived beneath the canopy of God Himself, hearing the Voice, talking with the Lord as Adam must have in the Garden of Eden.

Aaron was in awe of Moses, proud to be of his flesh and
blood. Aaron, too, heard God's voice, but for Moses, it would
always be different. His brother spoke to the Lord and God listened as a father would listen to his child. God was Moses'
friend.

As night came and the pillar of fire glowed, the scent of
Jethro's burnt offering filled the air. While they all partook of
Jethro's feast of roasted lamb, dates, and raisin cakes, Moses
spoke of all the things the Lord had done in bringing His people
out of Egypt. There were bread and olive oil in which to dip it.
Wine flowed freely. Nadab and Abihu held up their cups for
more each time a servant passed near.

Surely, this is what life would be like when they reached the
Promised Land. Ah, but Canaan would be even better, for the
Lord Himself had said it would be a land of milk and honey. To
have milk, there must be herds of cattle and flocks of goats. To
have honey, there must be fruit trees and grapevines with blos-
soms where the bees could gather their nectar.

After centuries of slavery, Israel was *free*.

Aaron took another piece of lamb and some dates. This was
the life to which he wanted to become accustomed.

✦ ✦ ✦

Aaron's head ached from too much wine, and he had to force
himself to rise the next morning. Moses would need his help
soon. People would be clamoring for his judgment over whatever difficulties had arisen in the last twenty-four hours. Mediating and arbitrating went on from dawn to dusk. The people
scarcely gave Moses time to eat. With so many thousands living
so close to one another, clashes were inevitable. Each day had
new challenges, more problems. A minor infraction could lead
to heated arguments and fighting. The people didn't seem to
know what to do with their freedom other than fight with one
another and complain to Moses about everything! Aaron was
torn between wanting them to think for themselves, and seeing
the consequences when they did—trouble, out of which Moses
had to judge fairly between opposing parties.

More people stood waiting for Moses' attention than had yesterday. Squabbles between tribes, arguments between tribal
brothers. Maybe it was the heat that kept them from getting
along. Maybe it was the long days and deferred hope. Aaron
didn't have much patience today. He longed for his tent and
a rolled-up blanket under his head.

"Is it like this every day?"

Aaron hadn't noticed Jethro's approach. "Every day gets
worse."

"This is not good."

Who is he to talk? "Moses is our leader. He must judge the
people."

"No wonder he has aged since the last time I saw him. The
people are wearing him out!"

Two men shouted at one another while waiting in the line.
Soon they were shoving each other, involving others. Aaron left
Jethro quickly, hoping to curb the disturbance, calling on the

assistance of several of his relatives to help break up the fight and restore order to those waiting.

The men were separated, but not before one was injured.

"Go and have someone see to the cut over your eye."

"And lose my place in line? *No!* I was here yesterday waiting, and the day before that! I'm not leaving. This man took the bride-price for his sister and now won't let me have her as my wife!"

"You want a wife? Here! Take mine!"

While some laughed, another lost his temper. "Maybe the rest of you can stand around making jokes, but I've got serious business. I can't stand here until the next full moon waiting for Moses to hack off this man's hand for stealing my sheep and making it a feast for his friends!"

"I found that mangy animal caught in a bramble! That makes it my sheep."

"Your son drove it away from my flock!"

"Are you calling me a liar?"

"A liar and a thief!"

Aaron's relatives helped separate the men. Angry, Aaron called for everyone to listen. "It would be easier for everyone if you all tried to get along with one another!" He gripped his staff. Sometimes they acted like sheep, Moses as their shepherd, and other times, they were more like wolves intent on tearing each other apart. "Anyone else who causes trouble in the line will be sent back to their tents. They can go to the end of the line tomorrow!"

The silence was anything but peaceful.

Jethro shook his head, expression grim. "This is not good. These people are worn-out from waiting."

For all the pleasurable memories of the feast the night before, Aaron was annoyed that the Midianite felt free to criticize. "It may not be good, but it is the way things must be. Moses is the one with the ear of God."

"It is almost evening, and there are more people here now than there were when the day began."

Aaron could see no good reason for stating the obvious. "You are a guest. It is not your problem."

"Moses is my son-in-law. I would like to see him live long enough to see his grandsons." He went into the tent. "Moses, why are you trying to do all this alone? The people have been standing here all day to get your help."

Aaron wanted to hook Jethro with his shepherd's staff and haul him from the tent. Who did this uncircumcised pagan think he was to question God's anointed?

But Moses answered with grave respect. "Well, the people come to me to seek God's guidance. When an argument arises, I am the one who settles the case. I inform the people of God's decisions and teach them His laws and instructions."

"This is not good, my son! You're going to wear yourself out—and the people, too. This job is too heavy a burden for you to handle all by yourself. Now let me give you a word of advice, and may God be with you."

Moses rose and asked those present to leave. Aaron didn't listen to the arguments, but upheld Moses' decision, urging those inside the tent to leave. They would not lose their places, but would have the first hearing when Moses sat as judge again. He signaled his relatives to send the rest to their tents, and tried to ignore the rumble of discontent. Aaron drew the tent flap down and rejoined his brother and Jethro.

"You should continue to be the people's representative before God, bringing Him their questions to be decided." Jethro sat, hands spread in appeal. "You should tell them God's decisions, teach them God's laws and instructions, and show them how to conduct their lives. But find some capable, honest men who fear God and hate bribes. Appoint them as judges over groups of one thousand, one hundred, fifty, and ten. These men can serve the people, resolving all the ordinary cases. Anything that is too important or too complicated can be brought to you. But they can take care of the smaller matters themselves. They will help you carry the load, making the task easier for you. If you follow this advice, and if God directs you to do so, then you will be able to endure the pressures, and all these people will go home in peace."

Aaron saw that Moses was listening intently and weighing, measuring the merit of Jethro's words. Had Moses always been this way or had circumstances made him so? The Midianite's suggestion did seem a reasonable one, but was this a plan the Lord would approve?

Aaron did not need Jethro to point out the lines deepening in Moses' face, or how his hair had turned white. His brother was thinner, not for lack of food but for lack of time to eat it. Moses did not like to leave important matters to another day, but with the increasing number of cases coming before him, he could not manage them all before sundown. And unless the Lord instructed him to do so, Aaron had no intention of sitting in Moses' judgment seat. But something had to be done. The dust and heat frayed the most patient among them, and every time Aaron heard arguing, he was in fear of what the Lord would do to these belligerent people.

Over the next few days, Aaron, Moses, and the elders met together to discuss men best suited to serve as judges. Seventy were chosen, able men of faith, trustworthy and dedicated to obeying the precepts and statutes God gave through His servant Moses. And there was some rest for Moses and for Aaron as well because of Jethro's suggestion.

Still, Aaron was glad to see the Midianite depart and take his servants with him. Jethro was a priest of Midian, and had acknowledged the Lord as greater than all other gods, but when the invitation to stay had been given by Moses, Jethro chose to go his own way. He had rejected being part of Israel, and therefore, rejected the Lord God as well. For all the love and respect Moses and Jethro shared for one another, their people were on different paths.

Sometimes Aaron found himself longing for the simplicity of slavery. All he had to do then was make his quota of bricks for the day and not draw the attention of the taskmaster. Now, he had all these thousands and thousands watching his every move, making demands, vying for his attention and the attention of Moses. Were there enough hours in a day to do all the work required? No! Was there any escape from this kind of servitude?

Worn down and burned out, lying sleepless on his pallet, Aaron couldn't keep the betraying thought from entering his mind and taunting him: *Is this the freedom I wanted? Is this the life I longed to live?* Granted, he no longer worked in a mud pit. He no longer had to fear the taskmaster's whip. But the joy and relief he had felt when death passed over him were gone. He had marched out into the desert, jubilant and filled with hope, secure in the future God had promised. Now, the constant carping, complaints, and pleas of the people weighed him down. One day they were praising the Lord and the next whining and wailing.

And he had no right to condemn them when he heard his own words echoing back from the days he had traveled this land in search of his brother. He, too, had complained.

When God brought the people into the Promised Land, then he would have rest. He would sit beneath the shade of a tree and sip nectar made from his own vines. He would have time to talk with his sons and surround himself with his grandchildren. He would sleep through the heat of the day, untroubled by worry.

The cloud was his solace. He would look up during the day

and know that the Lord was near. The Lord was protecting them from the scorching heat of the sun. At night, the fire kept the darkness away. It was only when he was inside his tent, eyes closed, trapped in his own thoughts, assessing his own abilities, that his faith wavered.

In the third month after leaving Egypt, the cloud settled over Sinai and the people camped in the desert in front of the mountain where Aaron had found his brother, the mountain where the Lord had first spoken to Moses from the burning bush. The people were at the place where Moses had received the call. Holy ground!

As the Israelites rested, Aaron went up with Moses to the foot of the mountain. "Tend the flock, Aaron." From there, Moses went on alone.

Aaron hesitated, not wanting to go back. He watched Moses climb, feeling more bereft as the distance grew between them. Moses was the one who heard the Lord's voice most often and most clearly. Moses was the one who told Aaron what to say, what to do.

If only all men heard the Voice. And obeyed.

As I must obey. Aaron dug his staff into the rocky ground. "Come back soon, my brother. Lord, we need him. I need him." Turning away, Aaron went down to the camp to wait.

FOUR

"YOU'RE to come with me this time, Aaron." Moses' words filled Aaron with joy. He had wanted . . . "When I go up before the Lord, you will stand so that the people will not come up the mountain. They must not force their way through or the Lord will break out against them."

The people. Moses always worried about the people, as Aaron knew he must.

Moses had already climbed the mountain twice, and Aaron longed to go and see the Lord for himself. But he was afraid to ask.

Moses and Aaron gathered the people and gave them instructions. "Wash your clothes and get ready for an important event two days from now. The Lord will descend on the mountain. Until the shofar sounds with a long blast, you must not approach the mountain, on penalty of death."

Miriam greeted him with tears. "Think of how many generations have longed for this day, Aaron. Just think of it." She clung to him, weeping.

His sons and their wives and children washed their clothing. Aaron was too excited to eat or sleep. He had yearned for the Voice to come upon him again, to hear the Lord, to feel God's presence over, around, in, and through him as he had before. He had tried to make his sons understand, his daughters-in-law, his grandchildren, even Miriam. But he could not explain the sensation of hearing God's voice when all around were deaf to it. He had felt the Word of the Lord from within.

Only Moses understood—Moses, whose experience of God must be far more profound than Aaron could even imagine. He saw it in his brother's face each time he returned from the mountain of God; he saw the change in Moses' eyes. For a time, on that mountain with God, Moses lived in the midst of eternity.

Now, all Israel would understand what neither man could explain. All Israel would hear the Lord!

Awakening before dawn, Aaron sat outside his tent, watching and waiting. Who could sleep on a day like this? But few were outside their tents. Moses came out of his tent and walked toward him. Aaron rose and embraced him.

"You're shaking."

"You are the friend of God, Moses. I am only your spokesman."

"You were called to deliver Israel, too, my brother." They went out into the open to wait.

The air changed. Lightning flashed and was followed by a low, heavy roll of sound. People peered out of their tents, tentative, frightened. Aaron called out to them. "Come! It is time." Miriam, his sons, and their wives and children came outside, washed and ready. Smiling, Aaron followed Moses and beckoned the people to follow.

Smoke billowed as from a giant furnace. The whole mountain shook, making the ground beneath Aaron's feet shake. His heart trembled. The air grew dense. Aaron's blood raced as his skin prickled with sensation. The cloud overhead swirled like great waves of dark gray moving around the mountaintop. A spear of light flashed and was answered by a deep roar Aaron could feel inside his chest. Another spear of light flashed and another, the sound so deep it rolled over and through him. From within the cloud came the sound of the ram's horn—long, loud, recognizable and yet alien. Aaron wanted to cover his ears and hide from the power of it, but stood straight, praying. *Have mercy on me. Have mercy on me.* All the great winds of the earth were coming through the shofar, for the Creator of all was blowing it.

Moses walked toward the mountain. Aaron stayed close to him, as eager as he was terrified. He couldn't take his eyes from the swelling smoke, the streaks of fire, the brilliance amidst the gray churning cloud. The Lord was coming! Aaron saw the red, orange, and gold flickering light descending, smoke billowing up from the mountain. *The Lord is a consuming fire!* The ground shook beneath Aaron's feet. There was no hint of ash in the air despite the fire and smoke from the mountaintop.

The deep blast of the shofar continued until Aaron's heart ached with the sound. He stopped when he came to the boundary God had set and watched as Moses went up the mountain alone to meet with the Lord face-to-face. Aaron waited, breath shallow, arms outstretched so that the people would know to stay back. The mountain was holy ground. When he looked over his shoulder, he saw Joshua and Miriam, Eleazar and little Phinehas, and others. They all stood looking up, faces rapt with awe.

And then Aaron heard the Lord again.

I am the Lord your God, who rescued you from slavery in Egypt.

The Word of the Lord rushed in, through, and out of Aaron.

Do not worship any other gods besides Me. Do not make idols of any kind, whether in the shape of birds or animals or fish. . . . Do not misuse the name of the Lord your God. . . . Remember to observe the Sabbath day by keeping it holy. . . . Honor your father and mother. Then you will live a long, full life in the land the Lord your God will give you. . . . Do not murder. . . . Do not commit adultery. . . . Do not steal. . . . Do not testify falsely against your neighbor. . . . Do not covet your neighbor's house. Do not covet your neighbor's wife,

male or female servant, ox or donkey, or anything else your
neighbor owns.

The Voice overshadowed and shone through, and drew up
from the depths inside him and spilled out with unbridled joy.
Aaron's heart sang even as the fear of the Lord filled him. His
blood raced like a cleansing stream washing away everything in
a flood of sensation. He felt the old life ebb and true *life* rush in.
The Word of the Lord was there inside him, stirring, swelling,
blazing bright in his mind, burning in his heart, pouring from
his mouth. Pure ecstasy filled him as he felt the Presence, the
Voice within, heard without, all around him. *Amen! And amen!
Let it be! Let it be!* He wanted to stay immersed. *Reign in me,
Lord. Reign! Reign!*

But the people were screaming, "Moses! Moses!"

Aaron didn't want to turn away from what he was experi-
encing. He wanted to scream back at them not to refuse the
gift offered! *Embrace it. Embrace Him. Don't bring an end
to the relationship we were born to have.* But it was already
too late.

Moses came back. "Don't be afraid, for God has come in this
way to show you His awesome power. From now on, let your
fear of Him keep you from sinning!"

The people ran. "Come back!" Aaron called, but they had
already fled in terror and remained at a distance. Even his own
sons and their children! Tears of disappointment burned his
eyes. What choice had he now but to go to them?

"You tell us what God says, Moses, and we will listen," the
leaders called out. "But don't let God speak directly to us. If He
does, we will die!"

"Come and hear for yourself what the Lord says to you."

They cowered from the sound and wind. They would not
raise their heads and look up at the smoke and fire.

The thunder ceased and the wind died down. The shofar no longer sounded from the mountaintop. The earth grew still.

Aaron was in anguish over the silence. The moment was over, the opportunity lost forever. Did these people fail to understand what had been offered, what they had rejected? His throat was tight and hot as he held in his grief and disappointment.

Will I ever hear His voice again? Miriam said something to him, then to his sons. Aaron could not speak for the choking sorrow holding him where he was. He kept looking up at the glow of glory on Sinai. He had felt that fire burning within him, igniting his life with what it would mean to be like Moses. Oh, to hear the Lord daily, to have a personal relationship with God, the Creator of all things. And if all had heard, the heavy burden of responsibility for this multitude would be lifted from his back and from Moses'. Each person would have heard God's voice. Each person would know God's Word. Each would be made to understand and could then choose to obey the will of God.

The dream of it gripped him. Freedom from the responsibility of so many lives. And the people! No more complaining! No more grumbling! Every man in Israel would be equally yoked!

But the dream was already slipping away and the weight of God's call was on him again. Aaron remembered the days of his youth when he had no one to worry about but himself, no responsibility but to survive the slave masters and the Egyptian sun.

The fire on Sinai was a red-gold haze through his tears. *Oh, Lord, Lord, how I long to . . . to what?* He had no words, no explanation for what he felt. Just this pain at the center of his being, the ache of loss and longing. And he knew it would never really go away. God had called them to the mountain to hear His voice. God had called them to be His people. But they

had rejected the proffered gift and cried out instead for a man
to lead them: Moses.

+   +   +

"Do not be downcast, Aaron." Miriam sat with him and put her
hand on his head. "We could not help but be afraid. Such
sound. Such fury."

Did she think he was a little boy to be comforted? He stood
and moved away from her. "He is the Lord! You have seen the
cloud and the pillar of fire. My own family fled like frightened
sheep!" His sons and their wives and children had cried out for
Moses like the rest. Did his words to them mean nothing? Was
he still a slave? All these months he had tried to tell them what
it was like to hear the voice of the Lord, to know it was God
speaking and not some voice in his own imaginings. And when
their chance came, what did they do? They ran from God. They
shook inside their newly washed robes. They wept in terror and
cried out for Moses to listen to God's voice and speak the Word
to them.

"You're acting like a child, Aaron."

He turned on his sister. "You're not my mother, Miriam. Nor
my wife."

Blushing, she opened her mouth to retort, but he walked past
her out of the tent. There was no silencing her. She was like the
wind, ever blowing, and he was in no mood to listen to her
counsel, or her complaining.

Moses approached. "Gather the people and have them assemble at the foot of the mountain."

They all came, Aaron leading them. Joshua was already at
the foot of the mountain, standing beside Moses. Aaron was
annoyed that Eliezer and Gershom were not there to serve their
father. Why should it be this young man of the tribe of Judah
who stood near Moses rather than one of their own relations?

From the beginning of the journey out of Egypt, Joshua had stationed himself as near Moses as possible, serving him with every opportunity given. And Moses had embraced the young man as his servant. Even when Jethro had brought Eliezer and Gershom with Zipporah, Joshua remained at Moses' side. Where were Moses' sons this morning? Aaron spotted them among the people, standing on either side of their ailing mother.

"Hear the Word of the Lord!" The throng fell silent and listened as Moses told them all the words the Lord had given him, laws to keep the people from sinning against one another, laws to protect foreigners who lived among them and followed the way of the Lord, laws concerning property when it would be given to them, laws of justice and mercy. The Lord proclaimed three festivals to be celebrated each year: the Festival of Unleavened Bread to remind them of their deliverance from Egypt, the Festival of Harvest, and the Festival of the Final Harvest to give thanks for the Lord's provision. Wherever they lived in the Promised Land, all the men of Israel were to appear before the Lord at a place the Lord set during these three celebrations.

No longer would they be able to do whatever was right in their own eyes.

"The Lord is sending His angel before us to lead us safely to the land He has prepared for us. We must pay attention to Him, and obey all of His instructions. Do not rebel against Him, for He will not forgive your sins. He is the Lord's representative—He bears His name."

Aaron's heart raced as he remembered the Man he had seen walking in front of his brother. He had not been a figment of his imagination! Nor was the Man who had stood within the rock at Mount Sinai and from whom the water had flowed. They were one and the same, the Angel of the Lord. Leaning in, he drank in his brother's words.

"If you are careful to obey Him, following all of the Lord's instructions, then He will be an enemy to our enemies, and He will oppose those who oppose us." Moses spread his arms, palms up. "We must serve only the Lord our God. If we do, He will bless us with food and water, and He will keep us healthy. There will be no miscarriages or infertility among our people, and He will give us long, full lives. When we get to the Promised Land, we must drive out the people who live there or they will cause us to sin against the Lord because their gods are a snare." He lowered his hands. "And what do you say to the Lord?"

Aaron called out, "Everything the Lord says, we will do!" And the people repeated his words until over a million voices rang out before the Lord God of Israel.

Early the next morning, Moses built an altar of earth before the mountain of God. Twelve uncut stone pillars stood, one for each of the tribes of Israel. Young Israelite men were chosen to bring forward sacrificed young bulls as fellowship offerings to the Lord. Moses took half the blood of the bulls and put it into bowls. The other half he sprinkled on the altar. He read the Word of the Lord that he had written into the Book of the Covenant, and the people said again that they would obey the Word of the Lord. The air was filled with the scent of burnt offerings.

Moses turned to him. "Aaron, you and your two sons, Nadab and Abihu, and the seventy leaders are to come with me up the mountain." Aaron savored the command. He had waited for this moment, a time when he would not only hear the Word of the Lord, but stand in His presence. Joy mingled with fear as he followed his brother up Mount Sinai, the elders behind him.

The climb was not easy. Surely, it was the Lord Himself who had given Moses the strength to make this climb four times before! Aaron felt every day of his eighty-three years as he followed in his brother's footsteps, weaving his way upward along the rough path. His muscles ached. He had to pause for breath and start again. Above was the swirling cloud of the Lord, the fire on the mountaintop. When Aaron, his sons, and the elders reached a level space, Moses stood waiting. "We will worship the Lord here."

Aaron saw the God of Israel. Under His feet there seemed to be a pavement of brilliant sapphire, as clear as the heavens. Surely now, Aaron would die. He trembled at the sight before him and fell on his knees, bowing his head to the ground.

Arise and eat. Drink the water I give you.

Never before had Aaron felt such exultation and thanksgiving. He never wanted to leave this place. He forgot all those around him and those who waited on the plains below. He lived in the moment, filled up and fulfilled with the sight of God's power and majesty. He felt small but not insignificant, one among many, but cherished. The manna tasted of heaven; the water restored his strength.

Moses put his hand on Aaron's shoulder. "The Lord has called me up the mountain to give me the Law for His people. Stay here and wait for us until we come back."

"We?"

"Joshua is going up the mountain with me."

Aaron felt a cold wave of anger. He looked past Moses to the younger man. "He is an Ephraimite, not a Levite."

"Aaron." Moses spoke quietly. "Are we not to obey the Lord in all things?"

His stomach clenched tight. His mouth trembled. "Yes." *I want to go,* he longed to say. *I want be the one at your side! Why do you set me aside now?*

All the feelings he had as a lonely boy sitting in the reeds came rushing back. Someone else was being chosen.

Moses spoke to them all. "If there are any problems while I am gone, consult with Aaron and Hur, who are here with you."

Bereft, Aaron watched Moses turn away and take the high path farther up the mountain, Joshua close behind. Tears burned in Aaron's eyes. He blinked them away, fighting against the emotions warring inside him. *Why Joshua? Why not me?* Hadn't he been the one to find Moses in the desert? Hadn't he been the one God had chosen as Moses' spokesman? Aaron's throat closed, hot, tight, choking him. *It's not fair!*

As Moses and Joshua ascended, Aaron remained with the others, and the weight of people was heavier now than it had ever been before.

✦   ✦   ✦

For six days, Aaron and the others remained on the mountain, the cloud shrouding its top, Moses and Joshua within sight, but separated from them. And then on the seventh day, the Lord called to Moses from within the cloud. Aaron and the others heard the Voice, like low, rolling thunder. Moses rose and continued up the mountain, Joshua following for a ways and then remaining like a sentry on guard as Aaron's brother entered the cloud. A rush of sound came, and a blaze of fire flashed brilliant from the mountain peak. From below, they could hear people screaming.

"Aaron!" Hur cried out. "The people need us to reassure them."

Aaron kept his back to the others. "Moses said to wait here."

"The elders are going down."

"We were to wait!"

"Aaron!" Hur called out. "They need you!"

Aaron wept bitterly. *Why? God, why must I be left behind?*

"Moses said they were to come to us for counsel. If they cross the boundaries, the Lord will strike out against them!"

Aaron shut his eyes tightly. "All right!" His shoulders
sagged as he turned away. He started back down the mountain
pathway, fully intending to do what the Lord required of him.

Glancing back one last time, Aaron looked up. Joshua
stood in the haze at the edge of the cloud that shrouded the
mountain.

✦   ✦   ✦

The elders surrounded Aaron, frightened, confused. "It's been
ten days, Aaron! And the fire has burned constantly."

"The people believe Moses is dead."

"Would the Lord God kill His anointed?" Aaron said, angry.

"No man could live in the midst of that fire!"

"Nor has Joshua returned."

"Someone should go up and see if—"

Aaron rose, glaring at his sons. "No one is to go near the
mountain! Have you forgotten the boundaries God set? It is
holy ground! Any who come near will be struck dead by the
Lord!"

"Then surely Moses and Joshua are dead already."

"My brother is alive! The Lord Himself called him to the top
of the mountain to receive the Word. He will come back to us!"

Korah shook his head. "You are a dreamer, Aaron! Look up!
What man can survive such a fire?"

"That fire will consume *you* if you rebel against the Lord!"

They all spoke at once.

Aaron shouted, "Go back to your tents. Gather the manna
each morning as you have been instructed. Drink the water the
Lord has supplied. And wait as I wait!" He went back inside his
tent and yanked the flap closed. He sat on a cushion and covered his face. He didn't want to listen to their doubts. He had
enough doubts of his own. Moses said, "wait." *I have to wait.
God, help me wait!*

He thought of Joshua standing up there beside Moses. Joshua, the one his brother had chosen . . .

"Don't you think you should . . ."

He glared at his sister.

She sighed loudly. "I was just thinking . . ." She held his gaze for a moment and then lowered her head and went back to carding wool.

Even Aaron's sons plagued him with questions. "I don't know why he remains so long on the mountain! I don't know if he is well! Yes! He is an old man, and I am older still! If you keep on besieging me, you will wear me down to the grave with your demands!"

Only after a long, exhausting day of counseling and judging did Aaron stand alone. While the people slept, he looked up at the mountain and watched the consuming fire. How had Moses born such pressure? How had he listened to case after case and kept himself clear of sides?

I can't do this, Moses. You've got to come down off that mountain. You've got to come back!

Was Moses dead? He shut his eyes tightly at the thought, fear welling up inside him. Was that why there was no sign of him after so many days? And where was Joshua? Was he still waiting on that rocky slope? His provisions must be gone by now.

The people were like sheep without a shepherd. Their questions had become like bleats and *baaa*s. Aaron knew he was going to have to do something to keep the people from wandering off. Some wanted to go back to Egypt. Others wanted to take their flocks to Midian pastures. No one was content.

He couldn't sleep. He gathered the manna with everyone else, but could barely eat. Everywhere he went, he was met with the same questions:

"Where is Moses?" *On the mountain with God.*

"Is he alive?" *I am certain he is.*

"When is he coming back?" *I don't know. I don't know!*

✦   ✦   ✦

Thirty-five days went by, then thirty-six, thirty-seven. With each day that passed, Aaron's fear and anger grew.

It was hot inside the tent, but he didn't go outside. He knew the moment he did, people would clamor for answers he didn't have. He was sick of their grumbling and whining. How should he know what was happening on the mountain?

Moses! Why do you linger?

Did his brother have any idea what Aaron was going through with these complainers down here on the dusty plains? Or was Moses just basking in the presence of the Lord? Aaron knew if he didn't do something soon, these people would stone him to death and then scatter across the wilderness like wild donkeys!

Miriam looked at him gravely. "They're calling for you."

"I can hear."

"They sound angry, Father."

They sound ready to stone someone.

"You have to do something, Aaron."

He turned on Miriam. "What would you suggest?"

"I don't know, but they are past patience. Give them something to occupy them!"

"Have them make bricks again? Build a city here at the foot of the mountain?"

"Aaron!" The elders were outside his tent. *"Aaron!"* Korah was with them. Even Hur was losing faith. "Aaron, we must talk with you!"

He fought tears. His heart trembled. "God has abandoned us." Maybe the only one God cared about was Moses. For the fire still burned on the mountain. Moses was still up there alone with God. Maybe God and Moses had forgotten about him and the people. His breath shook as he exhaled. If Moses was still alive. Forty days had passed. An eighty-year-old man couldn't last . . .

The elders and people surrounded him when he came outside. He felt oppressed by their impatience. They were no longer worried about his brother. The tribes were ready to split off and go in a dozen directions rather than remain at the foot of the mountain. They were no longer willing to hear the words, "Wait here until Moses returns."

"This man Moses, who brought us here from Egypt, has disappeared. We don't know what has happened to him."

This man Moses? They saw the miracle God performed in Egypt! They saw Moses hold out his staff while God opened the Red Sea so they could cross over on dry land! And they could speak about Moses' disappearance with such indifference? Fear gripped Aaron. If they cared so little about his brother who had delivered them from Pharaoh, how long before they despised him too?

"You must lead us, Aaron."

"Tell us what to do."

"We can't stay here forever waiting for an old man who is dead."

"Make us some gods who can lead us!"

Aaron turned away, but there were more people behind him. He looked into their eyes. Everyone was talking at once, crying out, pushing. Some raised fists. He felt the heat of their fetid breath, the pull of their fear, the shove of their anger.

"Give them something to do," Miriam had said. *"Give them something to occupy them!"*

"All right!" Aaron shoved back, wanting distance between himself and the people. How he longed to be up on that mountain. Better dead in the flames of God than alive down here on the plain, with the dust and the rabble. He hated being pushed and shoved. He hated their demands and complaints. He hated their constant whining. "All right!"

When they fell silent, he felt relief and then pride. They were listening to him, leaning toward him, looking to him to lead.

To give them something to do.

Yes, I'll give them something to do. "Take off the gold earrings that your wives, your sons, and your daughters are wearing." He would not ask these men to give up their own ornaments. "Bring them to me."

They scattered quickly to do his will. Exhaling, he went back into his tent. Miriam stood, shaking in confusion. "What are you doing, Aaron?"

"I'm giving them something to do!"

"What are you giving them to do?"

Ignoring her, Aaron emptied baskets and set them out. People came with gifts and offerings. The baskets were soon overflowing. Every man and woman, boy and girl gave a pair of gold earrings. Everyone in the camp participated, even Miriam and his sons and their wives.

Now what?

Aaron built a fire and melted the earrings, taking the gold God had given them from the vanquished Egyptians. *How do you make something that represents the God of the universe? What would He look like?* Aaron looked up at the mountain. Moses was up there looking at God. And Joshua was with him.

Aaron made a mold and poured the molten gold into it. Weeping angrily, he fashioned a golden calf. It was ugly and roughly hewn. Surely, when the people looked on his effort— and then up at the mountain still ablaze with the glory of the Lord—they would see the difference between the false statues of Egypt and the living God who could not be shown by human hands. How could they not see?

"These are your gods, O Israel!" the elders called out. "These are the gods who brought you out of Egypt!"

Aaron shuddered as he looked up at the consuming fire still ablaze on Mount Sinai. Was God watching, or was He too busy talking to Moses? Did God understand what was happening down here? *Do not worship any other gods besides Me.*

Fear gripped Aaron. He tried to justify himself. He tried to rationalize why he had made the idol. Hadn't God always given the people exactly what they asked for and then disciplined them? Wasn't Aaron doing the same thing? They demanded water. God gave it. They demanded food. God gave it. And each time, discipline had followed.

Discipline.

Aaron's body went cold.

The people bowed down to the golden calf, oblivious of the cloud and the fire above them. Had they become so accustomed to the sight that they no longer noticed them? They chanted and moaned their reverence for the golden calf that could not hear, see, or think. No one looked up as he did.

Nothing happened. The cloud remained cool; the fire above, warm.

Aaron took his eyes from the mountain and watched the people.

An hour passed, then another. They grew tired of bowing down to the ground. One by one, they stood and looked at Aaron. He could feel the gathering storm, the low hum.

He built an altar of stones in front of the calf as it stood before the mountain, uncut stones as God required. "Tomorrow there will be a festival to the Lord!" He would remind them of the manna God provided. They would have rested by then. Things always looked better in the morning.

Laughing and clapping their hands, they scattered like children eager to make preparations. Even his own sons and their wives were eager for the next day to come as they laid out the finery of Egypt.

The elders presented the burnt offerings and fellowship offerings to the golden calf as the sun's glow lit the eastern horizon. With that formality completed, the people sat down to feast. Scorning the manna that rained softly, they slaughtered lambs and goats to roast. Nor did they drink the water that still flowed unceasingly from the rock near Mount Sinai. They drank deeply of fermented milk. Those with harp and lyre played the music of Egypt.

Sated and drunk, the people rose to indulge themselves in dancing. They became louder and more raucous as the day wore on. Fights broke out. People stood around, laughing as blood was shed. Young women eager to be caught ran laughing from the young men pursuing them.

Face red with shame, Aaron went inside his tent. His younger sons, Eleazar and Ithamar, sat in grim silence while Miriam huddled in the back with their wives and children, hands over her ears. "This isn't what I intended. You know it isn't!" Aaron sat grimly, head down as he listened to the shouting outside his tent.

"You have to do something to stop it, Aaron."

"It was your idea in the first place."

"My idea?! This isn't what I—" She clamped her mouth shut.

He covered his face. Everything was out of control. The people were running wild. If he tried to stop them now, they'd kill him, and nothing would change.

The people took pleasure anywhere and any way they wanted. They had not made this much noise when they left Egypt on the day after the Angel of Death had passed over them! It was up to the Lord now to deal with them. If the Lord remembered them at all. . . .

He heard a low rumble and felt cold. He held his breath until his lungs hurt and breathed slowly, quietly. His hands were shaking.

Nadab and Abihu entered the tent, swaying, skin containers limp in their hands. "Why are you in here? There's a celebration outside."

A man's voice wailed in the distance, and the sound echoed and grew louder in rage and anguish.

Aaron felt the hair on the back of his neck rise. "Moses!" He threw the tent flap back and ran out, relief filling him. His brother was alive! *"Moses!"* Pushing his way through the revelers, he ran toward the boundary at the foot of the mountain, eager to welcome his brother home. Everything would be all right now. Moses would know what to do.

When Aaron came near the mountain, he saw his brother high on the pathway, head thrown back as he wailed. Aaron stopped running. He looked back and saw the debauchery, the shameless parading of sin. When he looked up again, he wanted to back away, to run and hide in his tent. He wanted to cover his head with ashes. He knew what Moses saw from his high place.

And God could see too.

With a scream of rage, Moses raised two stone tablets above his head and hurled them. Aaron drew back, terrified the Lord would give Moses strength to bring the weight of those two slabs down on his head. But the tablets shattered on the ground, merely pelting Aaron with bits of stone and a cloud of dust. The loss hit him, and he covered his face.

Pandemonium prevailed around him as people scattered. Others paused in confusion, all talking at once. Some were too drunk and caught up in their debauchery to hear or care that the prophet of God had returned. Some had the audacity to call out greetings to Moses and invite him to join the celebration!

Aaron drew back into the crowd, hoping to hide his shame

among the others, hoping Moses would forget about him for the moment and not make his disgrace public.

His brother went straight through the throng and stood before the golden calf. "Burn it!" At Moses' command, Joshua tumbled the idol. "Melt it down and grind the gold into dust and scatter it over the water. Let them drink it!"

The crowd parted like the Red Sea as Moses walked toward Aaron. It took every ounce of Aaron's courage not to run from his own brother. Moses had once murdered an Egyptian in anger and buried him beneath the Egyptian sand. Would Moses now raise his hand against his own brother and strike him down? Moses' knuckles whitened around his shepherd's staff.

Aaron closed his eyes. *If he kills me, so be it. It's no less than I deserve.*

"What did the people do to you?" Moses demanded. "How did they ever make you bring such terrible sin upon them?"

"Don't get upset," Aaron replied. "You yourself know these people and what a wicked bunch they are. They said to me, 'Make us some gods to lead us, for something has happened to this man Moses, who led us out of Egypt.' No one knew what happened to you. It's been over forty days, Moses! I didn't know if you were alive or dead! What did you expect me to do?"

His brother's eyes flashed. "You accuse me?"

Mortified, Aaron whined, "No. I didn't know what to do, Moses. So I told them, 'Bring me your gold earrings.' When they brought them to me, I threw them into the fire—and out came this calf!" He felt the heat flood his cheeks, and he could only hope his beard covered the telltale color of his lie.

It didn't. The fury died in Moses' eyes, but the look that came in its place filled Aaron with shame far deeper than any fear he had felt. He would have felt better if Moses had beaten him with his staff. Eyes filling with tears, Aaron bowed his head, unable to look at Moses. The people were running wild,

and Aaron knew it was his fault! He had not had the strength
to shepherd this wayward flock. As soon as Moses was out of
sight, he had begun to weaken. Was Israel now a laughingstock
to the nations watching them? The people wouldn't even listen
to Moses! They were out of control!

Moses turned his back on Aaron and went back to stand at
the entrance of the camp. Facing in, he shouted. "All of you
who are on the Lord's side, come over here and join me."

Aaron ran to his brother. "What are you going to do,
Moses?"

"Take your place at my side."

Moses did not look at him, but surveyed the riotous Israelites. Aaron knew that look and shuddered. Aaron saw his sons
and relatives among the throng. Fear filled him for their sake.
"Come on! Hurry! Stand with Moses!" His sons came running
and so did his uncles and cousins and their wives and children.
"Hurry!" Would fire come from the mountain?

Eliezer and Gershom raced to their father, taking their places
behind Moses. Even Korah the troublemaker came. The Levites
stood as one with Moses. Joshua, an Ephraimite, stood firm
beside his mentor, grim-faced when Moses' and Aaron's relatives continued to ignore Moses' command.

Moses raised his staff and spoke to the Levites. "This is what
the Lord, the God of Israel, says: 'Strap on your swords! Go
back and forth from one end of the camp to the other, killing
even your brothers, friends, and neighbors.'"

Joshua drew his sword. Standing in horrified silence, Aaron
watched as he cleaved the head of a man mocking Moses. Blood
sprayed as the body sank lifeless to the ground.

The hair rose on the back of Aaron's neck. "Moses! I am more
guilty than these wretched people! It's my fault they behave
like sheep without a shepherd."

"You're standing with me."

"Let the blame fall on me."

"It is for the Lord to decide!"

"Perhaps they didn't hear over the din." The screams of the dying tore at Aaron's heart. "Have mercy! How can I kill them when it's my own weakness that has brought this upon them?"

"They've shunned their opportunity for salvation!"

"Speak to them again, Moses. Shout louder!"

Moses' face darkened. "Be silent! They will learn—*as you will learn*—to heed the Word of the Lord when it is spoken."

Obey or die.

Joshua and the others waded into the throng. A man red-faced with rage, shouting blasphemies, ran at Moses. "No!" Aaron drew his sword and hacked the man down. Rage such as he had never before experienced flooded his body.

The sheep he had been left to tend had become attacking wolves barking obscenities. A drunken man shouted curses at the mountain of God, and Aaron silenced him forever. The smell of blood and death filled his nostrils. His heart pounded. Another man laughed hysterically. Aaron swung his sword and took off the man's head.

Sounds of terror filled the camp. Women and children scattered. Men turned this way and that. Those who rose up were cut down. Aaron went through the camp with the Levites, killing any who stood against the Lord. Those who cried out for the Lord's mercy and prostrated themselves, he left alive in the dust.

The battle ended swiftly.

Silence fell.

All Aaron could hear were moans and the rushing blood in his ears. He stood among the dead, his shepherd's robes stained with blood. Dazed, he looked around, his pulse slowing. Anguish filled him . . . and guilt too heavy to bear.

Oh, Lord, why am I yet alive? I am as guilty as any of them. More so.

His arm lost strength as he surveyed the carnage.

These people needed a strong shepherd, and I failed them. I've sinned against You. I don't deserve Your mercy. I don't deserve anything!

His bloodied sword hung at his side. His chest heaved.

Why have You spared me?

Sobbing, Aaron sank to his knees.

All the rest of the day, the tribes carried their dead outside the camp and burned them.

No one came near Aaron as he sat, and wept, and threw dust on his head.

✦   ✦   ✦

When Aaron entered his tent, Miriam was kneeling beside Nadab, wiping his ashen face. Abihu was vomiting into a bowl. His sister looked up at him. "How many?"

He saw no accusation in her eyes. "More than three thousand." The trembling had started, and his knees would no longer hold him. He sat heavily, his sword dropping beside him. Moses had praised the Levites and said they had been set apart to the Lord for what they had done today. They had fought and killed some of their own sons and brothers, and been blessed for it because they had chosen the Lord God of Israel over their erring fellowmen.

Aaron looked at his two elder sons and wanted to weep. If Eleazar and Ithamar had not found them and brought them inside the tent before Moses had returned to camp, they would be dead. But they had been found in time. Nadab and Abihu had come out and fought beside him, drink firing their courage. Sober now, they were aware of where they might have been had their younger brothers not dragged them away from their revelry. Aaron stared at them. How were they any different from those who had been killed? How was he any

different? At least, they shared his shame. They couldn't look
him in the face.

The next morning, Moses assembled his people. "You have
committed a terrible sin, but I will return to the Lord on the
mountain. Perhaps I will be able to obtain forgiveness for you."

Heartsick, Aaron stood in front, sons behind him, elders
around them. His brother would not even look at him. Turning
away, Moses headed back up the mountain. With Joshua.

Moses had only been gone a few hours when the plague hit,
and more died from sickness than had died by the sword.

✦   ✦   ✦

Aaron stood in front of the repentant multitude, watching
Moses make his way down the mountain path. It had been his
sin that had brought death on so many, his weakness that
allowed them to stray. He fought tears, overwhelmed with relief
that his brother had come back so soon. Moses came toward
him, staff in hand, his face filled with compassion. Aaron's
throat closed and he hung his head.

Moses put his hand on Aaron's shoulder. "We are to leave
this place, Aaron." He stepped away and addressed the people.
"We are to leave this place!"

Aaron realized then that Moses no longer needed him. Where
once he had been helpful, now he had proven himself unworthy to act as spokesman. Was this the cost of his sins? To be cut
off from fellowship from the one he loved most in the world?
How could he bear it?

Moses stood alone before the people, Joshua at a distance,
watching. "We are to go up to the land the Lord solemnly
promised Abraham, Isaac, and Jacob. He told them long ago
that He would give this land to their descendants. And He will
send an angel before us to drive out the Canaanites, Amorites,
Hittites, Perizzites, Hivites, and Jebusites. Theirs is a land flow-

ing with milk and honey. But the Lord will not travel along
with us. . . ."

Tearing his robes, Aaron fell to his knees, weeping in
anguish. This, then, was the cost of his weakness. All the people would be cut off from the Lord who had delivered them
from Egypt!

"The Lord will not travel along with us, for we are a stubborn, unruly people. If He did, He would be tempted to destroy
us along the way."

The people wailed and threw dust on their heads.

Moses did not weaken. "Remove your jewelry and ornaments
until the Lord decides what to do with us!"

Aaron was first to strip off his earrings and gold bracelets. He
rose and left them at the boundary near the foot of the mountain. The people followed his example.

Remaining in camp, Aaron grieved as he watched Moses go
to the tent he had pitched at a distance. If Moses ever spoke to
him again, it would be more than he deserved. Aaron watched
as the cloud moved from the mountaintop and came down
before the entrance of Moses' Tent of Meeting. He stood at the
entrance of his own tent with his sons and daughters-in-law, his
grandchildren and Miriam, and bowed low, worshiping the
Lord and giving thanks for his brother, God's messenger and
the people's mediator. Aaron and all those who belonged to him
did not leave the front of their tents until the pillar of cloud
returned to the mountaintop.

And the people followed his example.

+   +   +

When Moses did not return to camp, Aaron gathered his courage and went out. He found his brother on his knees chiseling
rock. Aaron went down on one knee beside him. "Can I help
you?"

"No."

Nor did it appear could Joshua, who stood at the entrance of the tent where Moses met with God. Even when Moses came into the camp, Joshua remained at the Tent of Meeting, as it had come to be called.

"I'm sorry, Moses." His throat was so tight and hot he had to swallow hard before he could say more. "I'm sorry I failed you." He had not been strong enough to serve the Lord faithfully. He had let his brother down.

Moses' face was gaunt from days of fasting and praying on the mountaintop, but his eyes glowed with an inner fire. "We have all failed, my brother."

My brother. Forgiven, Aaron's knees buckled. He knelt, head down, tears streaming. He felt Moses' hands on his head and then his kiss.

"And could I condemn you when the tablets I threw at the people from the mountain were God's workmanship? It is not the first time I have allowed anger to rule me, Aaron. But the Lord is merciful and gracious. He is slow to anger and rich in unfailing love and faithfulness. He shows this unfailing love to many thousands by forgiving every kind of sin and rebellion." The weight of Moses' hands lifted. "But even so, He does not leave sin unpunished. If He did, the people would scatter wild across the desert and do whatever was right in their own eyes." Moses gripped Aaron's shoulder. "Now, go back to camp and watch over the people. I must finish chiseling out these tablets by morning and carry them back up the mountain."

Aaron wished the Lord had given him some act of penance for his sins. A whipping might make him feel better. Leaving him in charge brought the full weight of his failure down on his shoulders. Joshua was looking at him, but Aaron saw no condemnation in the younger man's eyes.

Aaron rose and left his brother alone. He prayed that the

Lord God of Israel would give Moses strength to do as the Lord commanded. For the sake of them all.

Without the Lord, the Promised Land would be an empty dream.

+   +   +

Eleazar ran inside the tent. "Father, Moses is coming down the mountain."

Aaron hurried outside with his sons and hastened toward the boundary line, but when he saw Moses' white hair and glowing face, he drew back in fear. Moses did not look like the same man who had gone up the pathway days ago. It was as though the Lord Himself was coming down that pathway, the Law He had written on two stone slabs tucked beneath His arm.

The people ran.

"Come and hear the Word of the Lord!" Moses' voice carried across the plain.

Stomach clenched with fear, Aaron obeyed. Others followed, tentative, ready to flee at the first sign of threat.

This is my brother, Moses, Aaron told himself in order to have the courage to stand before the mountain. *My brother, the chosen prophet of God.* Was the Shekinah glory of God inhabiting Moses? Or was this merely a reflection of the Lord? Sweat beaded and ran down the back of his neck. Aaron didn't move. He opened his heart and mind to listen to every word Moses said, promising himself he would live by it, no matter how hard it was.

"On these tablets I have written the Word the Lord gave me, for He has made a covenant with me and with Israel." Moses read for all to hear the Law God had handed down from Mount Sinai. He had spoken the words once, but now they were written in stone and could be kept as a perpetual reminder of God's call on their lives.

When Moses finished speaking, he surveyed the multitude. No one spoke. Aaron knew Moses was waiting for him to come near, but he did not dare. Joshua remained at Moses' side—a silent, solemn sentry. Moses spoke to him quietly. Joshua said something in response. Taking the thin shawl from around his shoulders, Moses veiled his face.

Aaron approached him cautiously. "Is all well now between us, Moses?"

"Don't be afraid of me."

"You are not the same man you were."

"As you are changing, Aaron. When you receive and obey the Word of the Lord, you cannot help but change when you stand in His presence."

"My face does not glow with holy fire, Moses. I will never be as you are."

"Do you wish for my place?"

Aaron's heart drummed. He decided on truth. "I did. And I led like a rabbit rather than a lion." Perhaps it was because he couldn't see his brother's face that he felt free to confess. "I have envied Joshua."

"Joshua has never heard the voice of God as you have, Aaron. He is close to me because he longs to be close to God and do whatever God asks of him."

Aaron felt the envy rise. Here it was again. Another choice. He let his breath out slowly. "There is no other like him in all Israel." Strange that in the wake of that confession, he felt affection for the younger man, and hope that he would stand firmer than his elders had.

"Joshua is wholeheartedly for God. Even I wavered."

"Not you, Moses."

"Even I."

"Not as greatly as I did."

Moses smiled faintly. "Will we compete over whose sin is

greatest?" He spoke gently. "We all sin, Aaron. Did I not plead with God to send someone else? The Lord called you, too. I needed a spokesman. Don't ever forget that."

"You don't need me anymore."

"You are needed, Aaron, more than you realize. God will use you yet to serve Him and lead His people Israel."

Before Aaron could ask how, others interrupted. He was not the only one who yearned for personal contact with the only man in the world who spoke to God like he would to a friend. To be close to Moses made them feel closer to God. Veiled, Moses moved among them, touching a shoulder here, stroking the head of a child there, speaking to everyone tenderly, and always of the Lord. "We are called to be a holy nation, set apart by God. The other nations will see and know that the Lord, He is God and there is no other."

God's promise to Abraham would be fulfilled. Israel would be a blessing to all nations, a light to the world so that all men might see there was one true God, the Lord God of heaven and earth.

Aaron walked with his brother whenever he came into camp, relishing what time they had together, listening to Moses' every word as though the Lord Himself were speaking to him. When Moses spoke, Aaron heard the Voice come through his brother's words.

Moses pleaded with the Lord for the people's sake, and God stayed with them. Everyone knew it was for the sake of Moses that God changed His mind, for had the Lord left them, Moses' gray head would have gone down to the grave in grief. God knew Moses loved the people more than he loved his own life.

Each time Moses spoke, Aaron saw the gap between the ways of God and the ways of men. *Be holy because I am holy.* Every law was aimed at removing sin from their lives. God was the potter, working them like clay and reshaping them into something new. All the things they had learned and practiced in Egypt, and still practiced in the hidden recesses of their tents and hearts, would not go unpunished. God would not allow compromise.

Every time Moses came out of the Tent of Meeting, he came with more laws: laws against the abominations of Egypt and the nations around them; rules for holy gifts, holy convocations; crimes that required death; Sabbath days and Sabbath years; Jubilee and the end of slavery; prices and tithes. Every part of their lives would be governed by God. How would they ever remember it all? The laws of God were in complete opposition to everything they had ever known and practiced in Egypt.

Through the Law, Aaron realized how deeply immersed his own family had become in practicing the ways of the people around them. He and his brother and sister were children of incest, for their father had married his aunt, sister to his own father. The Lord said Israelite men were to marry outside their immediate families, but within their own tribes to keep the inheritance He would give them from being cut apart. And never were they to take women from other nations as their wives. Aaron wondered how Moses had felt when he heard the Lord say this, for he had taken a Midianite to be his wife. Even their ancestor Joseph had broken this law, marrying an Egyptian, and Joseph's father, Israel, had given his favorite son, Joseph, a double blessing, acknowledging Manasseh and Ephraim.

All those years, the Israelites had not known how to please the Lord other than to believe He existed, that His promise to Abraham, Isaac, and Jacob remained, and that one day He would deliver them from Egypt. Even during the years of living under the shadow of Pharaoh, and following too many of the ways of their oppressors, the Lord blessed them by multiplying their numbers.

The seventy elders once again mediated cases, referring only the most difficult to Moses to resolve. Aaron longed for more time with his brother, but when Moses was not hearing cases, he was hard at work writing down all the words the Lord gave him so that the people would have a permanent record.

"Surely, the Lord will let you rest for a little while." Aaron worried about his brother's health. Moses hardly ate and he slept little. "We can't survive without you, Moses. You must take care of yourself."

"My life is in God's hands, Aaron, as is every life in Israel, and all the earth for that matter. It is the Lord who has told me to write His words down. And write them I will, for words spoken are quickly forgotten, and ignorance will not be accepted as an excuse by the Lord. Sin brings death. And what does God consider sin? These things the people must know. Especially you."

"Especially me?" Living with the magnitude of the sin he had committed in allowing the people to have their way, and the number of lives that sin had cost, Aaron did not dare hope the Lord might use him again.

Moses finished the brush strokes of the last few letters on the papyrus scroll. He set the writing tools aside and turned. "Once the Law is written, it can be read many times and studied. The Lord has set the Levites aside as His, Aaron. Remember the prophecy of Jacob: 'I will scatter their descendants throughout the nation of Israel.' The Lord will scatter our brothers among the tribes and use them to teach the Law so the people can do what is right and walk humbly before our God. The Lord has called you to be His high priest. You will bring the atonement offering before Him, and one of your sons—I don't know which one yet—will begin the line for the high priests to follow in the generations to come. But all this must be explained to everyone."

High priest? "Are you certain you heard right?"

Moses smiled gently. "You confessed and repented. Were

you not the first to run to me when I called for those who were for the Lord? Once we have confessed them, the Lord forgets our faults and failures, Aaron, but not our faith. It is always His faithfulness that lifts us to our feet again."

As they went outside, Aaron remembered the entire blessing Jacob had given, if blessing it could be called:

"Simeon and Levi are two of a kind—men of violence. O my soul, stay away from them. May I never be a party to their wicked plans. For in their anger they murdered men, and they crippled oxen just for sport. Cursed be their anger, for it is fierce; cursed be their wrath, for it is cruel. Therefore, I will scatter their descendants throughout the nation of Israel."

Did not Aaron's family suffer from hot tempers, Moses included? Hadn't it been his temper that brought about the murder of an Egyptian? And lest he cast stones at Moses, what about his own sins? He suffered bouts of fury as well. How easily his sword had been raised against his people, slaughtering sheep he had been left to lead!

In his heart, Aaron was in fear for what the future could hold when the priesthood rested in the hands of a tribe so bent on violence and self-service. "Oh, Moses, if I am to teach and lead the people, God must change me! Plead with Him for my sake. Ask Him to create in me a pure heart and upright spirit!"

"I have prayed for you. I will never stop. Now gather the people, Aaron. The Lord has work for them. We will see if their hearts are up to it."

MOSES received instructions from the Lord to build a tabernacle, a sacred residence where God could dwell among His people.

The instructions were specific: Curtains were to be made, and poles to hang them. A bronze basin for washing and an altar for burnt offerings would stand in the court of the Tabernacle. Inside the Tabernacle would be another smaller chamber, the Most Holy Place, where a table, a lampstand, and an ark would be placed.

Details on how everything was to be made were given to Moses and handed over to two men the Lord named to oversee the work: Bezalel son of Uri, grandson of Hur; and Oholiab son of Ahisamach, of the tribe of Dan. When they came forward, eager to do God's will, the Lord filled them with His Spirit, so that they had the skill, ability, and knowledge in all kinds of crafts. God even gave them the ability to teach others how to do the work required! All skilled in any craft came to help.

The people rejoiced to hear that their prayers and Moses' pleading had been answered. The Lord would remain with them! They returned to their tents and laid out all the gifts the Egyptians had given them, gifts that had come from hearts stirred by fear of the Lord God of Israel, and they gave the best of what they had to the Lord.

Aaron felt shame for having used gifts God had given the people to fashion the golden calf. God had lavished wealth on them before they left Egypt, and he had wasted a portion in worshiping a hollow idol. That gold had ended up burned, ground, and cast on the water that ended up as refuse in the latrines outside of camp.

Aaron took all the gold he had and gave it back to the One

who had given it to him in the first place. His sons and their wives and Miriam gave the best of what they had. They spread ram skins dyed red and piled up gold jewelry, silver, and bronze. Miriam filled a basket with blue, purple, and scarlet yarn and another with fine linen, excited that what she had to give might end up as part of the Tabernacle curtain.

Others in camp came with the hides of dugongs, jugs of olive oil, spices for the anointing oil, and fragrant incense. Some had onyx stones and other gems. The people brought their gifts before the Lord, waving them in offering, and placing them in baskets set out. Soon the baskets were filled with brooches, earrings, rings, and ornaments.

Groups of men went out into the desert and cut down acacia trees. The best pieces were set aside for the ark, the table, posts, and crossbeams. The bronze was melted down for the basin with its stand, the bronze grating for the altar and utensils. Everyone brought something, and everyone who was able worked.

Fires were kept burning so the bronze, silver, and gold could be melted down, impurities strained off, and then be poured into molds made under Bezalel's watchful eye. Women wove fine cloth and made garments for Aaron and his sons to wear when they began ministering in the sanctuary.

As the work progressed, more gifts poured forth. Every day, more piled up near the work sites until Bezalel and Oholiab left their work and went to Moses and Aaron. "We have more than enough materials on hand now to complete the job the Lord has given us to do!"

Aaron rejoiced, for surely the Lord would see how the people loved Him. He and his sons and their wives and Miriam brought offerings each day, eager to see God's plan accomplished, eager to have part in it.

Moses looked at Aaron, his eyes awash with tears. "Gather

the elders. Tell them no more offerings must be brought. We have all we need."

✦   ✦   ✦

By Moses' command, Aaron's son Ithamar recorded everything that was given and used for the main Tabernacle and the Tabernacle of the Testimony. Almost everyone in camp was busy on some aspect of building the Tabernacle. Aaron was happy. He looked forward to each sunrise, for the people were content in the service of the Lord. Their hands were busy and their hearts and minds set on carrying out the work God had given them.

Nine months after reaching Mount Sinai and two weeks before the second celebration of Passover, the Tabernacle was completed. Bezalel and Oholiab and the people brought everything that was made to Moses. Moses inspected the tent and all its furnishings, the articles to be placed in the Most Holy Place, and the clothing for the priests. Everything had been done exactly as the Lord had commanded.

Smiling, Moses blessed them.

Under Moses' watchful eye, the Tabernacle was set up on the first day of the month. The Ark of the Covenant was placed inside and a heavy curtain hung to veil it from sight. To the right was the table of the Bread of the Presence and to the left the golden lampstand of pure gold, six branches coming out from the center, three on the left and three on the right with flowerlike cups at the top. In front of the curtain, Moses placed the gold altar of incense. Heavy curtains were drawn around and over the Most Holy Place.

The altar of burnt offerings was placed in front of the entrance to the Tabernacle. The basin was placed between the Tent of Meeting and the altar and filled with water. Curtains were hung around the Tabernacle, the altar, and basin; and another more elaborate curtain hung at the entrance for the courtyard.

When everything was set up according to the Lord's instructions, Moses anointed the Tabernacle and everything in it with oil and pronounced it holy to the Lord. He then anointed the altar of burnt offerings and the basin and consecrated them to the Lord.

Aaron and his sons were called forward. Aaron felt the eyes of all on him as he entered the courtyard. Men, women, and children stood by the thousands behind him, just beyond the curtain. Moses removed Aaron's clothing and washed him from head to foot, then helped him slip on a fine woven white tunic and a blue robe with pomegranates of blue, purple, and scarlet yarn around the hem and gold bells between them. "When you enter the Most Holy Place, the Lord will hear the bells, and you will not die." Moses straightened Aaron's garment.

Stomach quivering, arms outstretched, Aaron stood still while Moses secured the ephod with the shoulder pieces, two onyx stones engraved with the names of the sons of Israel and mounted in gold filigree. "You will bear the names of the sons of Israel as a memorial before the Lord."

Upon the ephod rested the square chestpiece with four rows of precious stones mounted and set in gold filigree: a ruby, topaz, beryl, turquoise, sapphire, emerald, jacinth, agate, amethyst, chrysolite, onyx, and jasper, each engraved for a son of Israel. "Whenever you enter the Holy Place, you will bear the names of the sons of Israel over your heart." Moses tucked the Urim and the Thummim in the chestpiece over Aaron's heart. "These will reveal the will of the Lord."

Aaron shut his eyes as Moses placed the turban on his head. He had seen the plate of engraved gold: *Holy to the Lord*. It now rested snuggly against his forehead. Moses left him standing alone and went to prepare Aaron's sons.

Standing in the shadow of the cloud, Aaron trembled. His heart pounded. From this day forth, he would be high priest of Israel. He looked at the basin, the altar of burnt offerings, and the curtain that enclosed the holy pieces inside the Lord's Tabernacle, afraid he would faint. Never again would he be an ordinary man. The Lord had elevated him, and at the same time made him a servant. Every time he entered the courtyard, he would carry responsibility for the people. He felt the weight of them on his shoulders and over his heart.

When Nadab, Abihu, Ithamar, and Eleazar were dressed in their priestly garments, Moses stood before them and anointed them with oil, consecrating them to the Lord. Then he brought forward a young bull for the sin offering. Aaron remembered his sin in making the golden calf. Blushing, he laid his hand on the head of the animal whose blood would be shed for his sin. His sons placed their hands on the animal's head as well. Moses slit the throat of the bull and took some of the blood in a bowl and put it on all the horns of the altar. He poured out the rest at the base. He slaughtered the bull and placed the fat around the inner parts, the covering of the liver, and both kidneys as a burnt offering on the altar. The rest of the bull would be burned outside the camp.

The second offering for Aaron and his sons was the ram for the burnt offering. Again, Aaron and his sons laid their hands on the animal. Moses sprinkled the ram's blood on the altar and then cut the animal into pieces, washed the inner parts and legs, and burned the whole ram on the altar. The smell of roasting meat made Aaron's stomach clench with hunger. It was a pleasing aroma made to the Lord.

The third offering was another ram, this one for Aaron and his sons' ordination. Aaron placed his hand on the animal's head. At his nod, his sons followed his example. Moses cut the animal's jugular and collected the blood in a bowl. He came to Aaron and, dipping his finger into the blood, put it on Aaron's right ear. Moses dipped his finger again and anointed Aaron's right thumb. Kneeling, he dipped his finger one last time and put the blood on the big toe of Aaron's right foot. He did the same for Aaron's four sons, and then sprinkled blood against the altar on all sides.

The rams for Aaron and his sons were slaughtered, the pieces stacked with the washed inner parts, and a cake of bread made with oil and one wafer were placed on top. Moses placed the first in Aaron's hands. Aaron raised the sacrifice before the Lord and then gave it back to his brother, who placed it on the altar. Flames leaped up. Aaron's sons waved their offerings and gave them to Moses to place on the altar, and each time, the flames exploded around the slaughtered animal, taking it in the place of the sinful men who gave it as offering.

Aaron stood solemn and humbled as Moses sprinkled him first with the fragrant anointing oil and the blood of the sacrifice. Finally, his sons were anointed, from the eldest to the youngest.

Aaron felt the change in the air. The cloud swirled slowly, glowing strangely. His heart raced as the cloud compressed and moved down from the mountain. He heard the people behind him, drawing in their breath, holding it, releasing it in trembling fear. The cloud covered the Tabernacle. A thousand shimmering colors flashed and glowed from within the cloud, and then it poured into the chamber of the Most Holy Place, and the glory of the Lord filled the Tabernacle.

Even Moses could not enter.

The people moaned in awe and reverence and bowed low.

"Cook the meat remaining at the entrance of the Tabernacle and eat it there with the bread from the basket of ordination offerings. Then burn the rest of the meat and bread. Do not leave the entrance of the Tabernacle. You must stay here, day and night for seven days or you will die."

Aaron watched his brother walk away. When Moses reached the entrance to the courtyard, he looked back solemnly; then he drew the curtains closed.

Aaron faced the Tabernacle. He knew all had been done to cleanse this place and make it sacred. Even he had been washed and dressed in new garments so he could stand before the Lord. But he could not stop the trembling inside, the quiver of fear that the Lord was within feet of him, hidden only by curtains. And Aaron knew he wasn't worthy to be in this place. He wasn't clean, not inside. As soon as Moses was out of sight, he turned weak. Hadn't he allowed his jealousy of Joshua to taint him? Hadn't he let the people's fears rule over the commands given to him. Why would God appoint a man like him to be high priest?

Lord, I'm unworthy. You alone are faithful. I am only a man. I failed to lead Your people. Three thousand lost their lives because I was weak. And You spared my life. You appointed me Your high priest. Lord, such mercy is beyond me. Help me to know Your ways and follow them! Help me to be the priest You want me to be! Instruct me in Your ways so that I can serve Your people and keep them strong in faith. Oh, Lord, Lord, help me. . . .

When he was too tired to stand, Aaron knelt, praying that the Lord would give him the strength and wisdom to remember the Law and do everything the Lord commanded. When he became weak from hunger, he and his sons gave thanks, cooked the meat and ate the bread left for them. When he couldn't keep his eyes open any longer, he prostrated himself before the Lord and slept with his forehead on his hands.

Eleazar and Ithamar stood before the Tabernacle, arms outstretched, palms up as they prayed. Nadab and Abihu knelt, sitting back against their heels when they tired.

Each day that passed softened Aaron's heart until he thought he heard the Lord's voice whispering to him.

I am the Lord your God, and there is no other.

Aaron lifted his head, listening intently, content.

Nadab stretched and yawned. "So begins the fourth morning."

Abihu sat cross-legged, forearms resting on his knees. "Three more to go."

Aaron felt a coldness in the pit of his belly.

✦   ✦   ✦

On the eighth day, Moses summoned Aaron, his sons, and the elders of Israel. Moses gave them the instructions of the Lord.

Aaron took a bull calf without defect and offered it as sacrifice to atone for his sins. He knew every time he did this, he would remember how he had sinned against the Lord by making a calf idol. Would his sons remember? Would their sons after them? Did the blood of this living calf really ransom him from the sin of making an idol?

More sacrifices followed. When he had made atonement for himself, he would be ready to stand and make the sin offering, burnt offering, and fellowship offerings for the people. The ox fought against the rope, kicking Aaron. He thought he would pass out from the pain, but kept his feet. His sons held the animal more firmly as Aaron used the knife. Next he killed the ram. The sight and smell of blood and the sound of the dying animals filled him with loathing for the sins that brought death. And he thanked God that the Lord allowed these poor beasts to substitute for each man, woman, and child. For all sinned. None could stand before the Lord with a pure heart.

Aaron's hands were covered with blood, and the corners and sides of the altar dripped with it. Arms aching, he lifted the breasts and right thigh of the sacrifices before the Lord as a wave offering. When all the sacrifices were made, Aaron lifted hands shaking with exhaustion toward the people and blessed them. Then he stepped down.

Moses went with him into the Tabernacle. Aaron's heart thundered in his ears. His stomach clenched. He was thankful for the heavy curtain that hid the Lord from his sight, for he knew he would die if he ever saw God. If he washed himself in the blood of calves and lambs, it still wouldn't wash all the sin away. He prayed for himself. He prayed for the people. And then he went outside with Moses and blessed the people.

The air around them changed. He held his breath at the movement—silent, powerful. The glorious presence of the Lord appeared for all to see. He gasped and the people cried out in awe when fire blazed forth from the Lord's presence and consumed the burnt offering and the fat on the altar.

As sinful as he was, as sinful as these people were who stood trembling in fear, the Lord had accepted their offerings!

Aaron shouted joyfully, tears of relief streaming down his cheeks as he fell facedown before the Lord.

And the people followed his example.

✦   ✦   ✦

Aaron's service fell into a routine. Every day, offerings were given at dawn and dusk. The burnt offering remained on the altar hearth throughout the night till morning. Aaron wore his fine linen clothes when performing sacrifices, but changed into others when carrying the ashes of the offerings outside camp. The Lord had said, "The fire must never go out." And Aaron saw to it that it did not.

Still he worried about it. He dreamed about fire and blood. Even when he was clean, Aaron could smell smoke and blood. He dreamed of people screaming like animals because he had failed to perform his duties properly and appease the Lord's wrath. Even more disturbing, he knew people went on sinning.

Hundreds waited in line to take grievances to the elders, and
Moses was always busy with one case or another. The people
could not seem to live at peace with one another. It was in their
nature to argue, contend, and fight anything that curtailed
them in any way. They did not dare question God, but they
questioned His representatives without end. They were no different from Adam and Eve, wanting what was denied them, no
matter what harm would come in the having.

Aaron tried to encourage his sons. "We must be living exam-
ples of righteousness before the people."

"No one is more righteous than you are, Father."

Aaron fought the pleasure of Nadab's flattery, knowing how
quickly pride destroyed men. Hadn't it destroyed Pharaoh and
Egypt with him? "Moses is more righteous. And no one is more
humble."

Abihu bristled. "Moses is always in the Tent of Meeting, and
where are you? Out there serving the people."

"It seems to me we have the heavier workload." Nadab
leaned back on a cushion. "When was the last time you saw one
of our cousins lift a finger to help?"

Eleazar looked up from a scroll. "Eliezer and Gershom are
tending their mother." He spoke quietly, frowning.

Nadab sneered, pouring himself more wine. "Woman's
work."

Miriam stood over them. "Don't you think you've had
enough to drink?"

Nadab glanced at her before holding out his goblet. Abihu
refilled it before hanging the wineskin on its hook.

Aaron did not like the tension in their tent. "We are each
called to be where we are called to be. Moses is the one who
hears the voice of the Lord and brings us God's instructions.
We carry them out. We have been given a great honor by the
Lord to serve—"

"Yes, yes." Nadab nodded. "We know all that, Father. But it is boring to do the same thing day in and day out, knowing we will be doing it for the rest of our lives."

Aaron felt a wave of heat come up inside him and then sink into a cold lump in his stomach. "Remember whom you serve." He looked from Nadab to Abihu and then to his two younger sons, who sat silent, heads down. Did they feel as their brothers did? Aaron felt an urgency to warn them. "You will do exactly as the Lord commands. Do you understand?"

Nadab's eyes changed. "We understand you, Father." His fingers tightened on his wine goblet. "We will honor the Lord in everything we do. Just as you always have." He finished his wine and rose. Abihu followed his brother from the tent.

"You shouldn't let them talk to you that way, Aaron."

Irritated, he glared at Miriam. "What do you suggest?"

"Take them by the ear! Give them a whipping! Do something! They both think they're more righteous than you!"

He could think of a dozen men who were more righteous than he was, starting with his brother and his assistant, Joshua. "They will come to their senses when they think about it."

"And if they don't?"

"Let it be, woman! I have enough on my mind without your constant nagging!"

"Nagging? As if I haven't always had your best interest in mind!" Miriam yanked the curtain aside to the women's chamber. She pulled the curtain down behind her.

The silence was anything but peaceful. Aaron rose. "We have work to do." He was thankful it was time to return to the Tabernacle. He had no peace in his own tent.

Eleazar sat up. "We'll be along shortly, Father." He reached out a hand to help Ithamar.

Aaron let Eleazar and Ithamar precede him. "See that you are." He snapped the tent flap down behind him.

Eleazar walked beside Aaron. "You're going to have to do something about them, Father."

"Is it your place to speak against your brothers?"

"It's for their sake I speak."

As Aaron performed his duties, Eleazar and Ithamar worked with him. Disturbed, Aaron thought about what Eleazar had said. Where were Nadab and Abihu? Aaron could not understand his elder sons. There was nowhere Aaron wanted to be so much as in the courtyard of the Lord. To stand in God's presence was Moses' calling, but to be this close to the Lord filled Aaron with joy. Why could his elder sons not feel the same way?

Laughter startled Aaron. Who dared laugh inside the courtyard of God? Turning, he saw Nadab and Abihu at the entrance. Dressed in their priestly garments, they held censers in their hands. What did they think they were doing? Aaron started toward them, ready to take them to task when Nadab took a small bag from his sash. He sprinkled dust over the burning coals. Yellow, blue, and red smoke rose, the same kind that Egyptian priests had used in their pagan temples.

"No!" Aaron cried out.

"Relax, Father. We are only paying homage to our God." Abihu held his censer out and Nadab sprinkled particles into the coals.

"Would you desecrate God's holy—"

"Desecrate?" Nadab stood defiant. "Are we not priests? We can show honor to God as we want!" He and Abihu stepped forward.

"Stop!"

A stream of fire shot past Aaron and struck his two elder sons in the chest. The force knocked Aaron and his two younger sons off their feet. Aaron heard Nadab and Abihu screaming and clambered to his feet. The shrieks of their unbearable agony lasted only seconds before they were consumed by flames. They had fallen where they stood in defiance, burned beyond recognition.

With a cry, Aaron's hands went to his robe. A heavy hand grabbed his shoulder and jerked him back. "No." Moses spoke heavily. "Do not mourn by letting your hair hang loose or by tearing your clothes. If you do, you will die, and the Lord will be angry with the whole community of Israel."

Lungs aching, Aaron swayed.

Moses gripped his arm, steadying him. "Aaron, listen to me. The rest of the Israelites, your relatives, may mourn for Nadab and Abihu, whom the Lord has destroyed by fire. But you are not to leave the entrance of the Tabernacle, under penalty of death, for the anointing oil of the Lord is upon you."

Aaron remembered the law: No priest was to touch a dead body.

"This is what the Lord meant when He said, 'I will show Myself holy among those who are near Me. I will be glorified before all the people.' "

Aaron fought back tears, fought down the anguished cry that threatened to choke him. *The Lord is holy. The Lord is holy!* He fixed his mind on the Lord's holiness, bending to it. Eleazar and Ithamar lay prostrate before the Tabernacle, faces in the dust, worshiping the Lord.

Moses summoned Aaron's cousins Mishael and Elzaphan. "Come and carry the bodies of your relatives away from the sanctuary to a place outside the camp."

Aaron watched them lift the charred bodies of his two elder sons and carry them away from the front of the Tabernacle. He faced the Tabernacle and didn't look back. His chest ached, his throat burned. Would Nadab and Abihu be cast into the refuse for their sin?

The Voice spoke, still and quiet.

You and your descendants must never drink wine or any other alcoholic drink before going into the Tabernacle.

"Aaron." Moses was speaking to him, and Aaron tried to absorb his instructions. "Aaron." Aaron and his younger sons were to remain where they were and complete their duties. They were to eat the leftovers from the offerings of grain and the goat of the sin offering. Aaron did all Moses instructed, but neither he nor his two sons could eat. The smell of burning meat made Aaron's gorge rise, and he had to clench his teeth to keep from vomiting.

Moses' face was red with anger. "Why didn't you eat the sin offering in the sanctuary area?" he demanded. "It is a holy offering! It was given to you for removing the guilt of the community and for making atonement for the people before the Lord. Since the animal's blood was not taken into the Holy Place, you should have eaten the meat in the sanctuary area as I ordered you."

Aaron groaned. "Today my sons presented both their sin offering and their burnt offering to the Lord." He swallowed convulsively. "This kind of thing has also happened to me." He fought his rising emotions, trembling under the strain. "Would the Lord have approved if I had eaten the sin offering today?" When sin lurked so close at hand, waiting to prey on his shattered family and sink its teeth into his weakened heart? *My sons,* he wanted to cry out. *My sons! Have you forgotten my sons died today?* He would have choked on the meat of the sin offering and defiled the sanctuary.

Nadab's words had come back over and over to haunt him all day: *"We will honor the Lord in our own way, Father. Just as you have."*

With a golden calf and a feast day of pagan celebration.

Even after the atoning sacrifices, Aaron still felt his sins heavy upon him. *If only the Lord would erase them forever. If only . . .*

Moses looked on Aaron with compassion and said no more.

✦   ✦   ✦

Aaron was with Moses when Moses invited Hobab, Jethro's son, to go with them to the Promised Land. "Stay with us, Hobab. Make your life with God's chosen people, Israel."

When Hobab left the camp, Aaron had a sick feeling in his stomach that they would meet Hobab again, under less than friendly circumstances. All the while the Midianite remained camped close by, Aaron had wondered if Hobab was merely watching for their weaknesses and how to make use of them.

"I hope we do not see him again."

Moses looked at him and Aaron said no more. His brother had spent many years with the Midianites and had deep affection and respect for his father-in-law. Aaron could only hope Moses knew these people as well as he thought he did and no threat would come from them. For what would Moses do if he ever found himself torn between the Israelites and his wife's family? For forty years, the Midianites had treated Moses with love and respect, even making him a member of their family. The Israelites had given Moses grief, rebellion, constant complaints, and work; then they made him a slave to them.

Worry seemed a constant companion these days. Aaron worried about Moses' health, his stamina, his family. Zipporah was near death. The only good that had come of her illness was the softening in Miriam, who often tended her now. Aaron also worried about getting things right. So far, he had made one mistake after another. He studied the laws Moses wrote down, knowing they were straight from God. But sometimes, when he was tired, he would think of his dead sons and the tears would come up, quick and hot. He had loved them, even knowing their sins. And he could not help feeling he had failed them more than they had failed him.

The people were complaining again. They couldn't seem to remember from one day to the next what the Lord had already done for them. They were like children, whining with every discomfort. It was the Egyptian rabble who traveled with them that caused the most trouble now.

"We're sick of nothing at all to eat except this manna!"

"Oh, for some meat!"

"We remember all the fish we used to eat for free in Egypt."

"And we had all the cucumbers and melons we wanted. They were so good."

"And the leeks and onions and garlics."

"But now our appetites are gone, and day after day we have nothing to eat but this manna!"

Aaron said nothing as he gathered his portion of manna for the day. He squatted and picked up the flakes, putting them into his container. Eleazar was scowling. Ithamar moved a little farther off.

Miriam was red-faced. "Maybe you should have stayed in Egypt!"

A woman glared. "Maybe we should have!"

"Fish and cucumbers," Miriam muttered under her breath. "We were lucky to have enough to eat at all. Just enough to keep us *working*."

"I am sick of eating the same thing every day."

Miriam straightened. "You should be thankful. You don't have to work for your food!"

"You don't call this work? We're down on our knees every morning, grubbing around for flakes of this stuff."

"If only we had meat to eat!" An Israelite joined in the complaining.

"Oh, Mama, do we have to eat manna again?"

"Yes, poor baby, you do."

The child began to whine and cry.

"Surely we were better off in Egypt!" The man spoke in a loud voice, knowing Aaron would hear.

Miriam glowered. "Aren't you going to say something, Aaron? What are you going to do with these people?"

What did she want him to do? Call down fire from the mountain? He thought of his sons again, and his throat closed hot and dry. He knew Moses heard the people complaining. He saw what it was doing to his brother. "Don't make more trouble than we already have, Miriam." He was weary of all of them.

"*I* make trouble! If you'd listened to me about . . ."

He rose, staring at her. Did she realize how cruel and thoughtless she could be at times? The fire went out of her eyes. "I'm sorry." She lowered her head. He loved his sister, but sometimes he could not abide her. He took his container and walked away.

Moses came outside the Tabernacle. Aaron went to him. "You look tired."

"I am tired." Moses shook his head. "So tired of trouble I asked the Lord to kill me and have done with it."

"Do not speak so." Did Moses think Aaron would do any better? God forbid Moses should die. Aaron never wanted to be left in charge again.

"You need not worry, my brother. God said no. The Lord has given instructions that seventy men be chosen, men known to us as leaders and officials among the people. They are to come here before the Tabernacle, and the Spirit of the Lord will fall on them and they will help lead God's people. We need help." He smiled. "You are older than I, my brother, and showing every day of your eighty-four years."

Aaron laughed bleakly, and savored the relief. Two men

could not bear the burden of six hundred thousand men on foot, not counting their wives and sons and daughters!

"And the Lord will send meat."

"Meat?" *How? From where?*

"Meat for a whole month, until we gag and are sick of it, because the people have rejected the Lord."

Sixty-eight men came to the Tabernacle. As Moses laid hands on each man, the Spirit of the Lord came on each new leader and he spoke the Word of the Lord as Moses did.

Joshua came running. "Eldad and Medad are prophesying in the camp! Moses, my master, *make them stop!*"

"Are you jealous for my sake? I wish that all the Lord's people were prophets, and that the Lord would put His spirit upon them all!"

Aaron heard the sound of wind coming out from the cloud over the Tabernacle. He felt the warmth of it lift his beard and press his priestly robes close to his body. And then it moved above and away. Aaron returned to his duties in the Tabernacle, but kept apprehensive watch on the sky.

Quail flew in from the sea, thousands of them. The wind drove them in a flurry of feathers straight down into the camp until they were piled up three feet deep on the ground. All that day and night, the people gathered birds, ringing their necks and stripping them of feathers in their haste for meat. Some didn't even wait to roast the quail before sinking their teeth into the flesh they craved.

Aaron heard the groans and feared he knew what was coming. Groans turned to wails as men and women sickened before the meat was even consumed. They fell to their knees, bent over, vomiting. Some died quickly. Others, as they suffered, cursed God for giving them the very thing they had demanded. Thousands repented, crying out to the Lord to forgive them. But the quail kept coming as the Lord had prom-

ised. Day after day, until the people were silent and filled
with dread of the Lord.

✦   ✦   ✦

After a month, the cloud lifted from the Tabernacle. Aaron
entered the Most Holy Place and covered and packed the
lampstand, table of the Bread of the Presence, and the incense
altar. The Tent of Meeting and the Tabernacle were dismantled,
packed, and the clans of Levites carried what the Lord had
assigned to them. At Moses' signal, two men blew trumpets.
The people gathered.

"Rise up, O Lord!" Moses' voice boomed. "May Your enemies
be scattered; may Your foes flee before You!"

The Ark of the Covenant was lifted by four men. Moses
walked ahead, his eyes on the Angel of the Lord who led him.
The people left the place that had come to be called Graves of
Craving. They traveled day and night until the cloud stopped at
Hazeroth.

Moses held his arms up in praise. "Return, O Lord! To the
countless thousands of Israel."

The Ark of the Covenant was set down. The Tabernacle was
set up around it. Aaron placed the holy items in their proper
places, as his sons and the heads of the Gershon, Kohath, and
Merari clans of Levites finished putting up the poles and curtains, the altar for the burnt offerings, and the bronze basin.

And the people rested.

✦   ✦   ✦

Aaron wanted to close his eyes and not think about anything
for a little while, but Miriam was upset and would not allow
him any peace. "I've come to accept Zipporah." She paced, agi-
tated, cheeks flushed. "I've been the one taking care of her all
this time. I've been the one seeing to her needs. Not that she has

shown any particular appreciation. She has never tried to learn our language. She still relies on Eliezer to translate."

Aaron knew why she was upset. He, too, had been surprised when Moses told him he was taking another wife, but he had not seen fit to comment on it. Miriam had never had such inhibitions, though Aaron doubted she had spoken to Moses yet.

"He needs a wife, Miriam, someone who can see to the needs of his household."

"A wife? Why does Moses need a wife other than Zipporah when he has me? I saw to everything before that Cushite entered his tent. He welcomed my help in the beginning. So that I could take care of his wife! Zipporah couldn't do anything without help. And now that she's dying, he's taken another wife! Why does he need a wife at his age? You should've talked him out of this marriage before he took that foreigner into his tent. You should've said something to keep him from sinning against the Lord!"

Had Moses sinned? "I too was surprised when Moses told me."

"Just surprised?"

"He's not so old he doesn't need the comfort of a woman." Aaron sometimes wished he could take another wife, but after mediating between the mother of his sons and Miriam for years, he decided it was wiser to remain chaste!

"Moses seldom spent time with Zipporah, and now he has this woman." Miriam threw her hands in the air. "I wonder if he listens to what the Lord says. If he must have a wife—and I don't see why he must at his age—he should have chosen a wife from among the women of the tribe of Levi. Hasn't the Lord told us not to marry outside our tribes? Have you seen how foreign that Cushite is? She is black, Aaron, blacker than any Egyptian I ever saw."

Aaron had been troubled about Moses' marriage, but not for Miriam's reasons. The woman had been a slave to one of the

Egyptians who had come with the people out of Egypt. Her mistress had died during the festival of the golden calf, and the Cushite had continued to travel among the people. As far as Aaron knew, she bowed down before the Lord. But still . . .

"Why do you just sit and say nothing, Aaron? You are a servant of the Lord, aren't you? You are His high priest. Has the Lord spoken only through Moses? Didn't the Lord direct me when I spoke to Pharaoh's daughter? Did the Lord not give me the words? And the Lord called you, Aaron. You have heard His voice and spoken His word to the people more often than Moses! I have never known Moses to show so little wisdom."

Aaron hated when his sister was like this. He felt like a little boy again, ruled by his older sister, overpowered by her personality. She had a will of iron. "You should be pleased that you will have less work to do."

"Pleased? Maybe I would be if he hadn't married a *Cushite!* Don't you care that Moses brings sin on all of us by this unwholesome marriage?"

"What is unwholesome about it?"

"You have to ask?" She pointed angrily. "Just go out to his tent and look at her! She should go back to her own people. She does not belong among us, let alone have the honor of being the wife of Israel's deliverer!"

Aaron wondered if he should talk to Moses. Truly, he had been taken aback when Moses took a Cushite slave woman into his tent. Perhaps he should speak with some of the elders before he approached his brother. What did the people think of Moses' marriage? Miriam would not keep her thoughts to herself for long.

Doubts filled Aaron. Miriam had tried to warn him about Nadab and Abihu, and he hadn't listened to her. Was he making another mistake now by not listening to his sister and standing against Moses' decision to marry again?

Go out to the Tabernacle, all three of you!

The hair rose on the back of Aaron's neck. He raised his head, in fear of that Voice.

Miriam straightened and tilted her chin. Her eyes glowed. "The Lord has called *me* to the Tabernacle. And you as well, if I can tell by the look on your face." She walked out of the tent. Standing in the sunlight, she looked back at him. "Well? Are you coming or not?"

Moses was waiting for them, perplexed. The cloud swirled overhead and compressed, descending.

Miriam looked up, her face flushed and tense with excitement. "You'll see now, Aaron."

He shook as the pillar of cloud stood at the entrance of the Tabernacle, and the Voice came from within the cloud.

Now listen to Me! Even with prophets, I the Lord communicate by visions and dreams. But that is not how I communicate with My servant Moses. He is entrusted with My entire house. I speak to him face to face, directly and not in riddles! He sees the Lord as He is. Should you not be afraid to criticize him?

The pillar of thick mist rose, and Aaron felt the deep anguish of his sin once more. He hung his head, ashamed.

Miriam drew in her breath in a soft shriek. Her face and hands were streaked white like a stillborn baby coming from its mother's womb, her flesh half eaten away. She fell to her knees, screaming and throwing dirt over her head.

"Ohhhh!" Aaron wailed in terror. He turned to Moses, hands outstretched, shaking. "Oh, my lord! Please don't punish us for this sin we have so foolishly committed." Fear ran cold in his veins.

Horrified, Moses was already crying out to the Lord, begging for mercy on behalf of his older sister.

And the Voice came for all three to hear:

*If her father had spit in her face, wouldn't she have been
defiled for seven days? Banish her from the camp for seven
days, and after that she may return.*

Sobbing, Miriam fell to her knees and prostrated herself
before the Lord. Her outstretched sickly white hands became
strong and brown again, worn from years of hard work. She put
her hands near Moses' feet, but did not touch him. Aaron bent
toward her, but Miriam drew back sharply. "You mustn't touch
me!" She rose clumsily and backed away. The leprosy was gone,
but her dark eyes were awash with tears and her cheeks red
with humiliation. She drew her veil across her face and bent
toward Moses. "Forgive me, Brother. Please forgive me."

"Oh, Miriam, my sister . . ."

Aaron felt her shame like a mantle on his own back. He
should have told her to be silent, to stop gossiping about anyone, especially Moses, whom God had chosen to deliver Israel.
Instead, he had allowed himself to be swayed by her words and
had joined in her rebellion.

People had come out of their tents and stood staring. Some
came closer to see what was going on. "Unclean!" Miriam cried
out as she hurried toward the edge of the camp. "I'm unclean!"
The people drew back from her as though she carried plague.
Some wailed. Children fled for their mother's tent. "Unclean!"
Miriam ran, stumbling in her shame, but did not fall.

Aaron's throat tightened. Was he destined to fail the Lord, to
fail Moses in everything he did? When he didn't listen, Abihu
and Nadab died. When he did listen, his sister bore the leprosy
of his lack of perception. He should be the one living outside
the camp! He had known better than to heed her jealousy.
Instead, he had given in to her. He had allowed her to fan his
own unanswered dreams of leadership. Every time he tried to

step out ahead, disaster fell not only on him, but on those he loved.

"Aaron."

The tenderness in his brother's voice made Aaron's heart ache even more. "Why did God spare me when it was as much my sin as hers?"

"Would you have grieved as deeply if the discipline had fallen on you? Your heart is soft, Aaron."

"And so is my head." He looked at his brother. "I wanted her to sway me, Moses. I have struggled with my role as the older brother who must stand aside for his younger. I have not wanted to feel these things, Moses, but I'm just a man. Pride is my enemy."

"I know."

"I do love you, Moses."

"I know."

Aaron shut his eyes tightly. "And now, Miriam suffers while I go about my priestly duties."

"We will all wait until her time of quarantine is over."

Before the pillar of fire warmed the chill desert air, all the nation of Israel would know how he and Miriam had sinned.

It would soon be time for the evening sacrifice.

Lord, Lord, have mercy. My sins are heavy upon me.

✦ ✦ ✦

When the seven days had passed and Miriam returned to camp, the pillar of cloud rose and led the people away from Hazeroth. The cloud stopped over the wilderness of Paran and the people camped there at Kadesh. Aaron and his sons and the clans of Levites set up the Tent and the Tabernacle, and the tribes set up their camps in their designated areas around the Tent. Everyone knew their place and responsibility, and the people were quickly settled.

Moses received instructions from the Lord and gave Aaron a list of twelve men, one from each of the tribes of Israel, excluding Levi, whose duties centered around the worship of the Lord. Aaron sent for the tribal representatives and stood before Moses when the Lord's instructions were given.

"You are to go into Canaan and explore the land the Lord is giving us."

Aaron saw excitement flood Joshua's face, for he was the man chosen to represent the half tribe of Ephraim, son of Joseph. Some of the others looked frightened by their assignment. They had no provisions, no maps, no experience for spying out the strengths and weaknesses of their enemies. Most were young men like Joshua, but there was one other, older than the rest, and unshaken by the task before him: Caleb.

Moses walked among them, putting his hand on each man's shoulder as he passed by, his voice filled with confidence. "Go northward through the Negev into the hill country. See what the land is like and find out whether the people living there are strong or weak, few or many. What kind of land do they live in? Is it good or bad? Do their towns have walls or are they unprotected? How is the soil? Is it fertile or poor? Are there many trees?"

Moses paused when he reached Joshua. He clasped his hand, looked into the younger man's face. Releasing Joshua's hand, he turned to the others. "Enter the land boldly, and bring back samples of the crops you see."

Each man was given a water bag. They would not have manna during the time they were away from the camp. They would have to eat whatever the land of Canaan had to offer.

And the people waited.

✦   ✦   ✦

A week passed, then another and another. A new moon came, and still the spies did not return. How far had they gone? Had they met with resistance? Had some been killed? And if they had all been taken captive and executed, what then?

Aaron encouraged the people to be patient, to trust in the Lord to fulfill His promise. He prayed unceasingly for the twelve spies, Joshua often foremost in his mind.

He knew the younger man mattered greatly to Moses, for his brother often spoke of him with affection. "I know of no other like him, Aaron. He is dedicated to the Lord. Nothing will sway him."

How sad that Moses' own sons and brother should fall so short. Aaron no longer resented Joshua. He knew his own weaknesses and felt his age. Younger men would have to step into leadership if the people were to be hedged in and guided into their inheritance.

"They're coming! I see them! The men are returning!"

Excited cries filled the camp as family members surrounded the returning spies overladen with samples of what Canaan had to offer. Laughing, Joshua and Caleb had a pole stretched between their shoulders and on it was one cluster of grapes! Blankets were opened, spilling out bright red pomegranates and purple figs.

Joshua spoke first, directing his words to Moses. "We arrived in the land you sent us to see, and it is indeed a magnificent country."

Caleb raised his hands, jubilant. "It is a land flowing with milk and honey. Here is some of its fruit as proof."

Milk and honey, Aaron thought. That meant there were herds of cattle and goats, and fruit trees that flowered in the spring. There would be fields of wildflowers and plenty of water.

But the other spies focused on other things.

"The people living there are powerful."

"Their cities and towns are fortified and very large."

"We also saw the descendants of Anak who are living there!"

A low rumble of fear went through the listeners. The Anaks were giants, warriors who knew no fear and showed no mercy.

"The Amalekites live in the Negev."

Caleb turned. "They are cowards who attack from behind and kill those who are too weak to defend themselves."

"What about the Hittites? They are fierce warriors."

"The Hittites, Jebusites, and Amorites live in the hill country."

"The Canaanites live along the coast of the Mediterranean Sea and along the Jordan Valley."

"They are too strong for us."

Caleb's eyes blazed. "Is anyone too strong for the Lord? Let's go at once to take the land! We can certainly conquer it!"

Aaron looked to Moses, but his brother said nothing. Aaron wanted to cry out that the Lord had promised the land, and therefore, the Lord would see that they conquered it. But he had not been among the spies to see everything. He was an old man, not a warrior. And Moses was God's chosen leader. So Aaron waited, edgy, for Moses to decide. But his brother turned away and went into his tent.

Several spies shouted. "We can't go up against them! They are stronger than we are!"

Caleb's face was flushed with anger. "Canaan is the land God promised us! It is ours for the taking!"

"How can you be so sure? Hasn't God been killing us one by one since we left Egypt? With thirst and hunger and plagues!" Ten of the spies left and the people followed after them.

Caleb faced Aaron. "Why didn't Moses speak for us? Why didn't you?"

"I . . . I am only his spokesman. Moses always seeks the will of the Lord and then instructs me in what I'm to say."

"The Lord has already told us what He wills." Caleb pointed angrily. "Go and take the land!" He stalked away, shaking his head.

Aaron looked at Joshua. The younger man's shoulders were slumped and his eyes were shut. "Rest, Joshua. Perhaps tomorrow the Lord will tell Moses what we are to do."

"There will be trouble." Joshua looked at him. "Caleb is right. The land is ours. God has said so."

By the next morning, Aaron was hearing the rumors. The land would swallow up any who went into it. All the people living there were huge! There were even giants among them! The spies had felt like grasshoppers next to them! The people would be squashed like bugs if they dared enter Canaan!

But the Lord said . . .

No one was listening to what the Lord had said. No one believed.

"We wish we'd died in Egypt, or even here in the wilderness!"

"Why is the Lord taking us to this country only to have us die in battle?"

"We are not warriors! Our wives and little ones will be carried off as slaves!"

"Let's get out of here and return to Egypt!"

"Egypt is destroyed. There is nothing for us there!"

"The people fear us. We will be their masters for a change!"

"Yes! Let's go back!"

"Then we need a new leader."

Aaron saw the rage in their faces, their clenched fists. He was afraid, but less of them than of what God would do at the sight of this open rebellion. Moses fell facedown before the people, and Aaron dropped down beside him, close enough that if it became necessary, he could use his body to shield Moses. He could hear Caleb and Joshua shouting to the people.

"The land we explored is a wonderful land!"

"If the Lord is pleased with us, He will bring us safely into that land and give it to us!"

"It is a rich land flowing with milk and honey, and He will give it to us!"

"Don't rebel against the Lord."

"Don't be afraid of the people of the land. They are only helpless prey to us! They have no protection, but the Lord is with us!"

"Don't be afraid of them!"

The people grew more enraged with their words and shouted against them. "Stone them!"

"Who are you to speak to us, Caleb? You would lead us to death, Joshua!"

"Kill them!"

Screams rent the air. Aaron felt the strange prickling down his back once again and looked up. The glorious Presence rose into the air above the Tabernacle. Moses stood, head thrown back, arms raised. The people scattered, running for their tents, as if goatskins could hide them. Joshua and Caleb remained where they were, their beards whipped by the wind.

Moses stepped forward. "But Lord, what will the Egyptians think when they hear about it? They know full well the power You displayed in rescuing these people from Egypt."

Oh, Lord, hear his prayer! Aaron went down on his face again, for the lives of the people were at stake. *Lord, Lord, hear my brother.*

"Oh, Lord, no!" Moses cried out in horror. "The inhabitants of this land know, Lord, that You have appeared in full view of Your people in the pillar of cloud that hovers over them. They know that You go before them in a pillar of cloud by day and the pillar of fire by night. Now if You slaughter all these people, the nations that have heard of Your fame will say, 'The Lord was not able to bring them into the land He swore to give them, so He killed them in the wilderness.' Please, Lord, prove that Your power is as great as You have claimed it to be. For You said, 'The Lord is slow to anger and rich in unfailing love, forgiving every kind of sin and rebellion. Even so He does not leave sin unpunished, but He punishes the children for the sins of their parents to the third and fourth generations.' Please pardon the sins of this people because of Your magnificent, unfailing love, just as You have forgiven them ever since they left Egypt."

Moses fell silent. Aaron raised his head enough to peer up at his brother standing, arms still outstretched, palms up. After a long while, Moses' arms lowered to his sides and he let out a long, deep sigh. The glorious Presence came down once again and rested within the Tabernacle.

Aaron stood, slowly. "What did the Lord say?"

The only two men standing near were Caleb and Joshua, silent, terrified.

"Have the people gather, Aaron. I can only bear to say it once."

The people came quietly, tense and afraid, for all had seen the glorious Presence standing above, and had felt the heat of wrath. They remembered too late how easily God could take the lives of those who rebelled against Him.

And the Lord's anger was in Moses' voice as he spoke God's Word to the people. "The Lord will do to you the very things you said against Him. You will all die here in this wilderness! Because you complained against Him, none of you who are twenty years old or older and were counted in the census will enter the land the Lord swore to give you. The only exceptions will be Caleb and Joshua.

"You said your children would be taken captive. And the Lord says He will bring *them* safely into the land, and *they* will enjoy what you have despised! But as for you, your dead bodies will fall in this wilderness! And your children will be like shepherds, wandering in the wilderness forty years. In this way, *they* will pay for your faithlessness, until the last one of you lies dead in the wilderness! Because the men who explored the land were there for forty days, you must wander in the wilderness for forty years! One year for each day, suffering the consequences of your sins. You will discover what it is like to have the Lord for your enemy! Tomorrow we are to set out for the wilderness."

The people wailed.

The twelve men who had gone into the land to explore it were standing in the front lines of people. Ten of them groaned in pain and fell to their knees. Rolling in agony, they died where all could see them, near the entrance to the great tent that held the Tabernacle of the Lord. Only Caleb and Joshua remained standing.

Aaron wept in his tent, feeling he had somehow failed again. Would things have been different if he had stood with Joshua and Caleb? Was the Lord saying even he and Moses would never see the land promised? When Miriam and his sons tried to console him, he left them and went out to sit with Moses.

"So close." Moses' voice was filled with sorrow. "They were so close to all they have ever dreamed of having."

"Fear is the enemy."

"Fear of the Lord would have been their greatest strength. In Him is the victory."

Eleazar ran into the tent early the next morning. "Father! Father, come quickly. Some of the men are leaving camp."

"Leaving?" Aaron went cold. Did these people never learn?

"They say they are going into Canaan. They say they're sorry they sinned, but now they're ready to take the land God promised them."

Aaron hurried out, but Moses was already there, crying out at them to stop. "It's too late! Why are you now disobeying the Lord's orders to return to the wilderness? It won't work. Do not go into the land now. You will only be crushed by your enemies because the Lord is not with you!" Joshua and Caleb and others faithful had joined them, trying to block their way.

"The Lord is with us! We are the sons of Abraham! The Lord said the land is ours!" Heads high, they turned their backs on Moses and headed for Canaan.

Moses cried out one last time in warning. "The Lord will abandon you because you have abandoned the Lord!" When none turned away from certain disaster, Moses sighed wearily. "Prepare the camp. Go about your duties as the Lord has assigned. We're leaving today."

The Lord was taking them back to the place where they thought they had left Egypt behind: the Red Sea.

THE PEOPLE had not traveled a day when they started grumbling. Aaron saw the scowls and resentful looks. Wherever he walked, cold silence fell around him. The people did not trust him. After all, he was Moses' brother and had taken part in the decision to turn back the way they had come. Back to the hardship. Back to fear and despair. The Lord had issued the order because of their disobedience, but now the people sought a scapegoat.

As they continued to rebel against the Lord, Aaron felt the mounting weight of their sins being loaded onto his back. Conquering his fear, Aaron walked among the people and tried to fulfill the thankless responsibilities the Lord had given him to perform for their sake.

Stragglers returned from Canaan. Most had been killed. Those who had survived were driven back as far as Hormah.

"Those ten spies were telling the truth! Those people are too strong for us!"

Aaron knew trouble was ahead, and did not know how to turn these people's hearts toward God. If only they could see that it was their stubborn refusal to believe what God said that brought continued disaster on them.

They headed back because of their sin, but God continued to extend His hand to His people through Moses. When Aaron sat with his brother and heard the Word of the Lord, it flowed over him clearly and was so full of purpose and love. Every law given was meant to protect, to uphold, to sustain, to guide, to fix the people's hope on the Lord.

Even the offerings were meant to serve a purpose and build a relationship with Him. The burnt offerings made payment for sins and showed devotion to God. The grain offerings gave honor and respect to the Lord who provided for them. The peace offerings were to be given in gratitude for the peace and fellowship the Lord offered. The sin offerings made payment for unintentional sins and restored the sinner to fellowship with God, and the guilt offerings made payment for sins against God and others, providing compensation for those injured.

Every festival was a reminder of God's intended place in their lives. Passover reminded the people of God's deliverance from Egypt. The seven-day Festival of Unleavened Bread reminded them of leaving slavery behind and beginning a new way of life. The Festival of Firstfruits reminded them how God provided for them with Pentecost at the end of the barley harvest and beginning of the wheat harvest to show their joy and thanksgiving over God's provision. The Festival of Trumpets was to release joy and thanksgiving to God and the beginning of a new year with Him as Lord over all. The Day of Atonement removed sin from the people and the nation and restored fellowship with God while the seven-day Festival of Shelters was intended to remind future generations of the protection and guidance God provided in the wilderness and instruct them to continue to trust in the Lord in the years ahead.

Sometimes Aaron despaired. There was so much to remember. So many laws. So many feast days. Every day was governed by the Lord. Aaron was glad of that, but afraid that he would fail again as he had failed thrice before. How could he ever forget the molten calf, the deaths of two of his sons, and Miriam's leprosy?

I am weak, Lord. Make me strong in faith like Moses. Give me the ears to hear and eyes to see Your will. You have made me Your high priest over these people. Give me the wisdom and strength to do what pleases You!

He was all too aware of the pattern of faith. He would witness a miracle and follow God in abject sorrow and repentance.

God would seem to hide for a time and the doubts would begin. The people would start grumbling. Skepticism would spread. It seemed faith was strong when it suited the people's purposes, but waned quickly under the stress of hardship. God's divine presence was overhead in the cloud by day and pillar of fire by night, promising to carry them through defeat to victory, but the people grew angry because it wasn't soon enough to suit them.

Had any nation ever heard the voice of God speaking from fire as they had and survived? Had any other god taken one nation for Himself by rescuing it through means of trials, miraculous signs, wonders, war, awesome power, and terrifying acts? Yet that is what the Lord had done for them right before their eyes!

And still they complained!

It would take a bigger miracle than plagues and parting the Red Sea to change the hearts of these people. Not an outside miracle like raining manna from heaven or water from a rock, but something inside.

Oh, Lord, You've written the Law on stone tablets, and Moses has written Your Word on scrolls. Will it ever be written into our hearts so that we might not sin against You? Transform me, Lord. Change me because I'm hot and tired and irritated by everyone around me, by my circumstances. I hate the dust and the thirst and the hollow ache inside me because You seem so far away.

It was not the war ahead that threatened to defeat Aaron, but the daily step-by-step journey in the wilderness. Every day had its challenges. Every day had its tedium.

We've been this way before, Lord. Will we ever get it right?

+   +   +

Aaron sat in Moses' tent, resting in the congenial company of his brother. There would be no work today. No reading scrolls and going over instructions. No traveling. No gathering of manna. Aaron had been waiting for six days to have this one day of peace.

And now there was a commotion in the camp. He heard his name shouted. "What now?" He groaned as he rose. It was the Sabbath. Everyone was to rest. Surely, the people could leave him and Moses alone for one day out of the week!

Moses rose with him, tight-lipped and tense.

A gathering of men stood outside. One man was held between two others. "I didn't do anything wrong!" He tried to jerk free, but was held firmly.

"This man was found gathering wood."

"How do you expect me to make a cook fire and feed my family without wood?"

"You should have gathered wood yesterday!"

"We were walking yesterday! Remember?"

"Today is the Sabbath! The Lord said not to work on the Sabbath!"

"I wasn't *working*. I was *gathering*."

Aaron knew the Law was clear, but he didn't want to be the one to pronounce judgment on the man. He looked to Moses, hoping he would have a ready and just answer that would also be merciful. Moses' eyes were shut, his face tight. His shoulders slumped and he looked at the man in custody.

"The Lord says the man must die. The whole community must stone him outside the camp."

The man tried to fight free. "How do you know what the Lord says? Does God speak to you when none of us can hear Him?" He looked at the three men pulling and pushing him. "I didn't do anything wrong! Are you going to listen to that old man? He'll kill all of you before he's through!"

Aaron walked beside Moses. He didn't question what the Lord had said. He knew the Ten Commandments. *Remember to observe the Sabbath day by keeping it holy. Six days a week are set apart for your daily duties and regular work, but the seventh day is a day of rest dedicated to the Lord your God.*

The people gathered around the man. "Help me, brothers! Mama, don't let them do this to me! I didn't do anything wrong, I tell you!"

Moses took up a stone. Aaron bent to take up another. He felt sick. He knew he had committed greater sins than this man. "Now!" Moses commanded. The man tried to block the stones, but they came hard and fast from all directions. One hit him in the side of the head, another squarely between the eyes. He fell to his knees, blood streaming down his face as he screamed for mercy. Another stone silenced him. He fell face first into the dust and lay still.

The people surrounded him, crying out and weeping as they threw harder. It was his defiance that had brought them to this, his sin, his insistence that he do as he wanted when he wanted. If anyone turned away, they would be siding with him, siding with doing whatever they pleased in the face of God. Everyone must participate in the judgment. Everyone must know the cost of sin.

The man was dead, and still the stones came, one from each member of the assembly—men, women, children—until the body was covered over with stones.

Moses sighed heavily. "We must stand on higher ground."

Aaron knew the Lord had given his brother words to say. He walked with him and stood beside him. Raising his hands, Aaron called out. "Come, everyone. Listen and hear the Word of the Lord." He stepped aside as the people came and stood before Moses, their faces bleak. Children wept and clung to their mothers. Men looked less sure of themselves. God would not compromise with sin. Living had become a hazard.

Moses spread his hands. "The Lord says, 'Throughout the

generations to come you must make tassels for the hems of your
clothing and attach the tassels at each corner with a blue cord.
The tassels will remind you of the commands of the Lord, and
that you are to obey His commands instead of following your
own desires and going your own ways, as you are prone to do.
The tassels will help you remember that you must obey all My
commands and be holy to your God. I am the Lord your God
who brought you out of the land of Egypt that I might be your
God. I am the Lord your God!' "

The people moved off slowly, heads down.

Aaron saw the strain in Moses' face, the anger and the tears
brimming as the people walked away in silence. Aaron wanted
to comfort him. "The people hear the Word, Moses. They just
don't yet understand it."

Moses shook his head. "No, Aaron. They understand and
defy God anyway." He lifted his head and closed his eyes. "Are
we not called Israel? We are people who contend with God!"

"And still, He chose us."

"Don't become proud on that account, my brother. God
could have made these rocks into men and probably had better
luck with them. Our hearts are hard as stone, and we're more
stubborn than any mule. No, Aaron. God chose people beneath
the heel of man's power to show the nations that God is all-
powerful. It is by and through Him we live. He is taking a multitude of slaves and making them into a nation of freemen under
God so that the nations around will know *He is God*. And when
they know, they can choose."

Choose what? "Are you saying He is not just *our* God?"

"The Lord is the *only* God. Didn't He prove that to you in
Egypt?"

"Yes, but . . . " Did that mean anyone could come to Him and
become part of Israel?

"All who crossed the Red Sea with us are part of our community, Aaron. And the Lord has said that we are to have the same rules for Israelite and foreigner. One God. One covenant. One law that applies to all."

"But I thought He meant only to deliver us and give us a land that would belong to us. That's all we want—a place where we can work and live in peace."

"Yes, Aaron, and the land God has promised us is at the crossroads of every major trade route, surrounded by powerful nations, filled with people stronger than we are. Why do you suppose God would put us there?"

It was not a question that lightened Aaron's burdened heart. "To watch us."

"To see God at work in us."

And then to say God was not God would be to deny and defy the power that had created the heavens and the earth.

✦   ✦   ✦

Every day seemed to get worse, until Aaron found himself with Moses standing before an angry delegation formed by Korah, one of their own relatives! Korah wasn't content to stand against them by himself, but had brought Dathan and Abiram, leaders of the Reubenite tribe as his allies, together with two hundred and fifty leaders well-known to Aaron, men who had been appointed to the council to help Moses shoulder the load of leadership. And now, they wanted more power!

"You have gone too far!" Korah stood in front of his allies, speaking for all of them. "Everyone in Israel has been set apart by the Lord, and He is with all of us. What right do you have to act as though you are greater than anyone else among all these people of the Lord?"

Moses fell face to the ground before them, and Aaron threw himself flat on the ground beside him. He knew what these people wanted, and he was powerless against them. Even more terrifying was what the Lord might do in the face of their rebellion. Aaron did not intend to defend his position when he knew his faith was weak and his mistakes so many!

Korah shouted to the others, "Moses sets himself up to be king over us and makes his brother his high priest! Is that what we want?"

"No!" Moses rose from the dust, his eyes blazing. "Tomorrow morning the Lord will show us who belongs to Him and who is holy. The Lord will allow those who are chosen to enter His holy presence. You, Korah, and all your followers must do this: Take incense burners, and burn incense in them tomorrow before the Lord. Then we will see whom the Lord chooses as His holy one. You Levites are the ones who have gone too far!"

Korah lifted his chin. "Why should we do what you say?"

"Now listen, you Levites! Does it seem a small thing to you that the God of Israel has chosen you from among all the people of Israel to be near Him as you serve in the Lord's Tabernacle and to stand before the people to minister to them? He has given this special ministry only to you and your fellow Levites, but now you are demanding the priesthood as well! The one you are really revolting against is the Lord! And who is Aaron that you are complaining about him?"

Who am I that I should be high priest? Aaron wondered. Any time he had tried to lead, he had brought disaster. No wonder they did not trust him. Why should they?

Lord, Lord, whatever You will, let it be done.

"Let Dathan and Abiram come forward so that I can speak to them."

"We refuse to come! Isn't it enough that you brought us out of Egypt, a land flowing with milk and honey, to kill us here in this wilderness, and that you now treat us like your subjects? What's more, you haven't brought us into the land flowing with milk and honey or given us an inheritance of fields and vineyards. Are you trying to fool us? We will not come."

Moses raised his arms and cried out to the Lord, "Do not accept their offerings! I have not taken so much as a donkey from them, and I have never hurt a single one of them."

"Nor have you given us what you promised!"

"It is not mine to give!"

Korah spit in the dust at Aaron's feet.

Moses shook with rage. "Come here tomorrow and present yourself before the Lord with all your followers. Aaron will also be here. Be sure that each of your two hundred and fifty followers brings an incense burner with incense on it, so you can present them before the Lord. Aaron will also bring his incense burner. Let the Lord decide!"

Crushed in spirit, Aaron made his preparations. Had all these men forgotten the fate of Nadab and Abihu? Did they think they could make their own fire and stir in their own incense and not face God's wrath? He couldn't sleep thinking about what might happen!

The next morning Aaron went out with his censer. Breathing in the sweet scent of frankincense, he stood with Moses at the entrance to the Tabernacle.

Korah came, head high. The number of his followers had multiplied.

The air became denser, warmer, humming with power. Aaron looked up and saw the glory of the Lord rise, Shekinah streaming light in all directions. Aaron heard the indrawn breath from the Israelites who had come to see whom God would choose. Aaron knew they were disappointed, as they had fixed their anger on God's prophet and spokesman. They stood en masse behind Korah.

Aaron heard the Voice.

Get away from these people so that I may instantly
destroy them!

As God had put an end to Nadab and Abihu! Crying out,
Aaron fell on his face before the Lord, not wanting to see the
nation obliterated by fire. Moses fell down beside him praying
frantically. "O God, the God and source of all life, must You be
angry with all the people when only one man sins?"

The people talked nervously, looking this way and that,
looking up, edging back.

Moses came to his feet clumsily and shouted, "Move away
from the tents of Korah, Dathan, and Abiram!" He spread his
hands and hurried toward the people. "Quick! Get away from
the tents of these wicked men, and don't touch anything that
belongs to them. If you do, you will be destroyed for their
sins!"

"Do not listen to him!" Korah shouted. "Every man you see
standing with a censer is holy!"

Aaron stayed on the ground. *God, forgive them. They don't
know what they're doing!*

Nothing had changed within the people. They were the same
as they had always been—hard-hearted, stubborn, defiant. Just
like Pharaoh, who had forgotten the hardships of the plagues
each time God lifted His hand, these people forgot God's kindness and provision when hardship came. Just as Pharaoh had
clung to Egypt's ways and his pride, these people clung to their
longing for a self-indulgent life. They longed to return to the
idol-infested country that had enslaved them.

"Were we not ourselves chosen by God to lead as a council?"
Someone else called out in rebellion.

"What has this old man done for you? We will show honor
to God by leading you into the land God conquered for us. We
will return to Egypt, and we will be the masters this time!"

Moses cried out, "By this you will know that the Lord has sent me to do all these things that I have done—for I have not done them on my own. If these men die a natural death, then the Lord has not sent me. But if the Lord performs a miracle and the ground opens up and swallows them and all their belongings, and they go down alive into the grave, then you will know that these men have despised the Lord!"

The earth rumbled. Aaron felt the ground roll violently beneath him as if the Lord were shaking dust from a blanket. Aaron rose, spreading his feet for balance, holding tight to his censer. Rocks cracked and a chasm opened. Korah pitched forward, screaming, and fell headfirst into the gaping hole, his men after him. Down went his tent with his wife and concubines, his servants. All of those whom the Lord found guilty went down into the earth alive. The horrific screams that rose from the crevice sent the people scattering in terror.

"Get back! Get away! The earth will swallow us, too!"

The chasm closed, deadening the horrific sounds of pain and terror that came up from the earth.

Fire blazed forth from the Lord and burned up the two hundred and fifty men offering incense, turning them into charred corpses like Nadab and Abihu. They dropped where they stood, their bodies smoldering, blackened fingers still gripping the censers that clattered to the ground spilling out homemade incense.

Aaron alone remained standing before the entrance of the Tabernacle, the censer of incense still clutched in his hand.

"Eleazar!" Moses beckoned Aaron's son. "Collect the censers and hammer them into sheets to cover the altar. The Lord has said this will remind the people now and in the future that no one except a descendant of Aaron should come to burn incense before Him, or he will become like Korah and his followers."

All through the night, Aaron heard the echo of hammer

against bronze as his son obeyed the Word of the Lord. Far into
the night, Aaron prayed with tears streaming into his beard.
"According to Your will, Lord . . . as You will. . . ."

✦   ✦   ✦

Aaron thought he was still dreaming when he heard angry
cries. Exhausted, he rubbed his face. He wasn't dreaming. He
groaned as he recognized Dathan's and Abiram's voices. "Moses
and Aaron have killed the Lord's people!"

Would these people never change? Would they never learn?

He rose quickly, his sons Eleazar and Ithamar with him, and
met Moses before the Tabernacle. "What do we do?" The people were heading toward them.

The mob came, shouting accusations. "You two have killed
the Lord's people."

"Korah was a Levite just as you are and you killed him!"

"The Levites are servants of the Lord!"

"You killed them!"

"You two won't be satisfied until we're all dead!"

The cloud came down and covered the Tent of Meeting and
the Shekinah glory glowed from within the cloud.

"Come with me, Aaron." Moses went to the front of the
Tabernacle, and Aaron joined him there. Shaking, Aaron
heard the Voice fill his mind. He fell on his face, arms outstretched.

*Get away from these people so that I can instantly
destroy them!*

And what would the nations say then if the Lord could not
bring His people into the land He promised?

People screamed, and then Moses spoke. "Quick, take an
incense burner and place burning coals on it from the altar. Lay
incense on it and carry it quickly among the people to make

atonement for them. The Lord's anger is blazing among them—
the plague has already begun."

Aaron clambered to his feet and ran as fast as his aging legs
could carry him. Breathing hard, he took the censer and ran to
the altar. He took the golden utensil and scooped burning coals
into his censer. His hand shook. People were already dying!

Thousands fell on their faces, crying out to the Lord, crying
out to Moses, crying out to him. "Lord, have mercy on us. Have
mercy! Save us, Moses. Aaron, save us!"

He must hurry! Aaron sprinkled the incense onto the coals
and turned back. Huffing and puffing, heart pounding and pain
spreading across his chest, he headed straight into the midst of
men and women falling to the right and left. He held the censer
high. "Lord, have mercy on us. Lord, forgive them. Oh, God,
we repent! Hear our prayer!"

Dathan and Abiram lay dead, their faces stiff in agony.
Everywhere Aaron looked, men and women were dropping
from the plague.

Aaron stood in the midst of them and cried out, "Those who
are for the Lord, get behind me!" The people moved like the
tide of a sea. Others who stood their ground screamed and fell,
groaning in agony as they died. Aaron did not move from his
post, the living on one side and the dying on the other. He
stayed, arm trembling as he held the censer high and prayed.

The plague abated.

His breathing slowed. Bodies sprawled all over the camp,
thousands of them. Some lay close to the burned places where
the two hundred and fifty Levites had died only yesterday. Sur-
vivors clutched one another and wept, wondering if they would
be struck down by fire or die in agony of plague. Each body
would have to be lifted and carried for burial outside the camp.

Weary, Aaron walked back to Moses standing at the entrance
of the Tabernacle. Aaron looked into the stricken faces of the

people staring at him. Would another rebellion begin tomorrow? Why couldn't they see that he wasn't their leader? Even Moses did not lead them. When would they understand that *the Lord* directed their path! It was God's divine presence that would make them into a holy nation!

Lord, Lord, I am so tired. They look to me and Moses, and we are just men like they are. You are the one leading us into the wilderness. I don't want to go any more than they do, but I know You are training us for a purpose.

How long will we fight against You? How long will we bow down to our own pride? It seems such an easy thing to look up, to listen and live! What is it in our nature that makes us fight against You so hard? We go our own way and die, and still we don't learn. We are foolish, all of us! I, most of all. Every day I fight the battle within me.

Oh, Lord, You lifted me from a mud pit and opened up the Red Sea. You brought me through the desert. Not once did You abandon me. And still . . . still I doubt. Still I fight a battle within myself I can't seem to win!

These people wanted someone else to stand between the Lord and them, someone more worthy to offer atonement. He couldn't blame them. He wanted the same thing.

Moses spoke again, his voice calm and clear. "Each leader from each ancestral tribe will bring me his staff with his name written on it. The staff of Levi will bear Aaron's name. I will place them in the Tabernacle in front of the Ark of the Covenant, and the staff belonging to the man the Lord chooses will sprout. When you know the man whom God has chosen, you will not grumble against the Lord anymore."

The tribal leaders came forward and handed Moses their staffs, their names etched into the wood. Aaron stood to one side. In his hand, he held the staff that had become a snake before Pharaoh and swallowed the snakes created by the Egyptian sorcerers. This was the same staff he had held over the Nile when the Lord turned the waters to blood and then brought forth the frogs. The Lord had told him to strike the ground with this staff and then the Lord had sent a plague of gnats.

"Aaron." Moses held out his hand.

Tomorrow everyone would know if his staff was simply a gnarled piece of acacia wood that offered him support as he walked the desert road, or an emblem of authority. He gave it to Moses. If God willed it, let another more worthy be chosen to become high priest. As a matter-of-fact, Aaron hoped He would. These men didn't understand the burden that came with the position.

Next morning, Moses summoned the people again. He held each staff high and returned it to its rightful owner. Not one had sprouted so much as a nub. When he held Aaron's staff high, the people murmured in awe. Aaron stared, amazed. Not only had his staff sprouted leaves; it had budded, blossomed, and produced almonds!

"The Lord has said that Aaron's staff will remain in front of the Ark of the Covenant as a warning to rebels! This should put an end to your complaints against the Lord and prevent any further deaths!" Moses took Aaron's staff back into the Tabernacle and came out empty-handed.

"We are as good as dead!" The people huddled together and wept. "We are ruined!"

"Everyone who even comes close to the Tabernacle of the Lord dies."

"We are all doomed!"

Moses entered the Tabernacle.

Aaron followed. His heart ached with compassion. What could he say that would do any good? Only God knew what the days ahead would reveal. And Aaron doubted the way would be any smoother than it had been so far.

The people continued to cry in despair. "Pray for us, Aaron. Moses, plead for our lives."

Even in the shade of the Tabernacle, standing before the veil, he could hear their weeping. And he wept with them.

+   +   +

"Be ready." Aaron kept his sons close, watching over them. "We must wait on the Lord. The moment the cloud rises, we must move quickly."

As the sun rose, the cloud rose and spread out over the camp. He watched it and saw that it was moving. "Eleazar! Ithamar! Come!" They headed quickly for the Tabernacle. "Don't forget the cloth." His sons took up the heavy chest and followed him inside the inner chamber. Removing the shielding curtain, he covered the Ark of the Covenant with it, then covered it with heavy, protective hides and spread a solid blue cloth over it. He slid the acacia wood poles into the golden rings.

Feeling clumsy in his haste, Aaron tried to calm himself and remember the details of preparing for travel. At his instructions, Eleazar and Ithamar spread another blue cloth on the Table of the Presence and placed on it the plates, dishes, bowls, and jars for the drink offerings. The Bread of the Presence remained. Everything was covered by a scarlet cloth and then covered again with hides. The lampstand was covered in blue and wrapped, along with the wick trimmers, trays, and jars for the oil. A blue cloth was spread over the gold altar. As soon as the ashes were removed and properly deposited, the bronze altar was covered with a purple cloth, along with all the utensils. When each item was properly stowed for travel, Aaron nodded. "Summon the Kohathites." The Lord had assigned them to carry the holy things.

The Gershonites were responsible for the Tabernacle and tent, its coverings, and the curtains. The Merarite clans were responsible for the crossbars, posts, bases, and all the equipment.

The Lord moved out before them overhead. Moses followed, staff in hand. Those who carried the Ark followed Moses; Aaron and his sons came next. Behind them, the multitude gathered in ranks with their tribes and proceeded in order.

Eleazar watched the cloud. "Where do you think the Lord will take us, Father?"

"Wherever He wills."

They traveled until late in the afternoon and the cloud stopped. The Ark was set down. Aaron oversaw the rebuilding of the Tabernacle and the raising of the curtains around it. He and his sons unwrapped each item carefully and placed it where it belonged. Eleazar filled the seven-branched lampstand with oil, and prepared the fragrant incense. At twilight, Aaron made the offering before the Lord.

As night came, Aaron stood outside his tent and surveyed the arid land by moonlight. There was little pasturage here and no water. He knew they would be on the move again soon.

In the morning, the cloud rose again and Aaron and his sons set to work quickly. Day after day, they did this until Aaron and his sons moved with quick precision, and the people fell into order with a single blast of the shofar.

One day Aaron rose expecting to move, but the cloud remained. Another day passed and another.

When Aaron and his sons and the people settled easily, relaxing their vigil, the cloud rose again. As he walked, Aaron remembered the jubilance and celebration as they had left Egypt. Now, the people were silent, stoic as they began to realize the fullness of God's decree that they would wander in the wilderness until the rebellious generation had died.

They came to rest again.

After performing the evening sacrifice, Aaron joined Moses.

They ate together in silence. Aaron had spent the entire day at the Tabernacle, performing his duties from dawn to dusk, and overseeing that the others did as the Lord bade them. He knew his brother had spent his day reviewing difficult cases and bringing them before the Lord. Moses looked tired. Neither felt like talking. They spent their days talking.

Miriam served manna cakes. "Perhaps we will stay here for a time. There's plenty of grass for the animals and water."

The cloud rose just as Aaron completed the morning sacrifice. Aaron swallowed his sorrow and called out to his sons. "Come! Quickly!" His sons hastened to him. The people rushed to their tents to make preparations for travel.

They only traveled half a day this time, and then remained camped in one place for a month.

"Does God tell you beforehand, Father?" Eleazar walked beside Aaron, his eyes on the Ark. "Does God give you any indication that we will be moving?"

"No. Not even Moses knows the day and the hour."

Ithamar hung his head. "Forty years, the Lord said."

"We deserve our punishment, Brother. If we had heeded Joshua and Caleb instead of the others, perhaps . . ."

Aaron felt such a heavy sorrow inside that he could hardly breathe past it. It came upon him so strongly he knew it must be from the Lord. *Oh, God, God, do we understand Your purposes? Will we ever understand?* "It is not merely punishment, my sons."

Ithamar looked at him. "What is it then, Father? This endless wandering?"

"Training."

His sons looked perplexed. Eleazar looked acquiescent, but Ithamar shook his head. "We move from one place to another, like nomads with no home."

"We look at the outer purposes and think we understand, but remember, my sons: God is merciful as well as just."

Ithamar shook his head. "I don't understand."

Aaron sighed deeply, keeping his pace steady, his gaze straight ahead on the Ark and Moses in the distance. "We came through the Red Sea, but we brought Egypt with us. We have to let go of who we were and become what God intends us to be."

"Free," Eleazar said.

"I don't call this freedom."

Aaron glanced at Ithamar. "Do not question the Lord. You are free, but you must learn obedience. We must all learn. We became a new nation when God brought us out of Egypt. And the nations around watch us. But what have we done with our freedom but drag all the old ways with us? We must learn to wait on the Lord. Where I have failed, you must succeed. You must learn to keep your eyes and ears open. You must learn to move when God tells you to move, and not before. One day, the Lord will bring you and your children to the Jordan. And when God says, 'Take the land,' you must be ready to go in and take and hold it."

Ithamar raised his head. "We'll be ready."

The arrogant impetuousness of youth. "I hope so, my son. I hope so."

✦   ✦   ✦

The years passed slowly as the Israelites wandered in the wilderness. The Lord always provided enough pasture for the animals. He gave the people manna and water to sustain them. Their shoes and clothing never wore out. Each day, Aaron arose from his pallet and saw the presence of the Lord in the cloud. Each night before he entered his tent to rest, he saw the presence of the Lord in the pillar of fire.

Year after year, the people traveled. Every morning and evening, Aaron offered sacrifices and fragrant offerings. He pored over the scrolls Moses wrote, reading them until he had memorized every word the Lord had spoken to Moses. As the high priest, Aaron knew he must know the Law better than anyone else.

The people God had delivered from Egypt began to die. Some died at an early age. Others lived into their seventies and eighties. But the generation that had come out of Egypt dwindled, and the children grew tall.

Aaron never let a day go by without instructing his children and grandchildren in the law of the Lord. Some of them had not been born when God brought the plagues upon Egypt. They never saw the Red Sea parted, or walked on the dry land to reach the other side. But they gave thanks for the manna they received every day. They praised the Lord for the water that quenched their thirst. And they grew strong as they walked the wilderness and relied on the Lord for everything they needed to live.

+   +   +

"He's asking for you, Aaron."

Aaron rose slowly, his joints stiff, his back aching. His grief deepened each time he sat with an old friend who was dying—deepened and remained. There were so few left now, a mere handful of those who had worked in the mud pits making bricks for Egypt.

And Hur had been a good friend, one of those Aaron could trust to strive to do right. He was the last of the first seventy men chosen to judge the people, the other sixty-nine now replaced by younger men, trained and chosen for their love of and adherence to the Law.

Hur lay on a pallet in his tent, his children and grandchildren gathered around him. Some wept softly. Others sat in silence, heads bowed. His eldest son sat close beside him, leaning down to hear his father's final instructions.

Hur saw Aaron standing in the doorway of the tent. "My friend." His voice was weak, his body emaciated by age and infirmity. He spoke softly to his son and the younger man with-drew, making a place for Aaron. Hur raised his hand weakly. "My friend . . ." He squeezed Aaron's hand weakly. "I am the last of those condemned to die in the wilderness. The forty years are almost over."

His hand felt so cold, the bones so fragile. Aaron put his hands around his as though he were holding a bird.

"Oh, Aaron. All these years of wandering and I still feel the weight of my sin. It's as though the years have not diminished it, but removed my strength to endure it." His eyes were moist. "But sometimes I dream I am standing on the shores of the Jordan, looking across at the Promised Land. My heart breaks at the loss of it. It is so beautiful, not at all like this wilderness in which we live. All I can do is dream of the fields of grain and the fruit trees, the flocks of sheep and cattle, and hope my sons and their sons will soon sit under an olive tree and hear the bees humming." Tears trickled into his white hair. "I am more alive when I sleep than when I wake."

Aaron fought the emotions gripping him. He understood what Hur was saying, understood with every fiber of his being. Regret for sins committed. Repentance. Forty years of walking with the consequences.

Hur let out his breath softly. "Our sons are not as we were. They have learned to move when God moves, and rest when He rests."

Aaron closed his eyes and said nothing.

"You doubt."

Aaron stroked his friend's hand. "I hope."

"Hope is all we have left, my friend."

And love.

It had been a long, long time since Aaron had heard the Voice, and he uttered a sob of gratitude, his heart yearning toward it, leaning in, drinking. "Love," he whispered hoarsely. "The Lord disciplines us as we discipline our sons, Hur. It may not feel like love when we're living in the midst of it, but love it is. Hard and true, lasting."

"Hard and true, lasting."

Aaron knew death was drawing near. It was time to withdraw. He had his duties to perform, the evening sacrifice to offer. He leaned close once last time. "May the Lord's face yet shine upon you and give you peace."

"And you. When you sit beneath your olive tree, Aaron, think of me. . . ."

Aaron paused outside the tent, and let his mind wander to the past. He would always remember Hur standing on the hilltop with him, holding Moses' left hand in the air while he held his brother's right, and below them Joshua defeating the Amalekites.

He knew the moment Hur breathed his last. Clothes ripped, men sobbed, and the women keened. It was a sound oft heard in camp over the years, but this time it brought with it a sense of completion.

Their wandering was about to come to an end. A new day was coming.

+   +   +

Aaron stood in his priestly garb before the curtain that hid the Most Holy Place from sight. He shook as he always did when the Lord spoke to him. Even after forty years, he had not become accustomed to the sound within and without and all around him, the Voice that filled his senses with delight and terror.

You, your sons, and your relatives from the tribe of Levi will be held responsible for any offenses related to the

sanctuary. But you and your sons alone will be held liable
for violations connected with the priesthood. Bring your
relatives of the tribe of Levi to assist you and your sons as
you perform the sacred duties in front of the Tabernacle of
the Covenant. But as the Levites go about their duties under
your supervision, they must be careful not to touch any of
the sacred objects or the altar. If they do, both you and they
will die.

*Let it sink in and remain fresh in my mind, Lord. Don't let me
forget anything.*

I myself have chosen your fellow Levites from among the
Israelites to be your special assistants.

*Oh, Lord, let them be men whose hearts are fixed on pleasing
You! From the time of Jacob, we have killed men in anger. Cursed
is our anger. It is so fierce. And we tend to cruelty. Oh, Lord, and
now You are scattering us throughout Israel just as Jacob prophe-
sied. We are dispersed as priests among Your people. Make us a
holy nation! Give us tender hearts!*

I have put the priests in charge of all the holy gifts that
are brought to Me by the people of Israel. I have given
these offerings to you and your sons as your regular share.

Let my life be an offering!

You priests will receive no inheritance of land or share
of property among the people of Israel. I am your inheritance and your share. As for the tribe of Levi, your relatives, I will pay them for their service in the Tabernacle
with the tithes from the entire land of Israel.

Aaron surrendered to the Voice, listening, listening, drinking
in the words like living water.

The Lord commanded that a red heifer without defect or blemish and that had never been under a yoke be given to Eleazar to be taken outside the camp and slaughtered. Aaron's son would take some of the blood on his finger and sprinkle it seven times toward the front of the Tent of Meeting. The heifer was to be burned, the ashes collected and put into a ceremonially clean place outside the camp for use in the water of cleansing, for purification from sin.

So much to remember: the festivals, the sacrifices, the laws.

Aaron sat with Moses and looked out over the tents and flickering lights of thousands of campfires. "We are all that is left of the generation that left Egypt." Thirty-eight years had passed from the time they left Kadesh-barnea until they crossed the Zered Valley. The entire generation of fighting men had perished from the camp, as the Lord had sworn would happen. "Just you and me and Miriam."

Surely now, the Lord would turn them toward the Promised Land.

+ + +

The cloud moved and the whole community traveled with the Lord until He stopped over the Desert of Zin. The people made camp at Kadesh.

While Aaron studied the scrolls, Miriam laid her hand on his shoulder. "I love you, Aaron. I have loved you like a son."

His sister had spoken very little since the Lord had afflicted her with leprosy, healed her, and commanded her to spend the seven days of cleansing outside the camp. She had returned a different woman—tenderly patient, quiet. She served the family with her customary devotion, but kept her thoughts to herself. He was perplexed by her sudden need to say she loved him.

She went outside the tent and sat at the entrance.

Troubled, Aaron rose and went out to her. "Miriam?"

"It is our own pride that slays us, Aaron."

Aaron searched her face. "Shall I send for Eleazar's wife to tend you?" She looked so old and worn down, her dark eyes soft and moist.

"Come closer, Aaron." She cupped his face and looked into his eyes. "I have made terrible mistakes."

"I know. So have I." Her hands were cool, her fingers trembling. He remembered when she was robust and full of fire. He had learned long ago not to argue with his sister. But she was different now. Humiliated before all Israel, humbled before God, she had become strangely content when God had stripped her of the one thing she could not conquer—her pride. "And the Lord forgave us both."

"Yes." She smiled and took her hands from him. She folded them in her lap. "We contend with God and He disciplines us. We repent and God forgives." She looked up at the cloud moving in slow undulating circles overhead. "Only His love endures forever."

Aaron felt a niggling fear grow inside him. Miriam was slipping away. Fear gripped him. She was dying. Surely the Lord would allow Miriam to enter Canaan. If she was not spared, would he also die before they reached the Jordan River? He could not imagine life without his sister. She had always been there for him, from the time he was a little boy. She had been like a second mother, scolding and disciplining him, guiding and teaching him. At eight, she had been bold enough to approach Pharaoh's daughter. Her quick thinking had brought Moses home for a few years before he was taken into the palace.

He beckoned Ithamar. "Bring Moses." Ithamar took one look at his aunt and ran. Aaron took Miriam's hand and tried to warm it between his. "Moses will come." She was just tired. She would be better soon. She would be refreshed after a rest and rise again.

"Moses cannot stop what God has ordained, Aaron. Have I not been just as disobedient as the others of our generation who have died? It is just that I go the way of all flesh here in the wilderness."

And what about me?

The cloud changed from gray to gold and from gold to fiery orange and red as day became night. The Lord stood guard, giving them light and warmth by night, just as the Lord gave them shade during the heat of the day.

"I'm not afraid, Aaron. It's time."

"Don't talk that way." He rubbed her hand. "The forty years are nearly up. We are about to go into the Promised Land."

"Oh, Aaron, don't you understand yet?"

Moses hurried toward them, staff in hand. Aaron rose. "Moses. Help her. Please. She can't die. We're so close."

"Miriam, my sister . . ." Moses knelt beside her. "Are you in pain?"

Her mouth curved. "Life is pain."

The family gathered: Eleazar and Ithamar and their wives and children; Eliezer and Gershom sat with her. Moses' Cushite wife approached. Smiling, Miriam lifted her hand. They had long since made their peace and become dear friends. Miriam spoke in a whisper, her strength ebbing. The Cushite woman wept and kissed Miriam's hand.

Aaron was frantic with fear. This couldn't be happening! Miriam couldn't die yet. Hadn't she been the one to lead the people with songs of deliverance, songs of praise to the Lord?

It was near dawn when Miriam sighed deeply. She died with her eyes still open and fixed on the pillar of fire that now became the swirling gray cloud. Spears of sunlight came from it, making spots of light on the desert ground.

With an anguished cry, Aaron reached toward her, only to be pulled back by Eleazar. "You can't touch her now, Father."

A high priest could not allow himself to become unclean. He would be unfit to perform his duties for the people as their high priest! Sobbing, Aaron straightened with difficulty.

"Father?" Eleazar supported him.

"It is time for the morning sacrifices." Aaron heard the harshness in his own voice and did not regret it. Is this the kindness of God, to allow his sister to live so long and then have her die so close to the borders of the Promised Land?

You never forget our sins, do You, Lord? Never.

Grieving and angry, he walked away as his sons' wives and servants began the warbling scream of grief.

People nearby heard and came running. Soon the entire camp was wailing.

✦   ✦   ✦

No sooner was Miriam buried than the people complained again. A crowd stood before the Tabernacle and quarreled with Moses. "Why did you bring the Lord's community to this place?"

Aaron could not stop thinking about his sister. Every day he awakened with an aching heart. Every day he had to come here and serve the Lord, and every day these grown children turned out to be no better than their fathers and mothers!

"There's no water here!"

"Why did you make us leave Egypt and bring us here to this terrible place?"

Aaron stepped forward. "What do you know of Egypt? You were not even born when we left that place!"

"We've heard!"

"We have come close enough to look back and see the green along the Nile."

"What have we had in this desert?"

"There's no grain!"

"And no figs!"

"No grapes or pomegranates."

"And there is no water to drink!"

"We wish we had died in the Lord's presence with our brothers!"

Aaron turned away, so angry he knew if he remained, he would say or do something he would later regret. He looked at Moses, hoping to draw wisdom and patience from him, but his brother too was red with anger. Moses fell on his face at the entrance of the Tabernacle and Aaron went down beside him. He wanted to pound his fists on the ground. How long would the Lord expect them to lead these people? Did they think he and Moses had water to drink? How many times did these people have to witness a miracle before they believed that he and Moses were appointed by the Lord to lead them?

You are the one who brought us to this place! They always blame us! Is it Your plan that my brother and I die at their hands? They are ready to kill us! Lord, give them water to drink.

You and Aaron must take the staff and assemble the entire community. As the people watch, command the rock over there to pour out its water. You will get enough water from the rock to satisfy all the people and their livestock.

Moses rose and went inside the Tabernacle. He came out with Aaron's staff in his hand. "Gather those rebels!"

Aaron went out ahead of him and shouted at the people to gather together in front of the rock. "You want water? Come and see it pour from the rock!" They swarmed there, empty water bags in hand, still complaining.

Moses pushed Aaron to one side and stood in front of all of them, the staff in his hand. "Listen, you rebels! Must we bring you water from this rock?"

"Yes! Give us water!"

Moses took the staff with both hands and hit the rock.

"Water, Moses! Give us water, Moses!"

Face red, eyes blazing, Moses struck the rock again, harder this time. Water gushed forth. The people pressed forward, crying out, rejoicing, filling their cupped hands, filling their skin bags, laughing and cheering Moses and Aaron. Aaron laughed with them, exultant. See how water flowed when his staff was wielded.

"Blessings on you, Moses! May you be praised, Aaron!"

Moses stood apart from them, staff in hand, head high, watching.

Aaron cupped his hands and drank with the people. Aaron blushed with pleasure as people called out praise to him and Moses. The water continued to flow and the Israelites brought their flocks and herds to drink. And still the water came. Never had water tasted so good. He wiped the droplets from his beard and grinned at Moses. "They do not doubt us now, do they, my brother?"

Because you did not trust Me enough to demonstrate My holiness to the people of Israel, you will not lead them into the land I am giving them!

God spoke softly, but with a finality that made Aaron's blood go cold. The curse of the Levites was on him. He had lost his temper and given in to pride. He had forgotten the Lord's command. *Command the rock.* No, that wasn't true. He hadn't forgotten. He had wanted Moses to use his staff. He had cheered when water gushed from the rock. He had been proud and delighted when the people slapped him on the back.

How quickly he had fallen headlong into sin. And now, he would pay the consequences just like the rest of his generation, even Miriam who had repented and served others with gladness for almost forty years! He would not set foot in the land God had promised the Israelites either. Miriam had died, and now he would die, too.

Aaron sank down and sat on a boulder, shoulders slumped, hands limp between his knees. What hope had he of ever being any different than what he was: a sinner. Pride, Miriam had said. Pride slays men. Pride strips men of a future and a hope. He covered his face. "I have sinned against the Lord."

"As have I."

Aaron glanced up. His brother's face was ashen. He was bent like an old man, leaning heavily on the staff. "Not as I have sinned, Moses. You have always praised the Lord and credited Him with all righteousness."

"Not today. I allowed anger to rule me. Pride made me stumble. And now, I too will die on this side of the Jordan River. The Lord has told me that I will not enter the land He promised."

"No." Aaron wept. "I am more to blame than you, Moses. I cried out for you to give us water as loudly as any of them. It is right that I be denied a land of my own. I am a sinner."

"Sin is sin, Aaron. Let's not get into a quarrel over who has outdone the other in that regard. We are all sinners. It is but for the grace of God that we live and breathe at all."

"You are the one God chose to deliver Israel!"

"Do not let your love for me blind you, my brother. *God* is our deliverer."

Aaron held his head. "Let your one mistake be on my head. Wasn't I the one who fashioned the molten calf and let the people run wild? Did I not try to steal some of your praise just now?"

"We both stole glory from God, who gave the water. All I had to do was speak to the rock. And what did I do but make a show for their benefit? And why else but to gain their attention, rather than remind them God is their provider."

"You have been telling them that for years, Moses."

"It needed to be said again." Moses sat beside him on the boulder. "Aaron, are we not each responsible for our own sins? The Lord chastens me because I didn't trust Him. The people need to trust in Him, only in Him."

"I'm sorry."

"Why are you sorry?"

"The Lord called me to stand beside you, to help you. And what help have I been over the years? If I were a better man, a better priest, I would have realized the temptation. I would have warned you."

Moses sighed. "I lost my temper, Aaron. I didn't forget what the Lord commanded. I didn't think speaking would be . . . impressive enough." His fingers tightened on Aaron's knee. "We must not be discouraged, Aaron. Doesn't a father discipline a son in order to train him up in the way he should go?"

"And where will we go now, Moses? God has said we will never set foot in the Promised Land. What hope have we?"

"God is our hope."

Aaron could not stop his tears. His throat ached. His chest heaved. *Oh, God, I've failed You and my brother yet again. Was I destined to stumble through life? Oh, Lord, Lord, surely, of all men, Moses has been the most humble. Surely he deserves to cross the Jordan River and walk in the pastures of Canaan, even if only for a day.*

I understand why You are keeping me out. I deserve to remain in the desert. I deserved death for making that detestable golden calf! Am I not reminded of it every time I sacrifice a bullock? But, oh, Lord, my brother has been Your faithful servant. He loves You. No man is more humble than my brother.

Let the blame fall on me for being such a fool and being so weak a priest that I failed to see sin when it crouched ready to kill our hopes and dreams.

Be silent, and know that I am God!

Aaron swallowed hard, fear coursing through him. It would do no good to beg or argue. And he knew the rest as though spoken into his heart. The people had to know the cost of sin. In the eyes of God, all men and women were equal. Aaron was without excuse. And so was Moses.

Only God is holy and to be praised.

They returned together to the Tabernacle. Moses went inside and Aaron stood outside the veil, his heart heavy. He could hear Moses speaking softly, his words indistinct, his anguish clear. Aaron bowed his head, the pain in his chest suffocating.

My fault, Lord. My fault. What kind of high priest am I who fails at every turn of life and cannot see sin when it stands before him? Forgive me, Lord. My sins are ever before me. I have done what is evil in Your sight. You have judged me justly. Oh, if only You would purify me so that I could be clean like a newborn child. If only You would wash me clean of my sins and make me hear with renewed joy the promise of Your salvation!

He wiped his tears away quickly lest they fall on the chestpiece of his priestly garment. *I must be clean. I must be clean!*

Oh, God of Abraham, Isaac, and Jacob. God of all creation. How will I ever be clean, Lord? I am clean on the outside, but inside I feel like a grave of old bones. I am full of sin. And it poured over today, as from a fouled pot. Even when I offer the atonement sacrifice, I feel the sin in me. I fight against it, Lord, but it is still there.

Aaron heard Moses weeping. God had not changed His mind. The Promised Land was lost to both of them. Aaron covered his face, heartbroken.

Moses! Poor Moses.

Oh, God, hear my prayer. If You see me weaken, don't let me

succumb to sin again or cause trouble for my brother. Don't let me
stand up in pride and lead the people astray. Oh, God, I would
rather You took my life than I give in to sin again!

✦   ✦   ✦

Moses sent messengers to the king of Edom requesting permis-
sion to cross his land in order to lessen the distance to Canaan.
Moses promised that the Israelites would not go through any
field or vineyard, or drink water from any well. They would
turn neither to the right nor to the left until they reached the
trade route called the King's Highway.

The king of Edom answered that he would not give permis-
sion, and if the Israelites tried to cross his land, he would march
out and attack them with the sword. Moses sent messengers
again with assurances that they would only go along the main
road and would pay for any water their animals might need.
Again, the king of Edom denied them passage and came out
with a large army to make sure no attempt was made to cross
his land.

The cloud moved from Kadesh, and Moses followed the
Angel of the Lord along the boundary of Edom toward Mount
Hor. Aaron walked beside his brother, desolate. When they
camped, he performed the evening sacrifice. Depressed, he
returned to his tent and carefully removed his priestly garments. Then he sat in the doorway and stared out. All day,
while walking, he had felt the barrenness of the land around
him. And now, sitting here, he remembered the fields of wheat
in Egypt, the barley, the green pasturelands of Goshen.

We were slaves, he reminded himself. He thought about the
taskmasters. He tried to remember how many times he had felt
the lash on his back, and the heat of the desert sun beating
down on him.

And the green . . . the smell of water filled with silt washing along the banks of the Nile . . . the ibises tipping their beaks in and drawing out fish . . .

Raising his head weakly, he looked up at the pillar of fire. *God, help me. Help me.*

And he heard the Voice again, soft yet firm.

Aaron waited all night and then rose in the morning and put on his priestly garments. He went to the Tabernacle, washed, and performed the morning sacrifice as usual. And then Moses came to him, Eleazar at his side. Moses took a slow breath, but could not speak. Eleazar looked perplexed.

Aaron put his hand out and gripped his brother's arm. "I know, Moses. The Lord spoke to me, too. Yesterday, at sunset."

Eleazar looked between them. "What has happened?"

Aaron looked at his son. "We are to go up Mount Hor."

"When?"

"Now." Aaron was thankful his son did not ask why. Nor did he ask that they postpone the journey until the cool of the evening. Eleazar simply started out toward the foot of the mountain.

Maybe there was hope for Israel after all.

✦   ✦   ✦

The climb was difficult, for there was only a narrow pathway between and around rugged rock outcroppings. Up, up Aaron climbed until he was exhausted and every muscle in his body ached. He kept putting one foot in front of the other, praying the Lord would give him strength. It would be the first time the Lord had called him to the top of a mountain. And the last.

After long hours of travail, he reached the top. His heart was pounding heavily, his lungs burning. He felt more alive than he ever had before as he stretched out trembling hands and gave thanks to God. The cloud pressed in and rose, turning from gray to orange-gold, then flashing red. Aaron felt warmth course through him and then dissipate, leaving him weak. He knew if he sat down, he would never rise again, and he needed to stand a little longer.

So he stood alone for the first time in years and looked at the plain below, speckled with thousands of tents. Each tribe had its position, and in the center was the Tabernacle. Flocks of sheep and herds of cattle grazed on the outer edges of the camp, and the vastness of the wilderness spread out before him.

Eleazar helped Moses up the last few feet, and then the three stood together, gazing out over Israel. "You need to rest, Father."

"I will." *Forever.*

Moses looked at him and still could not speak. Aaron went to him and embraced him. Moses' shoulders shook and Aaron held him tighter and spoke softly. "Oh, my brother, I wish I had been a better and stronger man to stand at your side."

Moses did not let go of him. "The Lord sees our faults, Aaron. He sees our failures and frailty. But what matters to Him is our faith. We have both stumbled, my brother. We have both fallen. And the Lord has lifted us back up with the strength of His mighty hand and remained with us." He drew back slowly.

Aaron smiled. Never had he loved and respected a man as much as he did his younger brother. "It is not our faith, Moses, but God's faithfulness."

"What's going on?"

Aaron turned to his son. "The Lord has said the time has come for me to join my ancestors in death."

Eleazar flinched, his eyes darting from Aaron to his uncle. "What does he mean?"

"Your father is to die here on Mount Hor."

"*No!*"

Aaron felt the hair stand on the back of his neck. "Yes, Eleazar." He could see already the seed of rebellion in his son's eyes.

"This can't be."

"Do not question the Lord—"

"You have to go with us into Canaan, Father!" His eyes filled with angry tears of confusion. "You have to come!"

"Be silent!" Aaron gripped his son's arms. "It is for the Lord to say when a man lives or dies." *Oh, God, forgive him. Please.* He gentled. "The Lord has shown me more kindness than I deserve. He has allowed you to come and attend me." He would not die surrounded by all the members of his family as so many did. But he would not die alone.

Sobbing, Eleazar bowed his head. Aaron ran his hand over his son's back. "You must be strong in the days ahead, Eleazar. You must walk the road the Lord gives you and never depart from it. Cling to the Lord. He is our father."

Moses let out his breath slowly. "Remove your clothing, Eleazar."

Eleazar's head came up. He stared at him. "What?"

"We must fulfill the Lord's command."

Aaron was as surprised as his son. When Eleazar looked at him, he couldn't answer the silent question. "Do as you're told." He only knew he was to die here on top of the mountain. Beyond that, Aaron knew nothing.

Moses shrugged off the water bag he had carried. When Eleazar was undressed, Moses washed him from head to foot. He anointed him with oil and took new linen undergarments from another pack. "Put these on."

And then Aaron understood. His heart swelled until he felt it would burst with joy. When Moses looked at him, Aaron knew to remove his priestly garments. He laid them out carefully on a flat boulder, one piece at a time, until he was standing in his linen undergarments.

Moses took the blue robe and helped Eleazar slip it over his head, the tiny woven pomegranates and gold bells tickling at the hem. Next, he put the embroidered tunic on his nephew, then tied the multicolored sash snugly around his waist. He attached the blue, purple, scarlet, and gold ephod at Eleazar's shoulders with the two onyx stones, six tribes of Israel engraved on each. Eleazar would carry the nation on his shoulders every day for the rest of his life. Moses hung the chestpiece on which were the twelve stones representing the tribes of Israel. He took the Urim and Thummim and tucked them into the pocket over Eleazar's heart.

Tears ran down Aaron's face as he looked at his son. Eleazar, God's chosen high priest. The Lord had once told Aaron that the line of high priests for generations to come would descend from him, but he had been convinced he had spoiled all possibility of that great honor happening. How many times he had sinned! He had been just like the people, complaining of hardships, lusting after things he didn't have, rebelling against Moses and God, greedy for more power and authority, blaming others for trouble he brought on himself by his own disobedience, afraid to trust in God for everything. Oh, that golden calf, that wretched golden idol of sin.

And yet, God kept His promise.

Oh, Lord, Lord, You are merciful to me. Oh, Lord, You alone are faithful!

Even as the joy spread through him, sorrow was in its wake, for he knew Eleazar would struggle as he had struggled. His son would spend the rest of his life trying to learn and obey the Law. The weight of it would press him down, for he too would come to realize how sin dwelt in the secret dark places of his heart. He would try to crush its head with his heel, but he too would fail.

All eyes would be on him, listening to what he said, watching how he lived. And the people would see that Eleazar was merely a man trying to live a godly life. Every morning and every evening, he would perform sacrifices. He would live with the smell of blood and incense. Once a year he would pass through the veil into the Most Holy Place and put the blood of the atonement sacrifice on the horns of the altar. And his son would know then, as Aaron knew now, that he would have to do it again and again and again. Eleazar would be burdened by his sin forever.

God, help us! Lord, have mercy on us! My son will try, as I have tried, and he will fail. You have given us the Law so that we can live holy lives. But Lord, You know we are not holy. We are dust. Will there ever come a day when we will be one people with one mind and heart, one spirit, one in striving to please You? Wash us with hyssop, Lord. Cleanse us from iniquity! Circumcise our hearts!

Trembling and too weak to stand any longer, Aaron sank to the ground and rested his back against a stone.

Is that the reason for the Law, Lord? To show us we can't live it out perfectly? When we break one law, no matter how small it seems, we are lawbreakers. Even if we returned to our mother's womb and started over, we would sin again. We would have to be born again, made into entirely new creations.

Oh, Lord, save us. Send us a Savior who can do all You ask, who can stand before the Most Holy Place without sin, someone who can be our high priest and present the perfect sacrifice, someone who has the power to change us from within so that we can stand without sinning. We need a high priest who can understand our weakness; a high priest who has faced all of the same temptations we face, and yet has not sinned; a high priest who can stand near the throne of God with confidence so that we may receive mercy and find grace to help us when we need it.

Moses sat beside him and spoke softly. Eleazar came near, but Aaron lifted his hand, staying him. "No. For the sake of the people . . ." Aaron could see him struggle.

His son wanted to embrace him, but death was too close to risk reaching out and embracing one another one last time. A high priest must remain clean. Eleazar must not be defiled. Hands clenching and unclenching, Eleazar remained at a distance.

Another stood on the mountain with them. A Man. Yet not a man. Aaron had seen Him walking beside Moses and leading the people out into the desert. He had seen Him again standing within the rock of Marah when water had poured forth for the people.

Moses' friend.

He was wearing a long white robe with a gold sash across His chest. His eyes were bright like the pillar of fire. His feet were as bright as bronze refined in a furnace. And His face was as bright as the sun in all its brilliance. The Man extended His hand.

Aaron.

With a long, deep sigh, Aaron breathed out softly in obedience, *Yes, Lord, yes.*

DEAR READER,

We hope you enjoyed this fictional account of the life of Aaron, Israel's first high priest and brother of Moses. This finely woven tale by Francine Rivers is meant to whet your appetite. Francine's first and foremost desire is to take you back to God's Word to decide for yourself the truth about Aaron—his duties, dilemmas, and disappointments.

The following Bible study is designed to guide you through Scripture to *seek* the truth about Aaron and to *find* applications for your own life.

God called Aaron to encourage Moses. He got off to a great start, but stumbled along the way. Aaron was the middle child—caught between a bright, creative, gutsy older sister and a younger brother who from birth was considered "special." It's not hard to see how Aaron would be, by nature, a people pleaser. A peacekeeper—at all costs. His uncomplaining acceptance of God's timing for his death whispers of Aaron's desire to trust God as fervently in the end as when he started out on the journey.

May God encourage you as you seek Him for the answers to your life's challenges, dilemmas, and disappointments. And may He find you willing to walk with Him through it all.

Peggy Lynch

SEEK GOD'S WORD FOR TRUTH
Read the following passage:

Then the Lord said to Moses, "Go back to Pharaoh, and tell him to let the people of Israel leave Egypt."

"But Lord!" Moses objected. "My own people won't listen to me anymore. How can I expect Pharaoh to listen? I'm no orator!"

But the Lord ordered Moses and Aaron to return to Pharaoh, king of Egypt, and to demand that he let the people of Israel leave Egypt.

These are the ancestors of clans from some of Israel's tribes:

The descendants of Reuben, Israel's oldest son, included Hanoch, Pallu, Hezron, and Carmi. Their descendants became the clans of Reuben.

The descendants of Simeon included Jemuel, Jamin, Ohad, Jakin, Zohar, and Shaul (whose mother was a Canaanite). Their descendants became the clans of Simeon.

These are the descendants of Levi, listed according to their family groups. In the first generation were Gershon, Kohath, and Merari. (Levi, their father, lived to be 137 years old.)

The descendants of Gershon included Libni and Shimei, each of whom is the ancestor of a clan.

The descendants of Kohath included Amram, Izhar, Hebron, and Uzziel. (Kohath lived to be 133 years old.)

The descendants of Merari included Mahli and Mushi.

These are the clans of the Levites, listed according to their genealogies.

Amram married his father's sister Jochebed, and she bore him Aaron and Moses. (Amram lived to be 137 years old.)

The descendants of Izhar included Korah, Nepheg, and Zicri.

The descendants of Uzziel included Mishael, Elzaphan, and Sithri.

Aaron married Elisheba, the daughter of Amminadab and sister of Nahshon, and she bore him Nadab, Abihu, Eleazar, and Ithamar.

The descendants of Korah included Assir, Elkanah, and Abiasaph. Their descendants became the clans of Korah.

Eleazar son of Aaron married one of the daughters of Putiel, and she bore him Phinehas.   EXODUS 6:10-25

List everything you learn about Aaron from this Levitical lineage.

Read the following passages:

One day Moses was tending the flock of his father-in-law, Jethro, the priest of Midian, and he went deep into the wilderness near Sinai, the mountain of God. Suddenly, the angel of the Lord appeared to him as a blazing fire in a bush. Moses was amazed because the bush was engulfed in flames, but it didn't burn up. "Amazing!" Moses said to himself. "Why isn't that bush burning up? I must go over to see this."

When the Lord saw that he had caught Moses' attention, God called to him from the bush, "Moses! Moses!"

"Here I am!" Moses replied.   EXODUS 3:1-4

"Now go, for I am sending you to Pharaoh. You will lead my people, the Israelites, out of Egypt."

"But who am I to appear before Pharaoh?" Moses asked God. "How can you expect me to lead the Israelites out of Egypt?"
                    EXODUS 3:10-11

But Moses protested, "If I go to the people of Israel and tell them, 'The God of your ancestors has sent me to you,' they won't believe me. They will ask, 'Which god are you talking about? What is his name?' Then what should I tell them?"   EXODUS 3:13

But Moses protested again, "Look, they won't believe me! They won't do what I tell them. They'll just say, 'The Lord never appeared to you.'"   EXODUS 4:1

But Moses pleaded with the Lord, "O Lord, I'm just not a good speaker. I never have been, and I'm not now, even after you have spoken to me. I'm clumsy with words."   EXODUS 4:10

But Moses again pleaded, "Lord, please! Send someone else."
   Then the Lord became angry with Moses. "All right," he said. "What about your brother, Aaron the Levite? He is a good speaker. And look! He is on his way to meet you now. And when he sees you, he will be very glad. You will talk to him, giving him the words to say. I will help both of you to speak clearly, and I will tell you what to do. Aaron will be your spokesman to the people, and you will be as God to him, telling him what to say. And be sure to take your shepherd's staff along so you can perform the miraculous signs I have shown you."   EXODUS 4:13-17

Now the Lord had said to Aaron, "Go out into the wilderness to meet Moses." So Aaron traveled to the mountain of God, where he found Moses and greeted him warmly. Moses then told Aaron everything the Lord had commanded them to do and say. And he told him about the miraculous signs they were to perform.
   So Moses and Aaron returned to Egypt and called the leaders of Israel to a meeting. Aaron told them everything the Lord had told Moses, and Moses performed the miraculous signs as they watched. The leaders were soon convinced that the Lord had sent Moses and Aaron. And when they realized that the Lord had seen their misery and was deeply concerned for them, they all bowed their heads and worshiped. EXODUS 4:27-31

Contrast Moses and Aaron from these passages.

Discuss God's role and response from the same passages.

What roles did Moses and Aaron take/accept?

How did the Israelite people respond? What did they conclude about the two men?

What impact, if any, do you think Aaron had on Moses at this juncture? Why?

FIND GOD'S WAYS FOR YOU
How do you respond when God impresses you to do something?

Which of the two leaders (Moses or Aaron) do you identify with and why?

> The Lord is for me, so I will not be afraid. What can mere mortals do to me? Yes, the Lord is for me; he will help me. I will look in triumph at those who hate me. It is better to trust the Lord than to put confidence in people.   PSALM 118:6-8

What do you learn about God from these verses?

STOP AND PONDER

> Now glory be to God! By his mighty power at work within us, he is able to accomplish infinitely more than we would ever dare to ask or hope.   EPHESIANS 3:20

SEEK GOD'S WORD FOR TRUTH

Moses and Aaron both chose to obey God and return to Egypt to help deliver their relatives out of bondage. Read the following passage:

> So Moses and Aaron returned to Egypt and called the leaders of Israel to a meeting. Aaron told them everything the Lord had told Moses, and Moses performed the miraculous signs as they watched. The leaders were soon convinced that the Lord had sent Moses and Aaron. And when they realized that the Lord had seen their misery and was deeply concerned for them, they all bowed their heads and worshiped.
>
> After this presentation to Israel's leaders, Moses and Aaron went to see Pharaoh. They told him, "This is what the Lord, the God of Israel, says: 'Let my people go, for they must go out into the wilderness to hold a religious festival in my honor.' "
>
> "Is that so?" retorted Pharaoh. "And who is the Lord that I should listen to him and let Israel go? I don't know the Lord, and I will not let Israel go."
>
> But Aaron and Moses persisted. "The God of the Hebrews has met with us," they declared. "Let us take a three-day trip into the wilderness so we can offer sacrifices to the Lord our God. If we don't, we will surely die by disease or the sword."   EXODUS 4:29–5:3

What steps did Aaron and Moses take upon returning to Egypt?

What supporting evidence do you find that Aaron was an encouragement to Moses?

Read the following passage:

> After this presentation to Israel's leaders, Moses and Aaron went
> to see Pharaoh. They told him, "This is what the Lord, the God of
> Israel, says: 'Let my people go, for they must go out into the wil-
> derness to hold a religious festival in my honor.' "
>
> "Is that so?" retorted Pharaoh. "And who is the Lord that I
> should listen to him and let Israel go? I don't know the Lord, and
> I will not let Israel go."
>
> But Aaron and Moses persisted. "The God of the Hebrews has
> met with us," they declared. "Let us take a three-day trip into the
> wilderness so we can offer sacrifices to the Lord our God. If we
> don't, we will surely die by disease or the sword."
>
> "Who do you think you are," Pharaoh shouted, "distracting the
> people from their tasks? Get back to work! Look, there are many
> people here in Egypt, and you are stopping them from doing their
> work."
>
> Since Pharaoh would not let up on his demands, the Israelite
> foremen could see that they were in serious trouble. As they left
> Pharaoh's court, they met Moses and Aaron, who were waiting
> outside for them. The foremen said to them, "May the Lord judge
> you for getting us into this terrible situation with Pharaoh and his
> officials. You have given them an excuse to kill us!"
>
> So Moses went back to the Lord and protested, "Why have you
> mistreated your own people like this, Lord? Why did you send
> me? Since I gave Pharaoh your message, he has been even more
> brutal to your people. You have not even begun to rescue them!"
>
> "Now you will see what I will do to Pharaoh," the Lord told
> Moses. "When he feels my powerful hand upon him, he will let
> the people go. In fact, he will be so anxious to get rid of them that
> he will force them to leave his land!"
>
> Then the Lord said to Moses, "Pay close attention to this. I will
> make you seem like God to Pharaoh. Your brother, Aaron, will be
> your prophet; he will speak for you. Tell Aaron everything I say
> to you and have him announce it to Pharaoh. He will demand that
> the people of Israel be allowed to leave Egypt."
>
> So Moses and Aaron did just as the Lord had commanded them.
> Moses was eighty years old, and Aaron was eighty-three at the
> time they made their demands to Pharaoh.

Then the Lord said to Moses and Aaron, "Pharaoh will demand that you show him a miracle to prove that God has sent you. When he makes this demand, say to Aaron, 'Throw down your shepherd's staff,' and it will become a snake."

So Moses and Aaron went to see Pharaoh, and they performed the miracle just as the Lord had told them.

EXODUS 5:1-5, 19–6:2; 7:1-2, 6-10A

How did Pharaoh react to the demands of Aaron and Moses? How did the Israelites react to Pharaoh's demands?

What does Moses do when he is confronted by the Israelite foremen?

Just as God laid out His plan to Moses, what role did He give Aaron? Why?

Notice Moses' and Aaron's response to God's plan (7:8). Discuss the possible reasons for the change in their attitudes.

FIND GOD'S WAYS FOR YOU
Have you ever needed to "go back" in order to go forward? Explain.

Share a time when someone was willing to support you, stay by your side, through a difficult time.

> A person standing alone can be attacked and defeated, but two can stand back-to-back and conquer. Three are even better, for a triple-braided cord is not easily broken.   ECCLESIASTES 4:12

Discuss this verse in light of Moses and Aaron. Who is always there to form the triple braid?

STOP AND PONDER

> God has said, "I will never fail you. I will never forsake you." That is why we can say with confidence, "The Lord is my helper, so I will not be afraid. What can mere mortals do to me?"
>
> HEBREWS 13:5B-6

SEEK GOD'S WORD FOR TRUTH
Read the following passage:

The Lord instructed Moses: "Come up here to me, and bring along Aaron, Nadab, Abihu, and seventy of Israel's leaders. All of them must worship at a distance. You alone, Moses, are allowed to come near to the Lord. The others must not come too close. And remember, none of the other people are allowed to climb on the mountain at all."

When Moses had announced to the people all the teachings and regulations the Lord had given him, they answered in unison, "We will do everything the Lord has told us to do."

Then Moses carefully wrote down all the Lord's instructions. Early the next morning he built an altar at the foot of the mountain. He also set up twelve pillars around the altar, one for each of the twelve tribes of Israel. Then he sent some of the young men to sacrifice young bulls as burnt offerings and peace offerings to the Lord. Moses took half the blood from these animals and drew it off into basins. The other half he splashed against the altar.

Then he took the Book of the Covenant and read it to the people. They all responded again, "We will do everything the Lord has commanded. We will obey."

Then Moses sprinkled the blood from the basins over the people and said, "This blood confirms the covenant the Lord has made with you in giving you these laws."

Then Moses, Aaron, Nadab, Abihu, and seventy of the leaders of Israel went up the mountain. There they saw the God of Israel. Under his feet there seemed to be a pavement of brilliant sapphire, as clear as the heavens. And though Israel's leaders saw God, he did not destroy them. In fact, they shared a meal together in God's presence!

And the Lord said to Moses, "Come up to me on the mountain. Stay there while I give you the tablets of stone that I have inscribed with my instructions and commands. Then you will teach the people from them." So Moses and his assistant Joshua climbed up the mountain of God.

Moses told the other leaders, "Stay here and wait for us until we come back. If there are any problems while I am gone, consult with Aaron and Hur, who are here with you."

Then Moses went up the mountain, and the cloud covered it.

EXODUS 24:1-15

Who was invited to the mountain? What took place among them while they were there?

When Moses went up the mountain with Joshua, what were his instructions to the other leaders?

With all this in mind, read the following passage:

When Moses failed to come back down the mountain right away, the people went to Aaron. "Look," they said, "make us some gods who can lead us. This man Moses, who brought us here from Egypt, has disappeared. We don't know what has happened to him."

So Aaron said, "Tell your wives and sons and daughters to take off their gold earrings, and then bring them to me."

All the people obeyed Aaron and brought him their gold earrings. Then Aaron took the gold, melted it down, and molded and tooled it into the shape of a calf. The people exclaimed, "O Israel, these are the gods who brought you out of Egypt!"

When Aaron saw how excited the people were about it, he built an altar in front of the calf and announced, "Tomorrow there will be a festival to the Lord!"

So the people got up early the next morning to sacrifice burnt offerings and peace offerings. After this, they celebrated with feasting and drinking, and indulged themselves in pagan revelry.

Then the Lord told Moses, "Quick! Go down the mountain! The people you brought from Egypt have defiled themselves. They have already turned from the way I commanded them to live. They have made an idol shaped like a calf, and they have worshiped and sacrificed to it. They are saying, 'These are your gods, O Israel, who brought you out of Egypt.' "

Then the Lord said, "I have seen how stubborn and rebellious these people are. Now leave me alone so my anger can blaze against them and destroy them all. Then I will make you, Moses, into a great nation instead of them."

But Moses pleaded with the Lord his God not to do it. "O Lord!" he exclaimed. "Why are you so angry with your own people whom you brought from the land of Egypt with such great power and mighty acts? The Egyptians will say, 'God tricked them into coming to the mountains so he could kill them and wipe them from the face of the earth.' Turn away from your fierce anger. Change your mind about this terrible disaster you are planning against your people! Remember your covenant with your servants—Abraham, Isaac, and Jacob. You swore by your own self, 'I will make your descendants as numerous as the stars of heaven. Yes, I will give them all of this land that I have promised to your descendants, and they will possess it forever.' "

So the Lord withdrew his threat and didn't bring against his people the disaster he had threatened.

Then Moses turned and went down the mountain. He held in his hands the two stone tablets inscribed with the terms of the covenant. They were inscribed on both sides, front and back. These stone tablets were God's work; the words on them were written by God himself.

When Joshua heard the noise of the people shouting below them, he exclaimed to Moses, "It sounds as if there is a war in the camp!"

But Moses replied, "No, it's neither a cry of victory nor a cry of defeat. It is the sound of a celebration."

When they came near the camp, Moses saw the calf and the dancing. In terrible anger, he threw the stone tablets to the ground, smashing them at the foot of the mountain. He took the calf they had made and melted it in the fire. And when the metal had cooled, he ground it into powder and mixed it with water. Then he made the people drink it.

After that, he turned to Aaron. "What did the people do to you?" he demanded. "How did they ever make you bring such terrible sin upon them?"

"Don't get upset, sir," Aaron replied. "You yourself know these people and what a wicked bunch they are. They said to me, 'Make us some gods to lead us, for something has happened to this man Moses, who led us out of Egypt.' So I told them, 'Bring me your gold earrings.' When they brought them to me, I threw them into the fire—and out came this calf!"

When Moses saw that Aaron had let the people get completely out of control—and much to the amusement of their enemies—he stood at the entrance to the camp and shouted, "All of you who are on the Lord's side, come over here and join me." And all the Levites came.

He told them, "This is what the Lord, the God of Israel, says: Strap on your swords! Go back and forth from one end of the camp to the other, killing even your brothers, friends, and neighbors." The Levites obeyed Moses, and about three thousand people died that day.

Then Moses told the Levites, "Today you have been ordained for the service of the Lord, for you obeyed him even though it meant killing your own sons and brothers. Because of this, he will now give you a great blessing."

The next day Moses said to the people, "You have committed a terrible sin, but I will return to the Lord on the mountain. Perhaps I will be able to obtain forgiveness for you."

So Moses returned to the Lord and said, "Alas, these people have committed a terrible sin. They have made gods of gold for themselves. But now, please forgive their sin—and if not, then blot me out of the record you are keeping."

The Lord replied to Moses, "I will blot out whoever has sinned against me. Now go, lead the people to the place I told you about. Look! My angel will lead the way before you! But when I call the people to account, I will certainly punish them for their sins."

And the Lord sent a great plague upon the people because they had worshiped the calf Aaron had made.   EXODUS 32

Discuss the circumstances surrounding the creation of the golden calf: Who? What? When? Where? Why? How?

What did Moses find when he returned? What was his response?

Compare Aaron's response to the people's request in verses 2-4 with his reply to Moses' questions in verses 22-24.

Moses took drastic measures within the camp of Israel when he discovered their sin. He drew a line in the sand. Who crossed that line to join him in obedience? What might this also imply about Aaron?

FIND GOD'S WAYS FOR YOU

Both Aaron and Moses were put on the spot, each revealing himself
in his response. Share a time when you were put on the spot by
other people. What did you learn about yourself by the way you
handled it?

With whom do you identify now—Moses or Aaron? Why?

Discuss steps Aaron should have taken when the people came to him
for leadership.

STOP AND PONDER

We can gather our thoughts, but the Lord gives the right answer.
People may be pure in their own eyes, but the Lord examines
their motives. Commit your work to the Lord, and then your
plans will succeed.   PROVERBS 16:1-3

SEEK GOD'S WORD FOR TRUTH
Read the following passages:

> "Bring Aaron and his sons to the entrance of the Tabernacle, and wash them with water." EXODUS 40:12

The Lord said to Moses, "Now bring Aaron and his sons, along with their special clothing, the anointing oil, the bull for the sin offering, the two rams, and the basket of unleavened bread to the entrance of the Tabernacle. Then call the entire community of Israel to meet you there."

So Moses followed the Lord's instructions, and all the people assembled at the Tabernacle entrance. Moses announced to them, "The Lord has commanded what I am now going to do!" Then he presented Aaron and his sons and washed them with water. He clothed Aaron with the embroidered tunic and tied the sash around his waist. He dressed him in the robe of the ephod, along with the ephod itself, and attached the ephod with its decorative sash. Then Moses placed the chestpiece on Aaron and put the Urim and the Thummim inside it. He placed on Aaron's head the turban with the gold medallion at its front, just as the Lord had commanded him.

Then Moses took the anointing oil and anointed the Tabernacle and everything in it, thus making them holy. He sprinkled the altar seven times, anointing it and all its utensils and the wash-basin and its pedestal, making them holy. Then he poured some of the anointing oil on Aaron's head, thus anointing him and making him holy for his work. Next Moses presented Aaron's sons and clothed them in their embroidered tunics, their sashes, and their turbans, just as the Lord had commanded him. LEVITICUS 8:1-13

Discuss the anointing of Aaron. What stands out to you from this account?

What do you learn about God from this passage, especially in light of
the previous lesson?

After such a high point in Aaron's life, it is hard to conceive that he
would ever vacillate again. Read the following passage:

> While they were at Hazeroth, Miriam and Aaron criticized Moses
> because he had married a Cushite woman. They said, "Has the
> Lord spoken only through Moses? Hasn't he spoken through us,
> too?" But the Lord heard them.
> Now Moses was more humble than any other person on earth.
> So immediately the Lord called to Moses, Aaron, and Miriam and
> said, "Go out to the Tabernacle, all three of you!" And the three
> of them went out. Then the Lord descended in the pillar of cloud
> and stood at the entrance of the Tabernacle. "Aaron and Miriam!"
> he called, and they stepped forward. And the Lord said to them,
> "Now listen to me! Even with prophets, I the Lord communicate
> by visions and dreams. But that is not how I communicate with
> my servant Moses. He is entrusted with my entire house. I speak
> to him face to face, directly and not in riddles! He sees the Lord as
> he is. Should you not be afraid to criticize him?"
> The Lord was furious with them, and he departed. As the cloud
> moved from above the Tabernacle, Miriam suddenly became
> white as snow with leprosy. When Aaron saw what had hap-
> pened, he cried out to Moses, "Oh, my lord! Please don't punish
> us for this sin we have so foolishly committed. Don't let her be
> like a stillborn baby, already decayed at birth."
> So Moses cried out to the Lord, "Heal her, O God, I beg you!"
> And the Lord said to Moses, "If her father had spit in her face,
> wouldn't she have been defiled for seven days? Banish her from
> the camp for seven days, and after that she may return."
> So Miriam was excluded from the camp for seven days, and the
> people waited until she was brought back before they traveled
> again.   NUMBERS 12:1-15

What complaints did Aaron and Miriam have about Moses?

What did God have to say about these complaints?

Who do you think started the complaints and why?

What does this imply about Aaron? about his motives?

FIND GOD'S WAYS FOR YOU
What significance do you see for yourself that God continued to work with, work through, and use Aaron? Explain.

For our earthly fathers disciplined us for a few years, doing the
best they knew how. But God's discipline is always right and
good for us because it means we will share in his holiness. No
discipline is enjoyable while it is happening—it is painful! But
afterward there will be a quiet harvest of right living for those
who are trained in this way.

So take a new grip with your tired hands and stand firm on your
shaky legs. Mark out a straight path for your feet. Then those
who follow you, though they are weak and lame, will not stumble
and fall but will become strong.   HEBREWS 12:10-13

What is the difference between God's discipline and our earthly father's
discipline?

What benefits are there from God's discipline? For you? For others in
your sphere of influence?

STOP AND PONDER

If we confess our sins to him [Jesus], he is faithful and just to forgive us and cleanse us from every wrong.   I JOHN 1:9

SEEK GOD'S WORD FOR TRUTH

Read the following passage:

One day Korah son of Izhar, a descendant of Kohath son of Levi, conspired with Dathan and Abiram, the sons of Eliab, and On son of Peleth, from the tribe of Reuben. They incited a rebellion against Moses, involving 250 other prominent leaders, all members of the assembly. They went to Moses and Aaron and said, "You have gone too far! Everyone in Israel has been set apart by the Lord, and he is with all of us. What right do you have to act as though you are greater than anyone else among all these people of the Lord?"

When Moses heard what they were saying, he threw himself down with his face to the ground. Then he said to Korah and his followers, "Tomorrow morning the Lord will show us who belongs to him and who is holy. The Lord will allow those who are chosen to enter his holy presence. You, Korah, and all your followers must do this: Take incense burners, and burn incense in them tomorrow before the Lord. Then we will see whom the Lord chooses as his holy one. You Levites are the ones who have gone too far!"

Then Moses spoke again to Korah: "Now listen, you Levites! Does it seem a small thing to you that the God of Israel has chosen you from among all the people of Israel to be near him as you serve in the Lord's Tabernacle and to stand before the people to minister to them? He has given this special ministry only to you and your fellow Levites, but now you are demanding the priesthood as well! The one you are really revolting against is the Lord! And who is Aaron that you are complaining about him?"

Then Moses summoned Dathan and Abiram, the sons of Eliab, but they replied, "We refuse to come! Isn't it enough that you brought us out of Egypt, a land flowing with milk and honey, to kill us here in this wilderness, and that you now treat us like your subjects? What's more, you haven't brought us into the land flowing with milk and honey or given us an inheritance of fields and vineyards. Are you trying to fool us? We will not come."

Then Moses became very angry and said to the Lord, "Do not accept their offerings! I have not taken so much as a donkey from them, and I have never hurt a single one of them." And Moses said to Korah, "Come here tomorrow and present yourself before the Lord with all your followers. Aaron will also be here. Be sure that each of your 250 followers brings an incense burner with incense on it, so you can present them before the Lord. Aaron will also bring his incense burner."

So these men came with their incense burners, placed burning coals and incense on them, and stood at the entrance of the Tabernacle with Moses and Aaron. Meanwhile, Korah had stirred up the entire community against Moses and Aaron, and they all assembled at the Tabernacle entrance. Then the glorious presence of the Lord appeared to the whole community, and the Lord said to Moses and Aaron, "Get away from these people so that I may instantly destroy them!"

But Moses and Aaron fell face down on the ground. "O God, the God and source of all life," they pleaded. "Must you be angry with all the people when only one man sins?"

And the Lord said to Moses, "Then tell all the people to get away from the tents of Korah, Dathan, and Abiram."

So Moses got up and rushed over to the tents of Dathan and Abiram, followed closely by the Israelite leaders. "Quick!" he told the people. "Get away from the tents of these wicked men, and don't touch anything that belongs to them. If you do, you will be destroyed for their sins." So all the people stood back from the tents of Korah, Dathan, and Abiram. Then Dathan and Abiram came out and stood at the entrances of their tents with their wives and children and little ones.

And Moses said, "By this you will know that the Lord has sent me to do all these things that I have done—for I have not done them on my own. If these men die a natural death, then the Lord has not sent me. But if the Lord performs a miracle and the ground opens up and swallows them and all their belongings, and they go down alive into the grave, then you will know that these men have despised the Lord."

He had hardly finished speaking the words when the ground suddenly split open beneath them. The earth opened up and swallowed the men, along with their households and the followers who were standing with them, and everything they owned. So they went down alive into the grave, along with their belongings. The earth closed over them, and they all vanished. All of the people of Israel fled as they heard their screams, fearing that the earth would swallow them, too. Then fire blazed forth from the Lord and burned up the 250 men who were offering incense.

And the Lord said to Moses, "Tell Eleazar son of Aaron the priest to pull all the incense burners from the fire, for they are holy. Also tell him to scatter the burning incense from the burners of these men who have sinned at the cost of their lives. He must then hammer the metal of the incense burners into a sheet as a covering for the altar, for these burners have become holy because they were used in the Lord's presence. The altar covering will then serve as a warning to the people of Israel."

So Eleazar the priest collected the 250 bronze incense burners that had been used by the men who died in the fire, and they were hammered out into a sheet of metal to cover the altar. This would warn the Israelites that no unauthorized man—no one who was not a descendant of Aaron—should ever enter the Lord's presence to burn incense. If anyone did, the same thing would happen to him as happened to Korah and his followers. Thus, the Lord's instructions to Moses were carried out.

But the very next morning the whole community began muttering again against Moses and Aaron, saying, "You two have killed the Lord's people!" As the people gathered to protest to Moses and Aaron, they turned toward the Tabernacle and saw that the cloud had covered it, and the glorious presence of the Lord appeared.

Moses and Aaron came and stood at the entrance of the Tabernacle, and the Lord said to Moses, "Get away from these people so that I can instantly destroy them!" But Moses and Aaron fell face down on the ground.

And Moses said to Aaron, "Quick, take an incense burner and place burning coals on it from the altar. Lay incense on it and carry it quickly among the people to make atonement for them. The Lord's anger is blazing among them—the plague has already begun."

Aaron did as Moses told him and ran out among the people. The plague indeed had already begun, but Aaron burned the incense and made atonement for them. He stood between the living and the dead until the plague was stopped. But 14,700 people died in that plague, in addition to those who had died in the incident involving Korah. Then because the plague had stopped, Aaron returned to Moses at the entrance of the Tabernacle.

Then the Lord said to Moses, "Take twelve wooden staffs, one from each of Israel's ancestral tribes, and inscribe each tribal leader's name on his staff. Inscribe Aaron's name on the staff of the tribe of Levi, for there must be one staff for the leader of each ancestral tribe. Put these staffs in the Tabernacle in front of the Ark of the Covenant, where I meet with you. Buds will sprout on the staff belonging to the man I choose. Then I will finally put an end to this murmuring and complaining against you."

So Moses gave the instructions to the people of Israel, and each of the twelve tribal leaders, including Aaron, brought Moses a staff. Moses put the staffs in the Lord's presence in the Tabernacle of the Covenant. When he went into the Tabernacle of the Covenant the next day, he found that Aaron's staff, representing the tribe of Levi, had sprouted, blossomed, and produced almonds!

When Moses brought all the staffs out from the Lord's presence, he showed them to the people. Each man claimed his own staff. And the Lord said to Moses: "Place Aaron's staff permanently before the Ark of the Covenant as a warning to rebels. This should put an end to their complaints against me and prevent any further deaths." So Moses did as the Lord commanded him.   NUMBERS 16:1–17:11

What complaint did Korah, Dathan, and Abiram have? To whom did they complain? About whom were they really complaining?

What did God tell Moses and Aaron to do? What was their response?

Because of this insurrection, who else began to complain? What was their complaint?

Compare the way the Lord dealt with Korah to the way He dealt with the whole community. What role does Moses have? What role does Aaron accept?

Discuss how God settled the murmuring and complaining against the leadership.

What two warnings come from these rebellions? How are they memorialized?

FIND GOD'S WAYS FOR YOU

Remember a time when you were criticized for your leadership, position, or authority. What effect did it have on you personally? How did it affect those around you?

Now remember a time when you complained about someone else's leadership, position, or authority. How did it affect others? Looking back, have you gained any insights into yourself? your motives?

> In everything you do, stay away from complaining and arguing, so that no one can speak a word of blame against you. You are to live clean, innocent lives as children of God in a dark world full of crooked and perverse people. Let your lives shine brightly before them.   PHILIPPIANS 2:14-15

What are you to do about complaining and arguing? Why?

STOP AND PONDER

> I urge you, first of all, to pray for all people. As you make your requests, plead for God's mercy upon them, and give thanks. Pray this way for kings and all others who are in authority, so that we can live in peace and quietness, in godliness and dignity. This is good and pleases God our Savior, for he wants everyone to be saved and to understand the truth.   1 TIMOTHY 2:1-4

SEEK GOD'S WORD FOR TRUTH
Read the following passage:

In early spring the people of Israel arrived in the wilderness of Zin and camped at Kadesh. While they were there, Miriam died and was buried.

There was no water for the people to drink at that place, so they rebelled against Moses and Aaron. The people blamed Moses and said, "We wish we had died in the Lord's presence with our brothers! Did you bring the Lord's people into this wilderness to die, along with all our livestock? Why did you make us leave Egypt and bring us here to this terrible place? This land has no grain, figs, grapes, or pomegranates. And there is no water to drink!"

Moses and Aaron turned away from the people and went to the entrance of the Tabernacle, where they fell face down on the ground. Then the glorious presence of the Lord appeared to them, and the Lord said to Moses, "You and Aaron must take the staff and assemble the entire community. As the people watch, command the rock over there to pour out its water. You will get enough water from the rock to satisfy all the people and their livestock."

So Moses did as he was told. He took the staff from the place where it was kept before the Lord. Then he and Aaron summoned the people to come and gather at the rock. "Listen, you rebels!" he shouted. "Must we bring you water from this rock?" Then Moses raised his hand and struck the rock twice with the staff, and water gushed out. So all the people and their livestock drank their fill.

But the Lord said to Moses and Aaron, "Because you did not trust me enough to demonstrate my holiness to the people of Israel, you will not lead them into the land I am giving them!" This place was known as the waters of Meribah, because it was where the people of Israel argued with the Lord, and where he demonstrated his holiness among them.

While Moses was at Kadesh, he sent ambassadors to the king of Edom with this message:

"This message is from your relatives, the people of Israel: You

know all the hardships we have been through, and that our ancestors went down to Egypt. We lived there a long time and suffered
as slaves to the Egyptians. But when we cried out to the Lord, he
heard us and sent an angel who brought us out of Egypt. Now we
are camped at Kadesh, a town on the border of your land. Please
let us pass through your country. We will be careful not to go
through your fields and vineyards. We won't even drink water
from your wells. We will stay on the king's road and never leave
it until we have crossed the opposite border."

But the king of Edom said, "Stay out of my land or I will meet
you with an army!"

The Israelites answered, "We will stay on the main road. If any
of our livestock drinks your water, we will pay for it. We only
want to pass through your country and nothing else."

But the king of Edom replied, "Stay out! You may not pass through
our land." With that he mobilized his army and marched out to meet
them with an imposing force. Because Edom refused to allow Israel to
pass through their country, Israel was forced to turn around.

The whole community of Israel left Kadesh as a group and arrived at
Mount Hor. Then the Lord said to Moses and Aaron at Mount Hor on
the border of the land of Edom, "The time has come for Aaron to join
his ancestors in death. He will not enter the land I am giving the people
of Israel, because the two of you rebelled against my instructions concerning the waters of Meribah. Now take Aaron and his son Eleazar up
Mount Hor. There you will remove Aaron's priestly garments and put
them on Eleazar, his son. Aaron will die there and join his ancestors."

So Moses did as the Lord commanded. The three of them went
up Mount Hor together as the whole community watched. At the
summit, Moses removed the priestly garments from Aaron and
put them on Eleazar, Aaron's son. Then Aaron died there on top
of the mountain, and Moses and Eleazar went back down. When
the people realized that Aaron had died, all Israel mourned for
him thirty days.   NUMBERS 20

Describe the mood of the camp. What steps do Moses and Aaron
immediately take?

Compare the instructions God gave to Moses and Aaron with what the two men actually do. Any conclusions?

What instructions are given to Moses and Aaron when the whole community arrived at Mount Hor?

Contrast Moses' and Aaron's actions this time with their previous actions.

What reasons are given for Aaron's not getting to enter the Promised Land?

What evidence do you find that God kept His promise to Aaron about the priesthood being kept in his family? How would you characterize Aaron at the end of his journey?

FIND GOD'S WAYS FOR YOU

What are some reasons we fail to follow instructions?

How do you handle personal disappointments?

> God has not given us a spirit of fear and timidity, but of power,
> love, and self-discipline.   2 TIMOTHY 1:7

When we believe in Jesus, what is available to us for navigating though
life's dilemmas and disappointments?

STOP AND PONDER

> That is why we have a great High Priest who has gone to heaven,
> Jesus the Son of God. Let us cling to him and never stop trusting
> him. This High Priest of ours understands our weaknesses, for he
> faced all of the same temptations we do, yet he did not sin. So let
> us come boldly to the throne of our gracious God. There we will
> receive his mercy, and we will find grace to help us when we
> need it.   HEBREWS 4:14-16

FRANCINE RIVERS has been writing for more than twenty years. From 1976 to 1985 she had a successful writing career in the general market and won numerous awards. After becoming a born-again Christian in 1986, Francine wrote *Redeeming Love* as her statement of faith.

Since then, Francine has published numerous books in the CBA market and has continued to win both industry acclaim and reader loyalty. Her novel *The Last Sin Eater* won the ECPA Gold Medallion, and three of her books have won the prestigious Romance Writers of America Rita Award.

Francine uses her writing to draw closer to the Lord, that through her work she might worship and praise Jesus for all He has done and is doing in her life.

BOOKS BY BELOVED AUTHOR
FRANCINE RIVERS

OVER 2.5 MILLION SOLD!

A Lineage of Grace Series

Unveiled..ISBN 0-8423-1947-6

Unashamed...ISBN 0-8423-3596-X

Unshaken ....ISBN 0-8423-3597-8

Unspoken..ISBN 0-8423-3598-6

Unafraid ....ISBN 0-8423-3599-4

And the Shofar Blew

Hardcover..ISBN 0-8423-6582-6

Softcover..ISBN 0-8423-6583-4

Audio—CD...ISBN 0-8423-6585-0

Visit www. francinerivers.com